THEIR FINAL CRY

BOOKS BY DEA POIRIER

DEA POIRIER

THEIR FINAL CRY

bookouture

Published by Bookouture in 2022

An imprint of Storyfire Ltd.
Carmelite House
50 Victoria Embankment
London EC4Y 0DZ

www.bookouture.com

ISBN: 978-1-80314-847-2
eBook ISBN: 978-1-80314-846-5

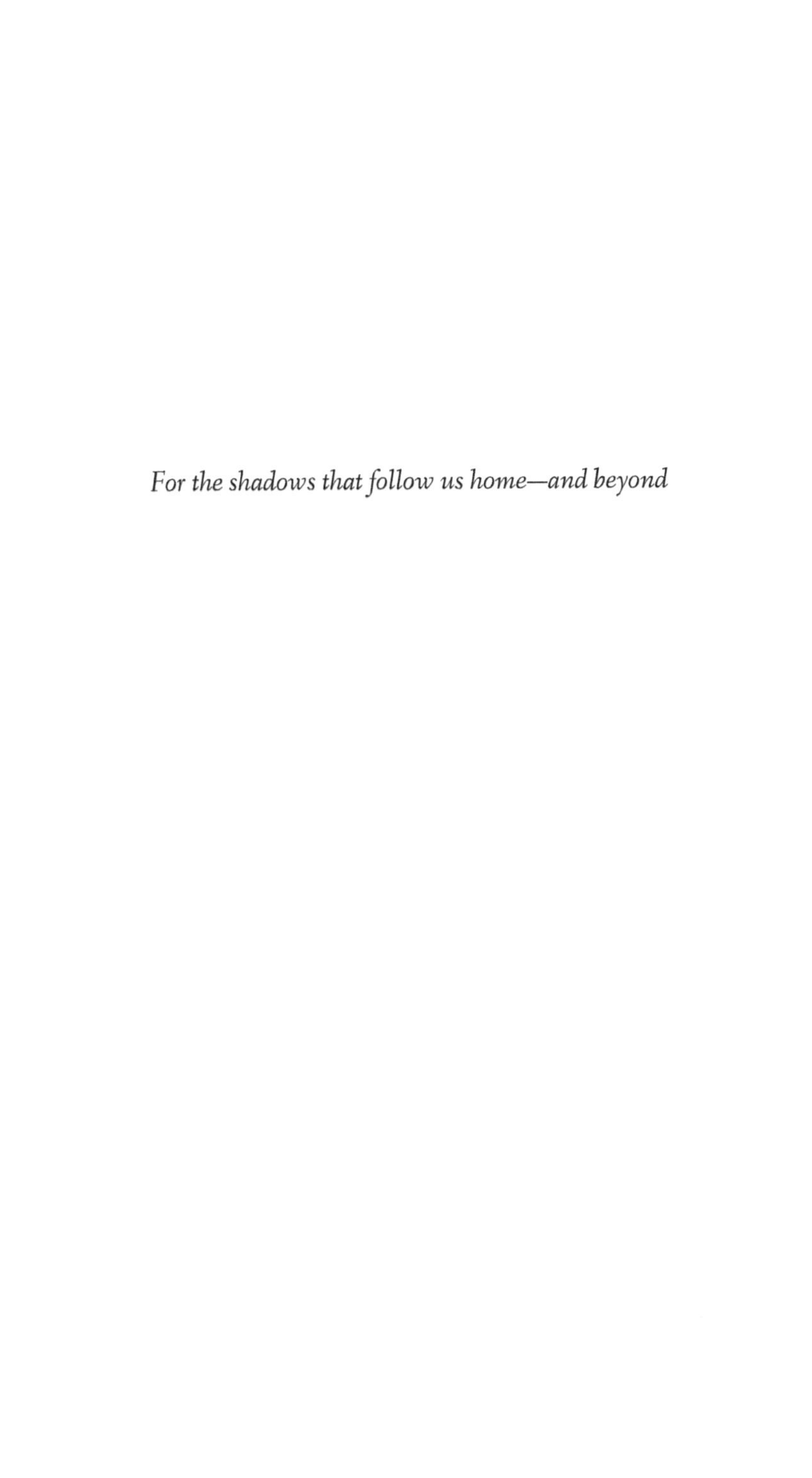

For the shadows that follow us home—and beyond

1

Sometimes I hear the whisper of death. In the breeze, in the quiet moments, in the beat of my own heart. I feel it ebbing and flowing, as life slowly ticks down. As it runs out. Most people take it for granted, the ignorance, the ability to forget mortality. But death is woven into my bones, the threads of it braided into my sinew, my soul painted with the blood of my father's victims. That's what happens when you're the daughter of a serial killer.

It's him I hear now, as I stand on the coast. On this nameless beach in Washington, the salty wind whips at my face. I couldn't escape him, no matter how far I ventured, no matter how hard I tried. There's a tether between us, my father and me. I'm back, standing at the edge of the world, where I was made to see if I can sever this connection for good, to bury my past so deep it would never be unearthed again. But what I see isn't hope, it isn't a future. In every shadow I see the darkness of my past. The words that follow me, the memories that haunt me. But I have to decide now if I will let them unmake me, if I will let those words, those demons, bring me down.

In my pocket, my phone vibrates, and I ignore it, as I have

for the past three months. My finger finds the button on the side by memory and presses it, ending the vibrations, killing the intrusion. I don't need to hear more about the unsolved cases of Officer Green and Chad Pearson. I wrap my arms around my midsection, holding my coat tighter as the cold wind reaches for me. But it does no good, this chill is too deep. It's already reached beneath my clothes, coiled against my flesh.

My feet crunch against the pebbles as I turn, my eyes following the rocky shore toward the line of pine trees that spring up as soon as the beach ends. Up and up the landscape goes, until it's all gobbled up by trees and I can't see anything other than a dark green blur of needles, moss, and branches. The difference between New York and Washington is stark, and I mark it in colors. In Washington, everything is green, save for the snow-topped mountain peaks the farther north you travel. While New York is gray, everything muted by a gauzy light that filters through endless clouds. Though the sky here is also clouded, the green shines through, brightening even the grimmest days somehow.

The vibration begins anew, and I sigh. This time I grab the phone, the cool metal hissing against my fingers. Sergeant Dirby's name flashes on the screen, and I accept the call. I promised during my sabbatical that at the very least, I would take his calls. And thus far, he's given me plenty of space.

"Durant," he says, unsteadily, as though he's not sure it's me that'll pick up the phone anymore. I pick apart his tone with more scrutiny, hoping to gather some evidence about his intrusion, but there's nothing.

"Sergeant," I say, in a tone that I hope puts him at ease.

"I need you to fly back to New York," he says, his words a cautious command. I imagine him behind his desk, his meaty brow furrowed as he contemplates how exactly to speak to me. Some men in law enforcement aren't sure exactly how careful they need to be with women on the force. I'd say Dirby is one of these men, as careful with me as he'd be with a quail's egg. But somehow from him it comes off as endearing, protective. It doesn't needle me the same way it does with others.

"Why?" I ask, needing more information to go on. I won't dig in my heels just yet and refuse him, but I wasn't planning to head back. I'm not done here.

"Lucas was working a cold case, and a new body was found in town, and he needs your help with it. He said that he's tried to call you several times—"

Lucas has actually tried to call me around a hundred times in the past month and a half, but I've ignored the calls. While I love my partner like a brother, *he* is not as careful with me as Dirby is, and I have half expected him to call me yelling, demanding that I come back and stop wallowing. Each time I've seen his name appear on the screen a kernel of anxiety has awoken inside me, and the only thing that extinguishes it is the little button on the side of my phone.

"Yeah, I know. I saw his calls," I say. I try to mask my sigh, but I'm sure he hears it on the other end of the call.

"So, will you come back? Needing help with the cold case was one thing, but we need you here—a girl died." There's pleading in his words, and guilt rises up inside me like the seafoam forming on the beach next to me. The waves push it closer to my boots, and I imagine each beat of my heart moving my guilt around my bloodstream in the same way.

I pause for a beat, then ask, "Does he really need me?" Lucas has a habit of not believing in himself. He's a very capable detective if he wants to be, but he has a codependent streak. Whether that's because his mother and grandmother disappeared when he was young, or because he lost the partner he had before me, I don't know.

"Yes, I'd say that he does. Two bodies were unearthed while a resort developer was breaking ground on a new hotel. Then, the body of a teenage girl was found dumped in front of the same piece of property. That's the only reason I agreed to step in here. If I thought that he could do this alone, I would have left you to whatever it is you're doing in Washington. But either you come back to help, or we we'll have to get someone else from the team to step in... Lucas really doesn't want that."

"Fine, I'll get on a flight as soon as I can," I say, wondering if he knew telling me about forcing a new partner on Lucas would light a fire under my ass. I of all people know how easily someone can be manipulated when you know what drives them.

I hang up the phone, my eyes sweeping the beach one more time. My past will have to wait. The shadows will have to follow me all the way back to New York.

2

NINETEEN YEARS AGO

There's a sickness inside me. The sour taste of it blooms from the pit of my stomach then pushes upward, propelled by the scene in front of me. The woman is bound to an old chair, the white paint flaking off the legs and the back, freckling the ground around her, like a bird that's lost its feathers. There's a gag in her mouth, though she struggles to scream around it, and the noise comes out strangled. Her nose is pointed, and curves downward like a beak. Tears stream down her face, drip, drip, drip from the tip of her nose. Her eyes are as wild as her dark hair, flitting from me to my father. And though I think I can hear her heart racing, it's probably just my own.

"Dad, please," I say, the words burning my throat on the way out. He asked me to save her. And I know what that means. When my father *saves* someone, he kills them because he thinks they're beyond the reach of anything else. In his twisted mind, putting these women out of their misery is saving them from something else, something worse.

"Harley, honey, it's the only way. She came to me for help, we need to save her. If we don't, she may be beyond saving one day."

Something cold and wooden meets my palm, and I look down to see a knife he's shoved into my hand. The weight of it hits me, hard. No knife should be so heavy, and I wonder if it feels weightier because of the choice he's trying to force upon me. A hard pebble of indecision forms in my throat and sticks there. Cold sweat prickles around my neck. I don't want to do this. And more, I don't want a father that tries to make me do this. I should have run as far away from here as I could when I had the chance.

The woman mumbles, her voice trapped by the cloth wedged in her mouth. At the corners it's wrinkled from all the attempts to speak, to scream. She sounds like a trapped animal and the sound of it claws at my mind. Tears spring to my eyes, and I imagine what she must feel like—what all my father's victims must have felt like. The smell of ammonia fills the room and liquid splashes onto the floor beneath the woman.

"I can't do this," I say, pushing the knife back toward my father.

He grabs my hand and holds it steady. I hadn't realized how much it was shaking. His grip is too hard, and I whine, afraid that my hand might crack beneath the pressure.

"You must, Harley Jane," he says, his words more of an order now. I look up at him, the ferocity in his eyes. There's a hunger there that scares me. And I wonder if someday I might end up on the sharp end of his knife, beneath his grip as he decides that it's time to *save* me.

"I can't do this. I can't," I say, trying to wrench my hand away, but he holds it so tight my bones aches beneath his grip.

He takes a step toward the woman, dragging me along with him. My eyes are fixed on the dirt floor and the puddle there. Soon, it'll be flooded with blood. My heart feels strangled as he tugs at me. Tears stab my eyes.

The woman sucks in a sharp breath as we grow closer, and I hiccup a sob. My chest tightens, and I wish I'd just let my dad leave. I should have just stayed with my mother and endured her hatred. Despite all her flaws, my mother would never thrust a weapon in my hand and ask me to kill someone. She'd never do *this*.

"Dad, please," I beg again, hoping that this time it'll do something. That somehow I'll be able to snap him back to reality. But deep down, I know I can't. My father is the one that can't be saved. He's too far gone. Depravity took him long ago when his blood was tainted by his first victim. I don't know who she is, who she was. But one day, I will learn all their names. And I will never forget them or what he did.

"Harley, I'll help you. It'll all be fine. I promise. The first few times, it's scary, but then it gets so much better. The adrenaline, the power. You'll see. And once you do, you'll understand that you are truly my daughter, that you and I are one and the same."

There's a madness in his eyes that scares me. Internally, I shrink away from it, because my body is frozen. With the grip he's got on my hand, I know I can't slip away. I can't even recoil. He raises the knife, our hands intertwined with the blade between them. The woman tries to scream, her voice smothered beneath the cloth, then it turns to sobs. Tears stream down her face. And I nearly choke on my own. She lets out a guttural noise, and her breaths come so quick, she sounds like an animal caught in a trap.

"Please, please, please, please," I beg, trying to yank my hand from his. But he won't free me.

My father's other arm wraps around my waist as he practically drags me forward. Something inside me snaps. Maybe it's a cord that's been fraying since I found out. This man urging me forward with a knife in our hands, this isn't my father. This is a broken shell of a man. Someone who has become twisted, and evil, and wrong. I need to get away from him, to run from this room and tell anyone who will listen what he's done.

The blade touches the woman's throat, and a sick smile appears on my father's lips. I screw my eyes shut, but the image of the woman, her terror, it's burned onto the insides of my eyelids. No matter how tightly I clench my eyes, I still see her. She may as well be tattooed there. She screams again, and warmth floods my hand. Finally, I'm able to wrench my fingers from my father's. I open my eyes, my fingers shining red. I stumble backward as the woman chokes.

I run up the stairs, my father's voice trailing after me. With my elbow, I turn on the kitchen sink, and plunge my hands under the water. A swirl of red water coils in the porcelain sink, and I wretch. My tears splash down too. I unleash it all. My guilt. My sorrow. My faith in this world.

He made me kill her.

3

It takes four separate planes to get from Washington back to New York to my apartment, just so I can pick up my things and then drive four hours south to New Paltz. Usually, New Paltz wouldn't be in our jurisdiction, but with homicides piling up, and the state being low on detectives, we're out on loan. This is as far south as I've been in New York, close enough to Manhattan that we could make a weekend trip out of it if we wanted to—not that we'll have time while we're working these cases.

From the info that was forwarded to me about Lucas's cold case, I've surmised that the skeletal remains of two women were uncovered from the ground on Ackert Farm a month ago. After searching the farm, they found evidence that the women may have been held captive on the property, in the root cellar. But the reason I was called out was because the body of a sixteen-year-old girl was found dumped in front of the farm two days ago.

I'm bone tired when I pull into the small motel. My new Jeep is low on gas, and so am I as I climb out and throw my duffel bag over my shoulder. At the other end of the lot, I notice Lucas's SUV, but I don't intend to see him until tomorrow. I'm still not in the right headspace. I feel like my demons rose to the surface in Washington and traveled all the way back here with me. If I see him now, I'll take my mood out on him—and though Lucas can handle me at my worst, he doesn't deserve that. Not after all he's been through. My eyes scan the lot and a bad feeling snakes up my spine. I feel like I'm being watched. I look up at the motel, trying to discern if someone is watching from a window. But nothing catches my eye.

Above me, the sky is gray, clotted with roiling clouds that warn of the rain to come. We're in the middle of July, and though I expected heat when I landed, the weather seems to be in the same mood I am. This time of year, upstate is a bit cooler, but the trees are all lush and full. I guess things are different the farther south you go. Full green maples and feathered pine trees flank the long building in front of me. A brick awning stretches from the front doors, and while I know it's supposed to look welcoming, it looks like the maw of a large creature, the two front teeth piercing the ground.

I approach the front desk, check in, and walk the seemingly endless hall to my room. The air smells like stale cigarette smoke, and somewhere in the distance the ice machine is churning. There's always a low hum in motels like this, whether it's the lights, the machines, or just the static of uncertainty that's in the air.

I unlock my door, throw my things on the bed, and glance around at my setup. All hotel rooms look nearly the same, especially when you're a detective that's given the bottom barrel of accommodations. The room opens to a small hallway. To my right is a bathroom, to my left a mini fridge and a microwave I'm sure doesn't work. Two queen beds are shoved up against the far-right wall, a nightstand with chipped paint standing in between them. The lights are all so yellow, I feel like I've stepped into the 1970s. Along the left side, I've got two chairs and a small table, a TV that's seen better days, and a desk.

As I grab my phone to consider my takeout options, it rings, a number I don't recognize flashing on the screen. The number is a New York area code, so I take the call, in case it's the New Paltz PD giving me a call.

"Detective Durant," I say as I slide the phone against my ear, then hold it there with my shoulder.

"Detective Durant, my name is Neal Lungrin. I'm an author, and I was hoping to speak with you," he explains.

"About what, exactly?" I ask, a bit taken off guard. In the past, I've had authors reach out to me to ask procedural questions for their upcoming novels, and I'm always happy to oblige if I have the time. But typically, I get an email. How did he get my cellphone number?

"I'm working on a book, and I was hoping to get your insight," he says easily, as if he's said this phrase a thousand times. How many other detectives has he called?

I plop down on the bed and take the phone away from my ear. I put it on speaker, then toss it onto the bed. If he's got questions about homicide work, this could take a while.

"Okay, what's the book about?" I ask. "And how exactly did you get my number?" I've always been careful with my cell, yet clearly some people manage to find it.

"I was a homicide detective in Washington and worked on your father's case. Well, it's about your father," he says. "And I was able to track down your number from a background check site."

I clear my throat as frustration ripples through me. "I'm sorry but I don't comment on works about my father," I say. This isn't the first call like this, and I know it won't be the last. By my count, there've been at least twelve books now about my father.

"Yes, I know you haven't in the past. But this is the first book that includes thoughts from your father's perspective. He talks about you a lot, so I wanted to give you the opportunity to give your side of the story."

Anxiety nags at me. What did he tell Neal? What did he say about our past? There are things that I've never told anyone, things that I'm not sure I could live with if they were made public. No one knows that I knew my father was a killer, that I saw him kill, that he tried to make me kill with him. Hell, he had my hand wrapped in his as he cut that woman's throat. I'm as guilty as him in her death. But no one knows that. I'd never be able to work again if anyone did.

"I could send you the manuscript…" When I don't respond, he adds, "Look, I have information in here that I'm sure you don't want public. If you don't work with me—"

I end the call and my rage grows. My breath catches, held tightly by anxiety. What do I do? I can't stop this book from coming out. But maybe I can control how much of the truth they learn about me.

4

There's a light knock on my door at seven in the morning. I've already been up for an hour, after a shitty night of sleep, waiting impatiently for one of the many coffee shops in town to open. A few times, I've almost been desperate enough to resort to the tiny coffee pot supplied by the motel, the bags of brown shards that look more like soil than coffee. But thus far, I've resisted and held firm. My body is out of whack from the time change, and I can only hope that the grip of jet lag releases me soon.

I look to the door, my eyebrow raised. Without opening it, I know who stands on the other side. I can imagine Lucas there, his hair a little longer, his face pinched as he glares at the peephole. This'll be the third case we've worked together. He's the only partner I've had this long, and it's become scary how well he knows me. I've never had anyone take my past well when they found out about it. That is, until I met Lucas. He found out about my father, what he did, and he didn't even bat an eye.

He knocks again, and this time I swear I can feel his exasperation in the gesture. I walk slowly toward the door, my mind going over what will happen. I unlock the door and open it, finding Lucas on the other side, his dark hair half in his eyes as he offers me a paper coffee cup with the name of a local shop splashed on the side.

"You come bearing gifts," I say as I take the cup. "How did you get this? They aren't even open."

"I know it's the only way to avoid dealing with your moods," he says darkly, but there's a hint of humor trailing on his words. "And yes, they are. This place opens at five. Your googling clearly was not thorough."

"You're hilarious." I test a sip of my coffee. It's rich and sweet, with the fiery taste of cinnamon. The velvety drink is enough to banish any of the dark thoughts I woke up with. That's the magic of caffeine.

"Thanks for coming back," he says, an edge to his voice. "But why were you avoiding my calls?"

I sigh and plop down on the bed, folding my right leg under me. "I just couldn't deal with anything from back here. I needed to focus on things. My head wasn't in the right place and I didn't want you to take it the wrong way." I was afraid I'd have to hear more about Chad and Officer Green.

"You don't give me enough credit," he says, and I know he's right.

I've spent my entire life building up walls, pushing people away, because at every turn, anytime I let anyone in, they completely abandon me or let me down. Everyone except for Lucas. He's been a constant, a good partner and friend. But old habits die hard, and I'm not sure even I know how to change at this point. My dad would say that if I built these walls, I can bring them down, but I'm not so sure. There's something addictive about control, about holding on so tightly that letting go feels foreign, wrong.

"Yeah, I know," I say softly. The admittance burns all the way up. "Want to talk about the case?" I ask, though I don't really have the energy yet. But I also can't talk about my failings anymore right now, or how I avoided him, or the minutia of why I avoided him.

"No, I want to talk about my new boyfriend, actually," he says, a lilt to his words. I turn around to face him. This is the first time Lucas has ever spoken to me about a boyfriend, minus the guy who broke his heart. I didn't even know he was dating; he rarely speaks about his personal life—and I understand why. Being a gay man of Korean descent on the force, it's not easy. The masculinity is so toxic in most stations it's incredibly off-putting.

"Well, tell me all about him," I say, waving my hand in the air for him to keep going when he doesn't spill all the details.

"We met online. I was nervous about meeting up with him because he's a little younger than I'd typically date. He's obsessed with *Law & Order*, so I was afraid he just wanted to feel like he was dating Stabler."

I laugh. "You're more of an Olivia."

He gives me a look. "Shut up."

"Totally something Olivia would say."

"Anyway," he snaps at me. "We're moving fast because it all just feels so perfect and right. So, obviously I'm waiting to screw it all up—since we know I inevitably will."

"Oh stop it, you will not."

He shakes his head. "Anyway... this case."

I take a sip of my coffee as I listen.

"Our vic, sixteen-year-old Mazie Winters, was found dumped in front of the farm where I've been investigating the cold case. It feels very... intentional. Like a warning," he adds. And I can't say that I disagree. It takes some major balls to dump a body at an active crime scene.

"What do you know about her so far?" I ask, taking mental notes.

"She was the sweetheart of this town. Sang in the church choir her whole life, daughter of the pastor, never got into any kind of trouble. I've talked to some of her friends and family, but no leads at all so far." He looks up at me. "And that's why you're here."

"Cause of death?"

"Still waiting on the official call, but it looks like she was strangled."

I nod. "Well, tell me about the cold case. I read the email, but what's your take?"

"It's really fucked up, Harlow. We believe these women were held captive for years. I don't even know for how long. There were newspapers in there from the nineties. We found the remains of children that look to be related to the woman that was held there buried nearby."

"Did you get DNA on the possible father from the children?"

He nods. "We logged the DNA, but so far we don't have any matches on it. One of the babies was buried as a newborn, and the DNA does not match the other children. So, we think she may have been pregnant with that baby when she was taken originally and trapped in the root cellar that was near the barn."

My heart sinks, and I cannot imagine what that woman must have gone through. "So, basically it looks like she was held captive for years, raped, and then had her children taken from her and killed?"

He nods slowly and sips his coffee again. "That's how it looks so far."

"Do we think this is the only time that he did this?" I ask.

"We're not certain on that. There's a lot of acreage, and it's very wooded. We're looking to see if there are any areas of interest where other bodies might be buried. However, a hotel bought the property. They're going to end up clearing all the trees and excavating most of the land. That should give us answers about what else might be buried there."

"Have they used GPR anywhere?" Typically in situations

like this, the forensics team would try to use ground-penetrating radar to see if there was anything else buried on the land. However, on a swath this size, that might not be realistic.

"Not yet, no." He shakes his head. "The team here doesn't have access, so we may need to call in a favor."

"Can we go out to the scene?" I ask.

He nods. "They don't start work out there until around nine, so we've got an hour to look at everything. There's not much left, but I can show you the pictures and then take you over there."

Lucas shows me the pictures on his phone, of a dark root cellar. It's clearly the basement of a barn. Then pictures of the inside. There's an old couch that looks like it's from the seventies shoved inside. There's a vent on the top of the shipping container, I'm guessing so that air could flow inside. A single light, the kind you'd usually see hanging from the ceiling in a mechanic's shop, dangles in the center. A tangle of extension cords twists across the floor, stretching to a space heater and a small fridge. The scene chills my blood, to know that someone was trapped in there and then buried.

"It looks like whoever was there was trapped for years," he says as I survey the images.

"God, that's awful," I say. He passes me another picture, next to the iron structure that marks the front of the farm. The pictures are of the newest victim, her dark hair splayed out around her, a purple gash across her pale throat.

"That's Mazie," he says, though I've already pieced it together.

As I stare at the victim, I wonder who would want to kill a girl like this, and dump her body—as what, a warning to us? A symbol of something far more sinister?

"What do we know about the farm?" I ask.

"It's odd. It's changed hands a lot. The farm is really the odd man out. All the others in the area have been owned by the same families for generations. A few were bought out by corporations. But this one has changed hands like an apartment. Brett Molina, one of the sergeants in town, his father owns the farm across from Ackert Farm," he explains.

"Did they see anything?" I ask.

He shakes his head. "They're all as surprised about the bodies turning up at the farm as anyone else. I spoke to all the adjacent farm owners and they're all really wondering why this is happening in this town."

That's what everyone thinks when murders happen in their small towns. No one ever thinks it can happen to them. But what I've learned, fast, is that this can happen anywhere.

It takes us about ten minutes to get from the hotel to Ackert Farm. We carve our way down a dirt road until it opens up to a gated property. An arch displaying the name of the property stands over the road. The wrought iron is aged, freckled with lichen. We stop and pull off the road, climbing out to survey a twenty-foot stretch of property that's cordoned off with caution tape. Tracks of footprints show me exactly where the teams moved, how they marked the crime scene, where her body lay when it was found. I take a few pictures with my phone, noting just how exposed this area is. Whoever dumped Mazie here, they wanted this body found fast—they wanted her seen. A killer that wants that much exposure, that's a very dangerous person. Another fact chills me to my core—the idea that if they're dumping bodies in plain sight, I don't think that type of killer is going to stop with one victim.

We climb back into the car and a chill prickles my spine as the pine trees tower above us on both sides, plunging the car into a flickering darkness. My Jeep sways as we roll over rocks and holes in the road. It feels like it takes forever for the road to open up, displaying a sprawling expanse of land. Directly in front of us, a large sky-blue house sprouts from the ground, the paint peeling, porches bowing like the entire structure is about to collapse. To the right of the farmhouse, there's a large barn, the doors yawning open.

To the left of the house, there's a path that leads to what looks like an orchard. Outside of the cleared yard that encircles the house, a forest rises up, gobbling up the rest of the land. Some of the trees have been cleared, an abandoned bulldozer standing at the edge of the tree line, like a sentinel.

"How did you connect the root cellar to the bodies?" I ask.

"We didn't at first. But the developer gave us permission to search the structures. I searched the house, then the barn, and realized there was something under it. It sounded very hollow when I was walking in there. In a stall, beneath some equipment, I found a trapdoor. I'll show you."

"Any chance that there are connections between the bodies found on the farm and the new vic?"

Lucas huffs out a sound of uncertainty. "Not likely, but it's way too early to know yet. A lot of years separate them though."

We walk together over the uneven ground. The sun is hot on the back of my neck, catching me off guard. The weather was much cooler in Washington. I've got to recenter my bearings—and adjust back to the difference. When we reach the barn, my feet thud hollowly against the wooden floor and I understand exactly what Lucas was talking about. Though the structure doesn't appear to have a basement from the outside, you can't hide the echo.

In the back corner, concealed in a stall, the door to the root cellar is wide open. A wooden ladder leads down into the darkness.

"Any power down there?" I ask. My real flashlight is back in the Jeep. My phone won't do much good if the space is huge.

"There are a few lights. It's dim, but there's enough to see," he explains.

I nod and head down the ladder first, then wait for Lucas to descend. He flips on the light and bathes the space in a soft orange glow. My eyes take a moment to adjust to the change. The walls down here are carved from dirt, the ceiling so low that I have to duck my head. Lucas is a full six inches taller than me, meaning he has to hunch down here to avoid hitting his head.

"Over here, that's where it looks like they spent the most time." He leads me to an alcove with an eighties-style floral couch, a dirt-covered shaggy rug, and a coffee table with only three legs. To the left of it, there's a mattress, and I inwardly flinch as I imagine our victims chained here. What horrors did these women live through? And more importantly, how many lived through it?

"Was there any blood on the shackles?" I ask.

"Yes. We swabbed it for DNA. It's been sent off to the team to match it, but as you know that's only useful if there's a sample in the database."

"Any missing women in town?" I ask as I look over a stack of *National Geographics* that are from nineties. I saw some of these in my library when I was in school.

He shakes his head. "Nope. This case isn't going to be that easy."

I was shocked to find how many open missing persons cases there were for women upstate when I took on my first case in Plattsburgh.

"You've searched the whole root cellar?" I ask.

"The forensics team did. I hung back while they searched. They didn't want me contaminating any evidence." He rolls his eyes.

"It's a dirty root cellar. This entire place is contaminated," I say, with an edge to my voice.

Whatever was here, whatever was found, even if there hadn't been years between when these women lived here and when they were buried—the entire place is so grimy, covered in dust, dirt, rat shit. If there was evidence here, it was lost a long, long time ago.

Back at the station, after lunch, Lucas's cell rings and he grabs it. After a short conversation, which I try not to eavesdrop on, he hangs up and looks over to me.

"Mazie's boyfriend wants to talk to us. He thinks that he may have some info about her death. I've got an interview set up with her best friend as well. She wanted to meet at a coffee shop downtown, so I'm going to have Langdon meet us over there," he explains.

I nod, feeling thankful that Lucas already set up some of these interviews. But as I think on it, I realize if he's already setting up these interviews, he probably didn't really need me here. I'm just acting more as a security blanket than anything else.

Twenty minutes later, we walk into the coffee shop, grab a couple lattes, and take our seats at a table in the back that'll be quiet enough for the interview. A few minutes after we sit down, a guy with shaggy blond hair comes through the door. He looks about sixteen, with rings in his nose and eyebrow. He's got jelly bracelets on his left arm, and a skull ring on his right hand. As he walks toward us, he straightens his button-up shirt—it looks like he dressed up specifically for our conversation.

"Are you the detectives?" he asks as he looks between the two of us.

"Yes, take a seat. I'm Officer Parks and this is Officer Durant," Lucas says as he introduces us, then motions for Langdon to sit across form us.

"Thanks for coming," I offer as he sits down. "Do you want anything to drink?"

He shakes his head. "I haven't really wanted to eat or drink anything since…" He trails off and his eyes lose focus.

"It will get better," I say. The first few weeks are the worst. That's what I hear anyway.

"I doubt that," he says.

"Do you mind if we ask you a few questions before you tell us what you know?" I ask. When he nods, I continue, "How long had you and Mazie been dating?"

"Since we were thirteen," he says.

I'm surprised that they'd been together for so long at such a young age. That's not common, and usually the early relationships are the most tumultuous.

"How did you meet?" Lucas asks before taking a sip of his coffee.

"Our parents were best friends. We grew up together. I've known her my entire life." He laces his hands together atop the table and stares down at them. I get the sense that he's trying to keep himself from crying. Desperately trying to hold himself together.

"Was Mazie having trouble with anyone at school? Did anything happen in the weeks before her death that was unusual?" I ask. I take a few notes on the little bit that we've gotten already. Though Langdon's keeping his emotions bottled up, I can tell exactly how torn up he is about her death—it's written all over his face.

He shakes his head. "No. Mazie got along with everyone. She wasn't fighting with anyone or anything like that."

"Any issues in your relationship?" Lucas asks, raising a brow as he appraises Langdon.

He shrugs one shoulder. "No."

The rest of his answers have been a bit more verbose, so this short answer catches me off guard. "Are you sure? Anything that you could tell us now will help us track down what happened to Mazie. That's what you want, isn't it?"

He looks up, his eyes red. "Of course that's what I want. But I have no idea what happened. That night we went to a party, and I heard that she was talking to some other guy—but I never found her. I checked the whole house. I searched for her. But I couldn't find her. If you check her phone, I texted her like fifty times trying to figure out where she was," he explains.

"Had you ever had problems with Mazie disappearing and talking to other guys before?" I ask. Mazie being unfaithful could be a motive.

He shakes his head. "No, that wasn't like her at all. I mean, she talked to her friends from school. But apparently no one knew who this guy was," he explains.

I make note of that. A strange man that no one else has seen?

The door jingles and a man strolls through. He's tall, broad, with dark hair and dark eyes. A thick beard covers his square jaw. His eyes are a little too wide set on his head. He glances from Lucas, to me, to Langdon before he strolls over.

"Langdon, what are you doing here?" he asks as he approaches.

"Dad, I was just answering a few questions about Mazie—"

"You're questioning my son without my permission?" he asks, the question clearly pointed at Lucas.

"Sergeant Molina, Langdon asked to speak with us. I understand he's eighteen, so we don't need—" Lucas is cut off by the sergeant raising his hand.

"It's a fucking courtesy to tell a fellow officer that you plan to question their kid." He reaches out and grabs Langdon by the collar and yanks him up from the chair. "We're leaving. Any other questions about my son need to go through me."

The two of them disappear through the door, and I take a sip of my coffee before I turn to Lucas. "Well, that could have gone better," I say.

"Did I miss some kind of unwritten rule?" he asks.

"An unwritten rule I didn't know about either," I add. Though I've never been in a situation where the child of a fellow cop was in a position to be interviewed. "You said their farm is across from Ackert Farm?"

He nods. "Yep, sure is."

"We should keep an eye on that then."

We wait at the coffee shop for Lily, Mazie's best friend, to arrive. Lucas elbows me when a tiny girl with a blue pixie cut comes in. She's got on a retro-style black dress with bright blue Converse high-tops. On her left wrist, she's wearing the same type of jelly bracelets that Langdon wore. She takes a seat across from us, her lips pursed as she sits down. Her whole body is taut as she adjusts herself atop the chair, her back too straight, her jaw locked. I'm used to seeing people look nervous before an interview with us—but she looks absolutely petrified.

I introduce myself and Lucas, then shift to some small talk to try and put her at ease. "Can I grab you something to drink?"

She shakes her head. "No, thank you. I just want to get this over with. How long will this take?"

"We'll try to keep it as short as possible," Lucas offers, and gives her a weak smile.

Though she keeps her hands in her lap, I can tell that she's fidgeting beneath the table. Her eyes dart between the two of us a few times before her gaze settles back on the table.

"How long had you and Mazie been friends?" I ask, figuring it's the easiest place to start.

"Our whole lives. No one new ever moves here. Everyone who lives here, I've known them forever," she says with an edge to her words.

"So would you say that you knew everything about Mazie?" Lucas asks.

She nods. "Of course I do. We didn't keep any secrets."

"Was she having any problems with Langdon?" The boyfriend is always the easiest place to start. Most women are typically attacked by a boyfriend, an ex, or someone else that was close to them.

"No. The two of them were a pretty boring couple," she says. "They didn't really fight. They never broke up. They'd been together the longest of anyone in our school."

"Langdon told us that the night of her death, Mazie was seen talking to a strange guy at a party. What can you tell me about that?"

Her eyes go a little wide. "No, there wasn't anyone strange at the party. It was at my house, and there were like twenty of us there. I'm in a lot of trouble with my mom right now because I had the party there—and I can't help but think that if I hadn't had the party, Mazie wouldn't be dead," she says, as she sniffles. Her eyes brim with tears.

I reach into my pocket, extricating a few tissues, then I pass them across the table to her. "None of this is your fault," I start.

"Asking yourself if you could have done something different, if you could have prevented this—it's not going to bring her back. And it's a very real possibility that it would have changed nothing. If someone had it in their mind already that they were going to hurt her, you couldn't have stopped them—not having the party wouldn't have changed anything, it just may have postponed it," Lucas says, picking up where I left off. He's always been better at soft skills.

She nods weakly and takes the tissues.

"So there wasn't anyone that you didn't recognize at the party?"

She shakes her head. "No, I would have noticed."

"Okay, can you tell me what you remember about the party then? Where Mazie was? Who she spoke to? Those sorts of things."

Lily sits a little straighter in the chair. "Well, she got to the party early. But she usually does so that we have time to talk first." She puts her hands atop the table and picks at her blue nail polish.

"What did you talk about?" I ask, making a few notes.

"She mentioned that she was a little stressed out. Her mom and dad had been fighting a lot. She was also annoyed because she was trying to get a part-time job at the burger shop and they told her that she didn't get the job," she explains.

"Anything else?" I press.

"Actually, she said she thought a car was following her on the way over. A pickup truck. But I think she was just being a little paranoid."

"Did she mention the color of the truck? A description of the driver?"

She shrugs noncommittally. "Not that I remember."

I run through the rest of my questions with Lily, but we don't really get anything else of note. She gives us a list of some of the other kids who attended the party so we can question them as well. I can't piece together yet who the strange man might have been that Langdon mentioned but didn't see himself —and who might have been following Mazie. The fact that a truck was following her on the way to a party before she died— that's not paranoia, that very well could have been her killer.

6

The next morning, we leave the city of New Paltz, driving east on highway 299 toward the Hudson River. Fields and rolling hills sprawl out between the small cities. It takes us twenty minutes, and a trip across the Mid-Hudson Bridge, to make it to the ME's office. This office is new to me. Our usual ME, Dr. Pagan, only services the northern counties. Down here, we have to go to Poughkeepsie. The office is hidden down a long drive, making it look more like we're going to someone's house for the holidays, rather than going to look at a body. After we twist down a winding road and pass several apartment complexes, we pull around the back to a squat brick building with a dingy roof.

The smell of astringent is so strong here I pick it up on the wind as soon as we step out of my Jeep. Lucas looks to me, his nose curling against the scent, and I know he smells it too.

"Lovely," he says with a sneer.

We've fallen back into step so quickly, as if I'd never left at all. We walk toward the ME's office, our feet thudding against the pavement. The chill in the air bites at me and takes my mind to my first case here in New York, the bodies found in the snowbanks. If we hadn't found the killer, this year might have brought more bodies hidden among the snow. I try to force the thoughts from my mind, but the image of a blue hand curling from beneath a pile of snow is burned into my mind, the women lost forever to the cold.

"You okay? You're really pale," Lucas says as he glances at me out of the corner of his eye. He stops me, his hand gripping my elbow as he drags me to a stop.

"It's nothing," I say, though I know I could tell him the truth. Lucas is the only person I've ever really opened up to who hasn't turned away, who hasn't abandoned me once he learned the truth about my past, where I really come from. I could dump my thoughts, my feeling on him. But then I'd just feel guilty, so I shake him off and decide to keep it to myself.

He puts a hand on his hip as he glowers at me.

I sigh and cross my arms. "Seriously, it's fine. Let's just go inside." When he doesn't turn toward the door, I walk in, knowing he'll follow me eventually.

The sliding doors open in front of me and a wave of astringent air hits me. It smells sterile, somehow stronger than most hospitals I've been inside. Lucas follows behind me as I walk into the waiting room. A receptionist checks us in, and a few minutes later Dr. Amelia Dushku comes to collect us. Dr. Dushku is a tall woman with tanned skin and large eyes. Beneath her open lab coat, she's got on a pink floral dress, which looks a little dressy for a morgue. She offers me a warm smile, then nods to Lucas like they know each other.

"Long story," he whispers to me as she waves for us to follow.

I follow behind Dr. Dushku until we turn into the morgue. In the middle of the room, there are three tables set up, with white cloths over each one. Though I can tell that there's something on the tables, two of them don't look like there's enough to be a body beneath the sheet. It's jarring. I haven't dealt with skeletal remains before.

"We'll start with the newest victim," she says, pulling the sheet back from Mazie's face. She exposes the corpse just enough to see her collarbones, shoulders, and face. Mazie has blonde hair, sharp cheekbones, and a nose that ends in a ball. A dark gash cuts across her neck, evidence of strangulation. Dr. Dushku confirms the details of Mazie's identity before moving on. "Initial cause of death is ligature strangulation."

"Any defensive wounds on the body?" I ask.

She shakes her head. "It doesn't look like she fought at all. Her blood alcohol wasn't high enough to account for blacking out or lack of struggle."

Could she have known her killer and that's why she didn't struggle? Did our killer come at her from behind?

"Anything else of note?" Lucas asks.

She shakes her head. "That's all we have so far. Should be a few more days before we rule the official cause of death and open her up. Let's move on to these." She motions to the other bodies.

Dr. Dushku gives us some of the details that we already know before pulling back the sheet on each table, revealing bones that are assembled into a skeleton atop the table.

"Obviously, as you can see, there's an advanced state of decomp here," she says as she signals to the bodies. "Both victims are women. The bones were still articulated, so we know that the bodies were not moved from their graves after decomp."

"What kind of timeline are we looking at here?" I ask.

"My best guess, these victims died at least ten years ago. So far, there's nothing indicative of their cause of death on the skeletons. No fractures, no head wounds." She looks over a clipboard as she lists off the details.

"Is it possible that they died of old age?" Lucas chimes in.

She shakes her head. "I don't think so with either of these victims. Based on the indicators we've got left from these skeletons, I'd say that they were both likely in their late twenties to thirties. It's hard to get more accurate than that since we're going off of degenerative elements on the skeleton."

"Does it appear that they were starved? Can we tell?" I feel a little out of my element here. I've never dealt with a case quite so cold that we were only dealing with bones.

"It doesn't appear so. The bones are in good condition. There's nothing indicative of starvation. They did find evidence inside the root cellar that the women were being fed and supplied."

"Is it possible that they were suffocated or strangled?"

"That could be possible, but it would be impossible to determine that with one hundred percent certainty with the evidence that we have," she explains. "There are indications on both skeletons that both women gave birth at least once before their deaths. There are no breaks. Nothing else really gives us much to go on."

I make a note of that. "Is there any indication of how long the bodies have been decomposing? Or when they might have been buried?" I ask.

"Unfortunately, the easy indications of time of death fade over time. Typically, if the remains have been buried for less than ten years, we'd likely still see some soft tissue remaining in areas of the skeleton. Especially with our hard freezes in the winter, that would slow down decomposition. Since we don't have those markers, my guess would be that we're looking at ten to twenty years based on the markers that I've found."

We finish up with Dr. Pagan and thank her for her time. The information will help us work out a timeline, but we've got a ten-to-twenty-year span of time that these women could have died within—and who knows how long before then they disappeared. How are we ever going to track down the identities of these women and find their killer?

7

All morning, Lucas and I talked to Mazie's parents. Tension and emotions were running too high, and we weren't able to get anything from them that was of any use. So, we've moved on, scouring the list of people that were at Mazie's party. We've gone through ten of them already, none of which saw the strange guy that Mazie may have left with—none of them saw a pickup truck either. We're holed up in the conference room, sitting at a table meant for twenty, but it's just the two of us taking up this enormous room. We dial the next number on the list, Jenny Hanson, a girl who goes to school with the rest of the bunch we've called. To my surprise, she answers on the first ring, like she was expecting us to call.

"Hello?" she says, tentatively.

I introduce myself and Lucas, then let her know that I've got her on speaker.

"Yeah, everyone told me that you've been calling. I figured it'd be my turn eventually. You're not going to tell my parents I was at the party—right?" she asks, and I hear her close a door. I imagine that she's giving herself a little more privacy in her room.

"No, we won't tell your parents about you being at the party. We'll do our best to keep you out of this as much as possible. We're just looking for leads on what happened to Mazie. Anything that you tell us could help, so it's very important that you don't leave out any details," Lucas says, laying it on thick. He's next to me, swiveling back and forth in his chair, his hand ready to take notes on a legal pad.

"Okay, good. I really appreciate that. Because they would kill m—" she starts, then gasps. "I mean... Oh God. I didn't mean... Ugh."

"It's okay. You don't need to be nervous," I say, trying to get Jenny to calm down a little bit.

"I'm sorry. I swear I can make myself calm down. This is just a lot." She pauses for a second, so I decide to jump in.

"Did you talk to Mazie the night of the party?" I ask.

"No, I saw her talking to Langdon and to Lily a few times, but I didn't talk to her. I was there with my boyfriend."

I make a few notes about that. "Did you see her having a fight with anyone?"

"No, I didn't see anyone fight with anyone else that night. It was a pretty low-key party. We barely had any booze."

"Did anyone mention that they were followed to the party?" Lucas asks.

She lets out a little laugh. "No, why would anyone be followed to a party?"

I skip over her question and continue. "Do you remember seeing any strangers at the party?"

"Of course not. That would have been weird," she adds, her voice getting a little shrill.

"Did you see Mazie leave?" I ask.

"Yeah, she got a ride with someone in a pickup truck," she explains.

My heart jumps at this. "Did you see what color the pickup truck was?"

"It was dark. Black, maybe? Or blue?"

"Did you happen to see who was driving it?" I ask, hoping that she at least saw enough to be helpful here.

"No, sorry." In the background, I hear someone calling Jenny's name. "Hey, I have to go. My mom needs me. But I hope that you find who did this. Sorry." She ends the call before I can ask anything else.

I look to Lucas, who raises a brow. "Well, at least we know it was a pickup truck."

We exhaust the rest of the list of the partygoers. A few others saw the truck, but no one else saw the stranger. I go over it all again and again in my mind. From what I've heard, Mazie didn't sound like the type to get into a car with a stranger. We need to get a list of all the pickup trucks in town.

8

Digging through land records first thing in the morning isn't my idea of a good time. But as we wait for the list of who owns pickup trucks in town, we don't have much other choice. In the basement of city hall, I feel entombed in dust. And I wonder if this is a bit like how the victims at the farm felt. It's not at all surprising that the town hasn't moved their land records online, but that doesn't make it any more convenient. Lucas coughs next to me and rubs his eyes.

"We have got to get out of here. I'm allergic to dust," he says, and I swear I can hear it in his voice. His words have become thicker, gruffer since we came down here an hour ago and started digging through the records. Lucas takes a sip of his coffee and clears his throat.

"It shouldn't take much longer," I say as I grab another box and shove the top off. So far, I've got the name of one property owner of Ackert Farm. But since we don't know how long ago exactly the women were held captive and died, I need to get all the records going back at least fifty years. That's the problem with cold cases. With years of owners, and so many possibilities about when these women might have been killed, it's going to be incredibly difficult to nail down a killer. Or even a timeline.

"So, what were you doing in Washington?" Lucas asks, and I can feel him staring at me as I flip through the files.

I raise a brow at him without looking up. I don't remember telling him that I went to Washington. I only told Sergeant Dirby. After solving two serial-killing cases for the New York State Crime Bureau, I felt like I'd earned the time off. Though that's not something I'd typically admit to Lucas. I've always tried to work the hardest, to prove that I'm more *in this* than everyone else. But where has it gotten me? The guilt hasn't subsided.

"Trying to find some closure," I say, the honesty surprising us both. For years, this is the kind of thing I'd bottle up, wouldn't tell anyone about. My sergeants always knew my history—because they had to. My name changes and frequent moves were detailed on all my forms. But I suffered through everything else myself. It still feels weird to let someone else share in my burden. I've always told myself this was something I had to do on my own. I didn't deserve help. There's blood on my hands, after all.

"Did you talk to him?" he asks as he sits up straighter in his chair. He leans closer to the table. His eyes are wide with interest.

I shake my head as I yank a file from the box and throw it on top of the growing stack on the table. A puff of dust flies toward Lucas, and seconds later he sneezes again.

"No, I haven't worked up the nerve yet. Maybe I don't need to talk to him," I say.

"Do you want me to go with you after this case is all over? I will," he offers, and I look up at him.

His words catch me off guard, and it takes me a few seconds to figure out what to say. "I don't know yet. Maybe. But thank you."

He nods but thankfully doesn't continue to press the issue or ask again.

"How's the boyfriend?" I ask.

He smiles widely, and I know I've asked the right question to get him off the topic of my dad. As I continue to dig, he gives me a brief overview of how he met his boyfriend and how close they've gotten in the last couple months. To me, it sounds like they're moving at light speed, but that may also be because I'm allergic to commitment.

"So, are you thinking that you're going to move in together or something?" I ask after he tells me that they're spending almost every day together anyway—or they were before this case.

He scoffs. "I don't know that I'm ready to settle down like that. It's going to take a lot for me to commit to having someone in my space all the time."

A smile cracks my lips. "Oh, so I'm not the only one with commitment issues."

He huffs a laugh. "I don't think there's anyone on this planet that would minimize what you've got going on"—he motions up and down my body—"and would call it issues. Oh honey, it is so much deeper than that. They could write a whole book on your situation." His statement makes me realize I haven't told him about the book. I gave him the Cliffs Notes about it.

I roll my eyes at him. If I didn't fully own the wall that I built around myself, I'd probably feel offended by his comments. But he's right. I learned early on that it's better to shut everyone else out, to protect yourself at all costs. Because I'd rather be the one to hurt myself than to let someone else do it. I won't give someone that power over me—not again.

Once my stack is several files high, I flip through the dates, and realize we've probably got enough to get started, but there are years missing. At the very least, this will give us a few people to question regarding the property. Because the farm hasn't been occupied in years, is it possible that someone was using the root cellar and the property owner didn't know?

"I think we've got enough to get started," I say as I scoop up the stack.

"Oh, so we're done talking about your commitment issues then?" He raises a brow at me.

"Yup. I guess you could say I'm not willing to commit to the topic right now." I shove the folders in my bag, then sling it over my shoulder. The weight of the files and my laptop makes it dig into my flesh. But I push through the discomfort as I walk toward the door. "We should probably look in the database too to see if there are any missing persons that could match the timeline of when these victims disappeared—once we nail down the timeline, that is," I say, as I start to make a mental checklist of all the things that I need to do.

Lucas and I finish up at city hall, but even once we're outside, I swear I feel a film of dust coating my skin. Drizzle ticks against the ground as we walk toward my Jeep. Lucas's pace keeps picking up. I know he hates getting wet—but I don't mind the light rain. Somehow it's comforting, maybe because this was the background static of my childhood. While nothing else remained constant, the gauzy gray sky and the light patter of rain was something I could always count on. Water droplets freckle the pavement as we walk.

"Cold cases are really something," Lucas says as we climb into the Jeep. He nestles himself into the passenger seat, buckling himself in.

I grunt acknowledgement to his comment before I push the start button and shift the vehicle into gear.

"I don't think I would have made any progress if you hadn't come back," he says, and I feel like he's pandering.

"Yes, you would have. It might have taken you a little bit longer, but you're a good detective. You don't *need* me here," I say, though the words needle me. It's times like this, I feel like Lucas is fishing for compliments because he doesn't have faith in his own skills. I'll prop him up however I can, but at the end of the day, he was right beside me solving our other cases. It wasn't all my work that did it.

He continues to talk about his uncertainty with the case as I carve a path across town back to the New Paltz PD headquarters. I turn up the long drive that leads to the squat police department. The building is much longer than it is tall, with gashes cut along the side where windows are inset. The style of the building is a departure from the historic architecture everywhere else in town. It looks like the type of building I'd see in Texas, meant to be a school auditorium, not a police department.

Once inside, we pass a small receptionist desk, then walk through the bullpen. I'm pleasantly surprised to find the team in New Paltz is more diverse than some of the other teams we've worked with farther upstate. There are four women on the team, one of which—Isabelle Ortega—is a sergeant. That, at least, I hope makes our time here a bit easier. There's always some tension working with other teams from different jurisdictions. Every team has its own dynamics, the way they like to do things, and when we are brought in from the state, it feels like we're intruding, we're taking something away from them. We deal with everything from general distrust to outright hate from these teams. But my hope is here, things might be a bit different. On the other side of the room, I see Brett Molina, looking out at us from his office. I'm still frustrated that he stopped our interview of Langdon, but so far, no one has said a single negative word about the kid—so for now, I'll leave it be.

We pass rows of desks with small cubical walls built between them. The bullpen is wide open, and right now it's about half-full. Along the outside walls, there are doors every fifteen feet or so, leading to what I imagine are offices, interrogation rooms, and conference rooms. There are a few officers congregating in the far-right corner, all talking to one another. But their attention isn't on us. Ortega is on the phone when we walk past, but she nods and offers me a smile.

When we get to the back-left corner, I find Lucas's desk, which has already been set up with a few of his things, and my desk, still empty. I throw my bag down and take a seat. Lucas looks at my sad station and frowns.

"I was going to get you a plant or something—"

"But you didn't, because you knew I'd kill it?" I ask, trying not to laugh. I'm not good at keeping things alive. I think it should be good enough that I'm keeping myself alive.

"Well... I didn't want to say it. But yeah."

I laugh as I extract my laptop from my bag. "Hopefully we won't be here long enough for that to matter," I say, though I don't know how hopeful I am that it'll be the case. Some cold cases sit unsolved forever, some take years. I'm not sure how long we'll be able to stick to this case before something new comes down the line for us. With Chad no longer being in the picture, and our team down to four detectives, the New York State Crime Bureau is running low on resources—we just have to do the best that we can with what we've got. "Okay, so we need to dig into the database to see what we've got on missing persons," I say as I log in on my laptop and pull up the database.

Lucas already has his laptop out and he's typing his login into the screen. "Okay, so what exactly are we looking for? What we've got from the ME..." he says as he pulls out his notebook and starts to skim over his notes. "Victims were possibly held from the seventies. These victims had been dead for at least ten years. So, we're looking for women that disappeared, when?"

"I guess if there's evidence from the eighties or nineties, we've got to just start there and work our way forward. Obviously, we're not looking at anyone that had a report filed after the late nineties, because the timelines wouldn't match," I say. Knowing exactly how many files we saw in Plattsburgh during the short time we were there a few months ago, I can only imagine how many files we're talking in a few decades' worth of time. Unfortunately, during the seventies and eighties, so many women disappeared, and they were completely written off. Many died, were killed, kidnapped—it was the height of so many serial killers—but it went largely ignored by law enforcement, because they thought nothing of women disappearing. Looking back at these files, I know we're going to see so many references to women *running away*.

"Want to start with the early eighties, and I'll start with the late nineties, and we can work our way toward one another?" he offers.

I nod. "That works for me," I say, relishing the fact that I have a competent partner. For years, I dealt with men who second-guessed every decision I made, did not pull their weight in investigations, or were downright assholes to me every chance that they got, so I will never take Lucas for granted. We might fight, but I'm thankful every day that I'm working with him and not some other asshole on the force. It was hard for me to trust Lucas in the beginning—I've never trusted anyone—but he has earned it.

We spend several hours pulling up all the missing persons files in a one-hundred-mile vicinity to New Paltz. Though it's possible that our killer traveled farther than that, for now, there are so many records to chase down this close to us, I think that it's best to start here and rule some of these women out before we move on to the next one-hundred-mile bucket. I pull up the DNA profile from the ME on our victims and rule out anyone that isn't within the racial group that we'd expect. That leaves us with about seventy possible victims that all disappeared in the eighties. That's still quite a few possibilities.

I glance around the room. Ortega is still on the phone, but

the group of officers that had been talking when we walked in has dispersed.

"I'm going to go see what they can tell us about the property," I say, as I motion to the front of the bullpen.

Lucas nods, then turns his attention back to the stack of printouts in front of him. He's shuffling through all the potential victims, cataloging them in his mind, I'm sure. Before I met Lucas and we worked our first homicide together, he worked in missing persons. Focusing on these women who've been missing for years, it ignites something different inside of him than it does me. It's much more personal for him, since his mother and grandmother disappeared when he was a kid. Every officer gets into this business for a different reason. For me it was trying to reconcile my father's crimes, trying to absolve my guilt; for Lucas, it's trying to make sure no other kid feels the same pain that he did. He's doing it for the right reasons; I'm like Constantine trying to buy his way back into Heaven.

Eyes follow me as I walk across the bullpen toward the other officers. They're all stationed at their desks, but they sit close together. From what Lucas has told me so far, these guys are Officers Nolan, Bryan, Chapman, and Warner. They all look so similar they look like carbon copies of one another. If you put these four men in front of me in a lineup, I'm not sure I'd be able to tell them apart. They've all got the same square jaw, close-cut haircut, hazel eyes that are a little too close together. In small towns like these, sometimes the features all start to become a little too homogenous, as if everyone has interbred too closely over the past two hundred years.

"Durant," one of the guys says as I approach. He nods to me before offering me what I assume is an attempt at a smile.

"We're working on the case over at Ackert Farm," I explain, though they already know what we're doing here.

They all nod, like bobbleheads. "Yeah, we know." The guy stands up and I see that he's got the name Nolan stitched onto his uniform. At least the name tags will help me tell them apart. "What do you need?"

"What can you tell me about Ackert Farm?" I ask. If I can get some background from the locals or their thoughts on the farm, that could at least point us in the right direction.

He crosses his arms as he leans against his desk. The other guys are silent as they look between me and Nolan. "It's been there forever. Not so much a farm as it is an apple orchard. I think that farm already existed when New Paltz was founded, honestly. It's been passed around a lot in the past thirty years or so. There was a guy who owned it when I was a kid, but he moved to Florida, I think? Since then, it's never really prospered. Different people keep buying the property trying to get it going again, but it's just never regained the glory it once had."

"It was an apple orchard?" I ask.

He nods. "Mostly, yeah. I think they tried a few other things, but apples were what grew best there."

I make a mental note of that. "Do you remember any stories of women that went missing here in town in the eighties or nineties?" I know I should probably ask some older members of the town, but for now, these guys will have to do. Every town has ghost stories, cautionary tales about how someone went missing, so hopefully they would have heard these stories.

The guys all shake their heads. "No, nothing like that. Nothing bad ever happens here," Chapman adds.

"Yeah, no one in this town is capable of *that*," Bryan pipes up. "I bet someone from another town came in and planted those bodies here, and just made it look like there was something fucked up happening here."

"Exactly, this is a nice, small town. Things like that don't happen here," Nolan says.

Frustration ripples through me. This right here is the difficult thing about working in these small towns. They think that they're somehow immune to the problems of big cities, that these things *can't* happen here.

"All right, thanks for your help, guys," I say, as I notice that Sergeant Ortega is finally off the phone.

I walk across the room to her desk, and she nods at me as I approach.

"Durant, I presume? I heard that you'd be in the office with Detective Park," she says as she gives me the quick once-over.

I nod. "Sergeant Ortega?" I verify, though I already know who she is. I looked over the directory of the officers here before coming to the town.

"That's me," she says as she leans back at her desk and pushes her chair back a bit. She's got long legs. She's wearing sleek chinos that flare at the bottom around her boots. "What can I help you with? I imagine the guys weren't much help." She glances over to them. They make eye contact with her, then turn around to face their computers.

I nod. "I was trying to get some background on the Ackert Farm. I wanted to know if there was anything we should know about the property or about the owners," I say.

"Let me guess, they think that no one in this town could have possibly held women captive and murdered them?" She raises a brow, and it looks like she's stifling a laugh.

"You're exactly right." I assume that she overheard part of the conversation while she was on the phone.

"Do you want to grab a cup of coffee? I can give you some background."

"Sure," I say, then motion toward my desk. "Let me just grab my jacket." It's still drizzling outside, and I need my wallet.

I grab my things, let Lucas know where I'm going, then meet Sergeant Ortega at the door. She's got on a leather jacket as she leans against the doorframe. We leave the station together, and she doesn't start to talk again until we're in the parking lot.

"Village Station is the best coffee around here, and it's about a five-minute walk, unless you'd like to drive?" She motions toward the gray sky.

I shrug. "I'm from Washington, so this is walking weather for me."

She lets out a laugh. "What brings you all the way out here?"

"Oh, you know, couldn't wait to get away from my parents when I was a kid, so I got as far away as I could," I say. It's not technically a lie, but it's enough of the truth that the words come out easily. It's a statement that I've found most people relate to enough that none of them really question me on it.

"I was the same way, but I grew up in Miami, moved to Manhattan when I was eighteen. I thought I was going to become a Broadway star." She rolls her eyes and lets out a little laugh aimed at her youthful naivety. "Can you imagine? I couldn't sing, I couldn't dance, yet somehow I thought I was going to be on Broadway? It was ridiculous." We weave our way through the parking lot toward a carved path that leads toward a street. "Anyway, I moved up here and lived with my aunt for a while, figured out pretty quickly that showbiz wasn't for me, and eventually found my way into law enforcement. I hated all the politics working in NYC, so I figured maybe moving upstate would improve things a bit."

We turn left onto a small street that's lined with brick buildings. Small storefronts stare out at us, a tailor, a bakery, a hobby shop. This must be the beginnings of the downtown stretch of New Paltz. On the corner a large wood-frame church stands overlooking the entire street, casting a jagged shadow across it.

"And did it?" I ask as I glance between the businesses, trying to take them all in and learn the lay of the land.

"It did a bit. I never would have made it to sergeant. It takes so much bullshit for women to succeed there. But at least here things are a bit better. Chief Davenport has been great to work for, so it's kept me around."

That gives me a bit of hope. Most of the offices I end up having to work in are testosterone-fueled cesspools that are incredibly toxic. They treat Lucas and me like shit, and do the absolute bare minimum to help us. You'd think with the haste they want us out of their towns that they'd put a few resources behind us, but that's never the way that it works out.

"How long have you been in New Paltz?" I ask.

"About seven years," she says. "Moved here around the time my daughter was born."

"Oh, you have a daughter?" I hadn't noticed any pictures on her desk.

She pulls out her phone and shows me a few pictures. "That's Ellie. She's one of the other reasons I moved here, but that's a long story. So anyway, I know the guys weren't helpful. What can I help with?"

I'm glad that she wasn't born in this town. I know that at least will make it more likely that she'll help us, and not believe the best of the town and the people that are in it.

"I was trying to find out if there'd been any stories about women going missing in town, any stories about the farm," I say, trying to sum up what I asked the guys about.

She nods. "I probably didn't hear a lot of the stories that they heard growing up, because obviously I didn't spend my childhood here. While I've been in town, I've never heard of anyone going missing. But back in the nineties there was a guy who was arrested. Vick Langley. He tried to kidnap a girl in town. It was pretty close to the farm actually. He sexually assaulted two girls that we know of, but I've suspected there were more."

That timeline could line up with when these women possibly disappeared. I've heard of nothing else like this and I find it interesting that the guys just glossed over it.

"That's terrible. What happened?" I ask.

She sighs. "Thankfully, the girl was able to get away. She went home and told her parents what happened and Vick was arrested."

"Where's he locked up?" I make a note of his name and the date. I'm going to need to talk to this guy if I can.

"He was over in Franklin County. He got moved a couple years ago. He got released recently. Not sure where he is now."

I raise a brow at that. "Released? When?"

"Two or three weeks ago. I think."

"Do you think he could have been responsible for the bodies on the farm?" I wonder if this could be related to Mazie. Was she a kidnapping gone wrong?

Her brows furrow as she considers. "It's possible. But I don't know if he was behind it. I was too young back then."

"Is there a way to find out where he is? I'd like to know if he was close enough to town to have the opportunity to kill Mazie," I say.

She nods. "I'll see if I can find anything on him."

The smell of coffee fills the street, and Isabelle opens the door to the coffee shop for me. In a few minutes, we leave with lattes and turn back out onto the street. But to my surprise, we don't head straight back to the station.

"There is something else I have heard from my daughter. I didn't really take it seriously. I thought it was just kid stuff. Now though, I have to wonder..." She trails off before taking a sip from her cup.

I take a swig of my coffee as I listen, and I'm pleasantly surprised by how strong the brew is. I'm anxious for her to continue, but I don't want to pressure her to spill the story. Isabelle looks like she's going to be a great resource for us, unlike the guys back in the station, and more than that, I have been desperate to find another woman in law enforcement to talk to.

"There were stories about the farm, urban legends that kids

talked about, that if at night you went into the woods and were quiet, you'd hear women crying. Sometimes they'd whisper. Sometimes they'd scream. They said if you were out too late at night, you'd become trapped in those woods," she says.

The story chills me because I wonder if it's rooted in some truth. Were they hearing the women that were trapped in the root cellar scream? Were they hearing their whispers, their cries? Did someone go missing in those woods long ago and they ended up trapped in that cellar? Stories like that always start somewhere, and I'm going to find out where this one began.

"I always thought it was just one of those campfire stories, you know?" she asks.

I nod in response, though I know she doesn't really need an answer from me. "Yeah, I don't know that I would have put much thought into a story like that either. It's like their version of Bloody Mary," I say.

"Exactly. But now I really wonder if there was something more."

Maybe tonight after dark I'll go out there, I'll listen, and see if I can hear anything in the woods.

Night thickens around me, and Lucas thinks that I've gone insane. We leave my Jeep at the end of the long road that leads up to the Ackert Farm, or what was the Ackert Farm before they began clearing the property out as they try to turn it into a resort. The moon is full above us, casting long shadows from the spindly trees around us on the ground. Though we're firmly in the middle of summer, there's still a bit of a chill in the air tonight. The cicadas trill in the trees, creating a strange chorus that rises and falls with the breeze.

"All the rain today made it so muddy," Lucas says as he pulls his boots from the mud. Every step he takes is loud, as the wet earth creates suction around his shoes.

"Yeah, I should have just driven up here," I say as I glance back at the winding path behind us.

"Well, at least I'll get my steps in," he says as he glances to his smartwatch. "What do you think we're going to find in here again?" he asks.

Ahead of us, the woods part, and there's a clearing. To the left stands what remains of the large farmhouse. An apple orchard stretches behind it. To the right, backhoes, tractors, and other large machinery sits abandoned—since this is all still a crime scene. For the moment, all construction has had to stop, at least until we're sure that we've gathered all of the evidence to be found here. I think we've got another week before they can begin clearing the property again. To our right, stretching beyond the clearing, is a thick forest of pines and evergreen trees. In total, the property is nearly three thousand acres, and while some of it was cleared for the apple orchard, most of the property remains heavily wooded. I stare out at the trees, wondering what secrets they're keeping. A breeze rustles them, tousling the feathered branches, as if they're trying to answer the questions that are forming in my mind.

"Sergeant Ortega told me that a guy who tried to kidnap a girl in the nineties just got released. I'm wondering if he had something to do with Mazie's death. She also told me some ghost stories about the property, so we're out here to see if there's any truth to it," I say, feeling ridiculous as I say the words out loud for what must be the fifth time. He's trying my patience, but I know why he's doing it. He wants me to know exactly how stupid he thinks all this is. And that's fine, because regardless, I would still be out here, investigating the information that was given to me.

"Uh-huh," he says, as we continue walking toward the clearing. "So are we going to walk the entire woods or..."

"No, we're not. We're probably just going to be out here for an hour. But if you don't be quiet, then we'll never get back to the hotel. So shush," I say. Lucas is the kind of person that needs to fill silence. Quiet makes him uncomfortable, so he's always asking questions, pushing to make noise. I'm the opposite, but maybe that's because of our childhoods. Mine was filled with noise, with arguing. His was filled with silence, sadness.

We carve a path around the barn, and I glance at the ground where I know the root cellar waits. I imagine the opening peeks out from under the house, looking like the maw of a beast. A chill sneaks under my skin as I think about it all again, the reality of what these victims lived through, how they suffered. We don't know for sure how long they were confined to that root cellar, the trauma they endured there. What kind of monster does that? Who holds women captive for years, abusing them? I think that's what scares everyone in town, the fact that they may have lived with someone capable of such evil, that a monster lived among them their entire lives, and they never noticed the evil that bloomed in their city, the darkness it harbored. In that way, killers always make us question ourselves. What else we may have missed? How close did we come to death? Mortality is a clock that one of us learned to read, but we can all hear the seconds ticking down.

I catch Lucas's eye before we turn toward the woods. And I finally pull a flashlight from my pocket. As we approach the line of trees, I click the light on, stretching the shadows in front of us, straining my eyes. We weave between the trunks of the trees, the pines tickling our arms as we pass.

Lucas stays behind me as I lead. The farther I walk, the more the cicadas rise in their harmony. And though I listen, I don't hear whispers. I don't hear cries. I wish that the voices of the victims would rise in the night and tell me their stories. I wish they'd tell me what happened to them, who did this to them. Their stories were buried with them, and I hope that in time I'll be able to unearth the truth.

9

NINETEEN YEARS AGO

I have to find out the truth. I need to know what he's done. These lies have lived inside me for so long that they've taken on a life of their own, and I don't know how to escape them. They've shaped me, and when I look at myself in the mirror now, I don't see the Harley I was before my dad put a knife in my hand. That blood spilled down my fingers, and it made me into someone else, a monster. I'm just like him, that's what he wants, and even if I don't want it—he's going to make me like him. He wants me to be a killer.

Sickness still wells inside me as I sit on my bed. They're both gone right now. At some fucking dinner party, trying to pretend like our lives aren't a trash fire. No one sees who he really is. No one but me. And it's slowly killing me. The truth, the blood, the bodies. Over the years, I've looked up a few of the women that my father *saved*, his patients. He's a psychologist and thinks that the only way to save some women is to kill them. He's putting them out of their misery, because if he didn't, they'd just suffer for the rest of their lives.

He's an angel of mercy. That's what I found on the internet, anyway. There are different types of killers, and doctors or nurses that kill their patients are a specific type of killer. I guess that's what he is. The thought of it, the reality of it all, still makes me nauseous.

There's an itch in the back of my brain. I need to know the truth, everything that he's done. Because I feel like somehow, if I see their names, if I see everyone he's killed, maybe that will change something. Maybe then I can convince everyone that he's a killer.

Guilt and sadness slice through me. Because I know what this really means. If I turn my father in, if I tell the police what he's done, he will go to prison. I'll never see him again, and I'll be stuck with my mother. My choice is blood on my hands or a mother that hates me. I guess I'll choose my mother.

I push up from the bed as my heart races. Sweat slicks my palms as thunder cuts the night. Thunderstorms in Tacoma aren't common, and it catches me off guard. I don't know if it's a warning or the universe cheering me on. Either way, I can't stop now. I have to do this. I have to. I stalk downstairs, into my father's office. My pulse is so loud it beats in my ears like a drum. They left an hour ago, so I know I should have two hours that are safe, two hours before they even think about leaving their friend's house. But anxiety eats away at me, the questions, the warnings in the back of my mind.

What if they leave early because my mom doesn't feel well? What if they leave because of the storm? What if... what if... what if he finds me? What if he kills me? What if?

I try to slow my breathing as the questions ricochet around in my mind. I can't stop them; I know that already. But if I can just slow them down so I can think, so I can focus... That's what I need to do. First, I check the drawers in my father's desk. Then his bookshelves, the closet. But there's nothing here. If nothing else, my father is fastidious, so I'm careful to put everything back exactly where I got it from. After I check all the obvious places, that's when my heart rate starts to slow, that's when my mind finally awakens.

I check under the couch, under the desk, behind the bookshelves. And then finally, I find it. In a hidden panel behind his TV, that's where it's stashed.

I run my hand along the cracked leather binding of a small, worn notebook. My mouth goes dry as I consider what's inside. I plop down on the floor, the book in my lap, and it feels so heavy. But how can something so small have so much weight to it? Half of me is desperate to know what's inside—while the other half of me just wants so badly for my father to be someone, anyone, else. Why can't he just be a normal father? Why does he have to be a killer?

Finally, I force myself to open the book, to look at the pages inside.

Names. It's all their names. And dates. They go back years, so many years. The first name is Brianna Addams, 13 July 1979. That's all that it says. The first one. I skim the dates, until I find the woman from the basement, Cassie Edwards.

My tears stain the page.

Death feels so different when you can attach a name to it. My mind wants to fill in the blanks. I want to know who she was, where she was from, and the life that she left behind.

When I see it laid out like this in front of me, I don't know how my father could have done it. He knew these women, he heard their stories, he knew about their lives. How could he have done it? How could he have killed these women?

10

There's something about sitting in an abandoned office that really makes it feel like the investigation is getting real. Maybe it's being alone with my thoughts, maybe it's something else. But with the stack of three names in front of me, the previous owners of the farm, I feel like we've got a path to walk down. We've run out of leads on Mazie, questioned all her friends, her family—but it's gotten us nowhere. Until we find out something about Vick, we've really got nothing to go on. And as of yet, Ortega hasn't found anything on him. There are several posts up online asking the public to come forward with details if they saw anything. Though I've requested the list of everyone in town with a pickup truck, it's taking forever to get that back.

Lucas shoves in through the conference room door. He's got coffee in each hand, sweat beading on his brow. The way he looks at me, you'd think he ran a marathon with the coffee. The fact that he went out to get us coffee at all is an improvement. When we first worked together in Plattsburgh, he wouldn't risk drinking coffee from a shop because the other guys on the force would give him shit for it.

"Doing all right?" I ask him as I raise a brow.

He shoves one of the cups toward me. Once I take it, he says, "You try climbing three flights of stairs with two cups of coffee."

"I offered—" I start, but he holds up his free hand, cutting me off.

"Yes, I know." He shakes his head. "It was my idea, so I'm just not going to complain." He takes a slow sip of his latte and sits in a seat across from me.

The conference room table stretches between us. On the wall, I've got my laptop screen projected, so Lucas and I can easily look at the same information as we go through the folders. Out in the bullpen, I hear the first signs of life, and I know that my secluded morning is over. There are only brief moments of quiet when you work in law enforcement, when there are shift changes, early in the morning, or too late at night. Otherwise, there's always a dull roar of chaos that's the background static of the station.

"Okay, so are we ready to get started?" Lucas asks as he taps on the folders.

Out in the bullpen, two phones start ringing simultaneously. I swig my coffee and try to prepare myself mentally to start questioning the owners of the farm. It's too early for us to know if we're looking for an owner of the property, or if something went on in this swath of land that the owner didn't know about or if this is even related to the kidnapping in the nineties. With a cold case like this, we can't make any assumptions. We've got to do the legwork and collect the evidence here.

I pull the first folder over to me and flip it open. I skim the pages and rattle off the details to Lucas. While we pulled the info out of city hall together, we haven't really looked into the owners yet, or their history. I'm hoping that talking to the owners will also give us an idea of who else may have had access to their property.

"So, here we've got Ben Fennick. He owned the farm for

just six months. Looks like he bought and sold it in 1992, so he owned the property likely after the time period that we think these women died, but I think it's still worth talking to him," I say. Yesterday, Officer Nolan, the officer assigned to us by Sergeant Ortega, pulled up the details about each person of interest we've got in the file. So, thanks to a little small-town policework, we've got a contact list to work from.

I grab my phone, dial the number for Ben Fennick, and throw the call on speaker. It rings several times before a gruff voice answers.

"Hello?" the man says, his Boston accent thick through the static.

I introduce myself and Lucas, before he loses patience. Though he's only said one word, it sounds like he's in a hurry. "We were hoping to talk to you about Ackert Farm. We saw in the records that you owned it back in the nineties," I say.

"Yeah, barely. I owned it for about six months." He clears his throat, and something rustles in the background. "What about it? It's been over thirty years since I owned that."

My guess is, Ben isn't the kind to watch the news. If he'd been keeping up with it, he would have heard about the bodies that were discovered on the farm.

Lucas jumps in and gives Mr. Fennick the background on the farm, what was found there.

"Huh, about time I guess," Ben finally says.

That response surprises me. It's almost like he expected them to eventually find bodies on the property. Did he see something while he owned it? Did he find something?

"You're not surprised..."

He lets out a low, humorless laugh. "No, not at all. Honestly, if you'd been out on that property, you'd understand. In the time I owned it, I only went out there once. The night that I bought the farm, when the keys were in hand, I went out there. And I swear, I heard voices in the woods, and as I walked,

I heard a woman crying. I'd heard rumors about the land, that it was cursed. Being out there at night, hearing it, I knew that it was true. I put it on the market the next day, and within six months it wasn't mine anymore. Took a loss on the land, but it was worth it. I don't need a curse following me," he says. By the tone of his voice, I know that he's being completely honest. That's one thing that you learn working in law enforcement for as long as I have: there are some things you just can't fake.

While I believe that Ben thinks that the land is cursed, I don't believe in curses. The look on Lucas's face tells me he doesn't believe in curses either.

"Mr. Fennick, would you mind coming in to talk to us a little more about the farm?" Lucas asks.

He lets out another laugh. "I'd love to, but I live in Ohio. Moved out here right after I put the farm up for sale. I just realized it was time for me to get out of that town," he explains.

I shift gears. If he's left town, then we need to wrap up our questioning on this call. While I think we can go ahead and rule this guy out—he didn't own the property long enough to be a suspect—he might be able to provide some information from his trip to the farm.

"Did you go into the house before or after you bought the property?" I ask.

"No, the realtor told me that the house was in bad shape, that it was basically a teardown. I bought the land to try and generate a profit from the apples. I never planned to live out there," he explains.

"Did you already own a home in town?" Lucas asks.

"No, I lived in Modena." Modena is a small town about ten minutes south of New Paltz. It's definitely close enough that he could drive if he had bought a farming property over here.

"When you went out to the property, how much of it did you walk?" I ask.

He takes a swig of something, pausing before he answers.

"It's been a long time. But I didn't go far. I parked near the house and then walked around the woods near it," he explains. "I'd like to say that I explored the woods and went farther in to try to make out the noises I'd been hearing—but growing up in this town, I'd heard the stories about the curse on the land. I thought it was all rumors, kid stuff. But once I heard those voices, the sobbing, something inside of me switched on and I had to get out of there."

I pause for a moment to reflect on what he said before continuing. "Would you say that you heard multiple voices out there or just one?" I can imagine how someone might have heard the victims talking from inside the root cellar. Maybe the talking resonated and carried through the woods, maybe it was his imagination after years of stories, or maybe it was just kids partying in the woods.

"Hard to say, but I know for sure that I heard a woman."

"Did it sound like the woman was the one crying or was it someone else?" Lucas asks, and I know he's trying to get the full picture of whether or not this man heard a child or just a woman. We can't lead him too much, otherwise he may stop giving us accurate testimony, especially after all this time. The longer it's been since someone experienced something, the more impressionable their memories become.

"Honestly, I don't know," he says, his words a bit rushed.

"Was there anyone that had easy access to the farm?" I ask.

He lets out a rough laugh. "Anyone in town had access to the farm, anyone driving by. It's not like it was surrounded by an electrified fence. Kids snuck out into the woods, I found squatters on the property. You name it."

My heart sinks. How are we going to find who did this if *everyone* had access and opportunity to get onto the farm?

"Look, I need to get going."

I'm annoyed that he's cutting our call short, but at the same time, he's not giving us much to go on anyway. "If you think of anything else, please give us a call back," I say.

"Yeah, sure," he says before ending the call.

When the line goes dead, I look to Lucas, and the look on his face says it all. He's just as disappointed as I am. We should know better. After all these years in law enforcement, you never get the answers that you're looking for on the first call—but that doesn't make it any less disappointing. Lucas and I chat a bit about the call, and I know what our next step needs to be. We need to track down someone who spent more time at the property.

I go through the files and find that the other two owners that we've got on our list are still in town. I'm dying to get out of the station, to do some real policework, so I run my plan past Lucas.

"Let's do it. Calling them into the station is going to make them jumpy, calling them gives them an easy out, and you know I'm always on board for swinging by and questioning someone," Lucas says. And this is exactly why I love working with him. We're absolutely on the same page.

Outside, the wind has kicked up, sweeping across the small parking lot of New Paltz PD. Trees sway back and forth, thrown about by the breeze, their branches popping and cracking from the force. On the horizon, thunderheads are blooming, warning of the storm that's sure to come in an hour or two. The thunderstorms up here are nothing compared to the ones I experienced in Texas. Down there, sometimes a violent energy fills the air. Somehow the clouds seem angry, like they've been waiting for their chance to rain down destruction on the plains. It's different out here now, the static in the air not quite violent—but there is something lingering, an energy I can't quite place.

Lucas climbs into the passenger side of my new Jeep, and I start the engine. I hope that we can finish our questioning before the storms really roll in. As we carve through the small city, we pass through the small downtown lined with brick buildings filled with small businesses and they begin to give away to Cape Cod and colonial houses. Finally, we pull into a small house at the edge of town. The lawn is overgrown, forgotten. Dandelions have taken over the grass, creating puffy white clouds between the tall stalks. It almost looks like tufts of snow.

White paint is peeling off the siding of the house, but otherwise, it seems to be in good shape as we approach. Lucas knocks on the door, and after a few attempts, a man in sweatpants and an old T-shirt answers the door. He looks between us, obviously trying to puzzle out who we are before Lucas introduces us.

"The cops? Why are you here?" He raises a brow but stands squarely in the doorway. I'm not sure that he's going to invite us inside. Asher Murphy is a large man with pale skin, probably six-foot-three. His shoulders are broad, and he's got a thick salt-and-pepper beard that covers most of his red cheeks. He's built wide, like a football player. But even as tall as he is, he's still shorter than Lucas.

"We're here to talk to you about Ackert Farm. We understand that you owned it for a while?" I ask.

He crosses his arms and nods slowly. "Yeah, I did. What's it to you?"

"Well, we were hoping that we could come in for a few minutes to talk to you about the farm," Lucas explains as he takes a step toward the door.

Asher narrows his eyes, but to my surprise he waves Lucas inside, and I follow after the two of them. The house looks like it was last updated in the early nineties, with striped wallpaper covering nearly every wall. Leather sofas sit in the living room, with sports memorabilia posted all around the room. A flat-screen TV hangs over the fireplace, a muted football game playing in the background, casting a flickering light around the room.

He waves for us to take a seat on the sofa, and he sits opposite us in a recliner that he shifts to face us, instead of the TV. "Want anything to drink?" he asks after he's already sitting down, so I shake my head. I want to dig into our questions, not wait for him to come back.

"Mind if we just get to it?" Lucas asks as he takes a notepad from his jacket pocket. I do the same, clicking my pen before I press the tip to the paper. While some detectives like to take notes on their phone, I feel like it's less personal. It makes witnesses feel like we're distracted by our devices, not like we're engaged in the questioning. I want anyone that we're speaking to to know that we're listening to the words that they're saying, that for better or worse, those words are important to an investigation. So many people assume if you're on your phone, you're scrolling on social media.

"So, yeah, I owned the farm, as you know. I bought it from Fennick in ninety-two or ninety-three, I think? Owned it for about five years. I sold it in ninety-seven to Thurston," he explains.

I nod. "Yeah, we pulled the property records. Did you see what happened down at the farm?" I ask. It's been all over the news. It's currently on the front of the paper—I don't know how he could have missed it. Unless, like Fennick, he's been away from the city and just returned.

"Yeah, they found a body out there," he says with a shrug. It always surprises me when someone is so unsurprised by a body being recovered on a property. But then again, not many details have been released to the public. We're holding information back—like we always do in any homicide case—so we can be sure if anyone comes forward with information, that what they're telling us aligns with the facts we've kept secret. It's a very common law enforcement technique to weed out the weirdos and people trying to get information out of us. So we have only told the media that one body was removed. And we haven't made it clear that homicide is suspected.

"They did," I explain. "So, we're trying to talk to anyone that lived on the property—"

"Because you think that I killed someone and buried their body there?" he asks, an edge to his voice. His wide jaw clenches as he glowers at me. I feel a bit taken aback by his tone. He was cordial enough when he was speaking to my partner. I glance to Lucas, hoping he'll take over. I want to be sure that we can actually get some information out of this guy and that he doesn't just kick us to the curb because he hates me. That'll make this investigation more difficult than it needs to be.

"No. From what we know about the body that was recovered, it was buried well before you owned the land—the timeline doesn't match up. So at this time, you're not a person of interest," Lucas says, smoothing the concern right over. We're not going to let it be known to any members of the public exactly when we think the bodies were buried, when these women were likely kidnapped, or anything like that.

"Why do you think that I know anything then?" he asks, leaning back in the recliner as he props his right ankle on his left knee.

"We'd just like to know your experiences at the farm since you lived there for five years. Did you see anything odd? Did you hear anything while you were out there?" Lucas asks. He's being careful to not lead Asher too much, but I can tell exactly what he's trying to get out of him. I want to know if he heard the women talking too, if someone might have been on that property still in the nineties. While the bodies we found were from the eighties or nineties, what if there were more? Maybe my brain is just too hardwired to think about serial killers at this point, but I can't help but wonder...

"For starters, I didn't really live there. The house on the property wasn't in good shape, so I only went out to check on the apples. The years that I owned it, the farm wasn't doing well. The trees all had a fungus that was causing problems. My arborist thought that we were going to have to cut most of the crop down and start over, which I didn't want to stick around for... What's the point in owning a big farm like that if it's not going to make any money?"

It seems no one really lived on the farm. Based on the state of the house when we went out to the property, I can't say I'm surprised. The paint was peeling, the porch looked like it was a swift wind away from caving in—but I hadn't realized that it's been over thirty years since anyone lived on the farm.

"Did you ever venture out into the woods?" I ask, hoping that Asher has shaken off some of the anger he previously directed toward me.

He shakes his head. "No, I didn't have any reason to. It's heavily wooded on the far side of the property. I'd heard that kids liked to party out there, so I didn't feel like traipsing around in empty beer bottles, cans, what have you. I stayed on the productive part of the land and that was about my involvement with it."

"So, you never heard anything then?"

He sighs and shakes his head. "I didn't say that. There were a few times that I heard voices in the woods, but again, there were kids out there. They liked to tell each other stories about how the woods were cursed. You know how kids are in small towns. There's nothing else to do, so they go scare each other in the forest." He lets out a low laugh.

"Do you think that the land is cursed? We've heard a lot of stories from locals about the farm," Lucas asks.

A strange look comes over Asher's face, and it's hard for me to place. He seems almost... spooked somehow.

"Part of me doesn't know. It's been pretty barren for so long. Maybe there is something wrong with the land. Maybe it's just a shitty farm. Who knows. But weird things do happen out there," he says.

"Weird things... like?" Lucas asks, urging him to continue.

"Sometimes—" He stops and shakes his head.

"It's okay, you can tell us," Lucas urges again.

"Sometimes when I was out there early in the morning, I swear I'd hear a baby crying. And a few times, in the early days, I'd find tire tracks leading into the woods, like someone had driven between the trees, but I never saw anyone out there. I never saw anyone on the property. For a while, I chalked it up to the kids—maybe they were out there hauling liquor back to the place in the woods where they liked to party. But I don't know, something about it felt off to me."

A baby crying? He's the second person to say that. The kids in the woods drinking, I suppose I can see that, especially since so many of the kids in town thought that the land had a curse on it. But why would someone bring a baby out into the woods? What doesn't make sense though, the body we found, the child, it would have been dead for at least ten years at the time they heard a baby crying in the woods. So that makes me wonder, who else was out there?

"Did anyone help you take care of the property? Did you hire anyone?" Lucas asks before I'm able to get to the question.

"Yeah, a few people helped me with the property. Calvin Porter spent more time out at the farm than I did. He lives right down the street," he explains.

I write down Calvin's name. Maybe we'll go talk to him before we speak to Mr. Thurston. We spend a few minutes wrapping up with Asher. I'm anxious to get moving, to keep the investigation on track.

Four houses down in a yellow Dutch colonial, we find Calvin Porter. He answers the door so quickly that I half expect that Asher called to tell Calvin about our impending arrival. In a town this small, that wouldn't surprise me at all. Calvin is the exact opposite of Asher. His ginger hair is long and dusts his shoulders. He's got on a thick plaid flannel shirt even though it's nearly ninety degrees outside. He rocks back and forth on his bare feet as he appraises me. His nose and cheeks are covered in freckles.

"You the cops? I heard there were cops in town." He looks at me harder, as if squinting at me hard enough may make me reveal my true form.

"We are. Can we come in and talk to you for a few minutes?" I ask.

He nods and waves us inside. The inside of his home feels like a cabin. It's disjointed from the outside. I'd expected more of a farmhouse to be waiting in here. He waves us into the kitchen and motions for us to take a seat at the kitchen table before heading to the coffee pot on the far end of a cluttered countertop.

"Want a cup?" he offers.

"Sure, thanks," Lucas says.

After a few minutes of fiddling with cups, he joins us at the table and slides steaming mugs in front of us. Mine is emblazoned with a Yankees logo, while Lucas's shows off the logo of the New York Giants. I test a sip and then dive into the questioning. This isn't a social call, after all.

"We were just over at Asher's house. We're investigating the body that was found out at Ackert Farm," I explain.

He nods. "I figured someone would come talk to me eventually. I worked out there for quite a while," he says before he scratches his nose, and then begins to swivel his coffee mug back and forth on the table. At least he doesn't seem to be as edgy talking to me as Asher was.

I grab my notebook. "When exactly did you start working there?"

He takes a long, slow sip of his coffee. "Honestly, since I was a kid. My grandpa was friends with Hershel; he owned the farm back then. So, I started doing basic farm work over there when I was around ten. I loved it and got pretty good at it, so I just kept it up."

"What kind of work did you do there exactly?" Lucas asks.

"Coordinating the apple picking, moving, making sure the house didn't fall down, equipment maintenance, that sort of thing. I also did deliveries for Hershel from time to time, picking up equipment or parts from God knows where all over the state for him."

"We've heard some stories that the farm is cursed," I say as I jot down a few notes about his history at the property.

He lets out a low laugh, his eyes glimmering with humor. "Oh yeah, I know those stories have circulated about the farm for as long as I can remember. Kids dare each other to come out into the woods at night. There was a story about how the original owner of the farm, Mr. Ackert, stole naughty kids, killed them, and buried their bodies in the foundations of his house."

I nod. Most towns have some kind of ghost story like this. But there's sometimes some truth to the stories. That makes me wonder if there's more sinister goings-on at this farm than we realized. We've got the bodies to prove it. "Did you ever hear anything strange when you worked out there?"

He shrugs. "Strange? No. Sometimes you'd hear kids in the woods. Someone would scream because a friend spooked them, that kind of thing."

I feel Lucas glance at me, then he asks, "Are you sure the screams were kids playing? Could it have been somebody else out there?"

"No, there wasn't anyone out in the woods, other than the kids. If there had been, I would have seen them," he says.

"So, you spent a lot of time in the woods, then?" Lucas follows right up, not giving me a chance to jump in. Though it annoys me, I try to remind myself how nice it is to have a competent partner. Even though he transferred to homicide from missing persons, and this is technically only his third homicide investigation, I feel like Lucas is a natural and he's picked it up incredibly quickly.

Calvin clears his throat, his bony fingers tightening on the cup resting on the table in front of him. The air in the room shifts slightly and outside pellets of rain begin hammering the roof. "I wouldn't say I spent a lot of time out there. There were times I had to gather firewood for Hershel before the winter, but I didn't go that far out into the forest." He shakes his head and looks down at the table. "To be honest, when I was young, I was incredibly afraid of the woods. I tried to avoid going out there if I could. It always gave me the creeps."

"Why is that?" I ask. Calvin seems spooked, and I'm not sure why but it makes me think he did see something in that forest and he doesn't want to tell us about it.

He shrugs and his demeanor shifts again. "The property was huge, probably about thirty-five hundred acres in total. There was no easy way for us to even get out into the woods. Hershel had an ATV, but he didn't let me use it because he said that his insurance wouldn't cover it if I got hurt on it." He plays with his cup again, his eyes seemingly mesmerized by the dark liquid swirling in his cup. "And I guess I was always scared of the woods. Maybe it was the stories, maybe it was something else—I don't know. I just didn't like it."

That strikes me as odd. It's not all adding up for me. It seems like Hershel was trying to keep Calvin on a specific part of the land only. But if the women were being held captive in the root cellar close to the house, what was Hershel hiding in the woods?

"How did you get out to the orchard? That's not close to the house," Lucas says.

"There's access to it from the road or I could get there from the back road that cuts around the house," he explains. "It's not paved or anything, but my truck would get through it without any problems."

I nod and lean my elbows on the table, toward Calvin. Something about our conversation just still doesn't feel right.

He's not telling us everything. So, I've got to figure out why exactly that is. "Look, Calvin, I've been doing this a long time," I say, letting the seriousness of the situation leach into my words. "And I can tell that you're keeping something from us. So, I'll say this: if you don't want to give us all the details, that's fine, but we will figure out everything that's going on here. And if I connect you to this somehow, it's not going to look good for you."

"It'll be much better for you if you're just upfront with us now," Lucas adds.

Calvin sighs and looks to the door, like he's contemplating kicking us out. "Look, it just might not mean anything," he says.

"It's still best if you just tell us. It's funny how sometimes information that doesn't seem helpful at all will end up being critical to an investigation," Lucas urges.

Calvin laces his fingers together atop the table, then looks down before he starts to speak. "When I was probably fifteen, I went out to the farm early in the morning. I wasn't supposed to be there yet. Hershel didn't like me to show up before nine, when he got there. But I had a date that afternoon. I had asked my crush—Macy Williams—to go to the movies with me. I needed to finish up with the chores at the farm early, so I could make it back to town in time. I got out of my dad's truck and went to grab a few things from the barn that I needed. As I walked past the house, I looked up and I swear I saw a woman staring down at me from the second-floor window," he says and shivers. His face has gone pale, slack.

I raise a brow to that. Thus far, I haven't heard of anyone staying at the farm. This could be a huge lead. "Did Hershel have a wife?" I ask.

He nods. "Yeah, he did."

"So, couldn't that have been his wife?" Lucas asks before I get the chance.

He shakes his head. "No, you don't understand. No one had

lived in that house since the seventies. The guy who owned it before Hershel, his wife died in the house. I think I saw her."

"Are you saying you saw a ghost?" I ask, trying to clarify the purpose of the story. My eyebrow is arched so high, it's probably touching my hairline.

Calvin throws his hands up. "I don't know what I saw. All I know is, she was there one second, then gone the next," he says, then his brows scrunch up. "But I did see her again, or I think I did at least."

I glance to Lucas, tiring of this ghost story.

"Where did you see her?" Lucas asks. His tone makes it clear that he's still entertaining the story at least.

"In the woods, probably six weeks later," he says.

"Did she try to talk to you?" Lucas tilts his head as he asks.

I take a sip of my coffee, hoping it hides how skeptical I'm sure my expression looks. All this talk about ghosts and curses has my rational side begging for real answers.

"No. She didn't speak. She was only there for a few seconds. I swear, I'm not the type to believe in ghosts, but I have no other explanation," he says.

"Is there anything else you can think of?" Lucas asks.

Calvin shakes his head. "No, I don't think so."

I text Sergeant Ortega about Hershel. Her response is almost immediate: he left New York and moved to Florida in the late nineties.

We finish up with Calvin and head back outside. Dark clouds have settled over New Paltz, but thankfully the rain has slowed for now. We climb into my Jeep and I start the engine, frustration still needling me that all we got from our conversation was a goddamn ghost story.

"So, what's your take?" I ask him as I roll down the street, dodging cars that have parked a little too far off the curb. It feels like trying to navigate an obstacle course.

"Honestly, I believe that he thinks that he's telling us the truth," he says as he looks out the window. I agree with him there. While it was clear that Calvin may not have told us everything, I don't necessarily think that he was trying to lie to us. But I also don't believe in ghosts.

"Do you think the woman he saw in the window was the woman whose body was found?" I ask.

Lucas shakes his head as I turn left onto Main Street and pull into the coffee shop. I dodge a few cars on the street, then we head inside. The door jingles overhead as we enter, and a barista with long blue and purple pastel hair gives us a little wave from behind the counter. Lucas orders for both of us while I grab my phone.

I text Ortega back, asking if there's any aerial footage of the farm, and I glance over my shoulder for a second to see a tall scrawny man with red hair and a beard a few shades lighter than his hair. I grind my teeth together. I recognize the man because I googled him after he called my first night here in New Paltz. Neal, the journalist writing the book about my father, strolls over, his eyes narrowed on me. Of course, he's not just here for coffee. No, he's actively trying to hunt me down.

"Harlow, I'm so glad I found you," he says, nearly out of breath, like he's been running, and even though I've got my back to him, I swear I can hear him smirking. I turn to face him, though I know I should probably just ignore him. But I can't. His presence needles me, forcing me to act.

"Why is that, exactly?" I ask as I cross my arms.

"I wanted to get your take on the news," he says as he pulls his phone from his jacket pocket. This guy always dresses like a smarmy journalist from a movie set in the seventies. I raise a brow, then grind my teeth again. He's dragging this out on purpose for dramatic effect. *Just say what the fuck you want and get out of here already.* I motion for him to continue, my movements sharper than usual, like I'm slashing the air.

He turns his phone toward me. A webpage showcasing an

article covers the screen. It takes me too long to process the words that I'm seeing.

Seattle Sleeper Reweds Ex-Wife.

Are you fucking kidding me? Without thinking, I grab his phone and skim the article.

In an interesting turn of events, ten years after the divorce that was splashed all over national headlines for over a year, Deirdre and Mitchell Edward Fisher, also known as the Seattle Sleeper, have announced they are reuniting. The pair exchanged their vows in the Washington State Penitentiary chapel three weeks ago, according to the wedding license that was filed with the state.

We've reached out to the pair for their comment on why they've reunited now, but we have not heard back.

Anger blooms inside me like a toxic cloud. I feel betrayed. During our last case, my mother was nearly killed by the McKenzie Mauler, but I saved her. And after everything, this is how she repays me? She decides to tie herself to a killer again. What the hell is wrong with her?

I shove the phone back into Neal's hands.

"So?" he urges when I say nothing.

"She has no comment," Lucas says. He grabs our coffees from the barista and pushes me toward the door.

Neal trails us, practically nipping at our heels. I'm so distracted, my rage clouding my thoughts, that I'm lucky muscle memory gets me back to my Jeep. Lucas opens my passenger-side door and I climb inside without thinking about it. When Lucas climbs in, he hands me a coffee, then starts the engine.

A year ago, I never would have let him or anyone else drive

my Jeep. But now, I know I can trust him with it. How's that for growth?

"Okay, let it all out," he says as he pulls off the curb and drives through downtown.

I swear my anger crowds my throat and it takes me longer than it should to figure out what to say. "I can't fucking believe her. What is wrong with her?" I finally seethe.

"Is she doing this so she can get something out of it? Can she cash in on this?" he asks. And that at least may make some sense. She is the type to do something like this for money, but if she was just going to get back together with him, why did she bother reconnecting with me in the first place?

"Maybe." I take a long swig from my coffee before continuing. "Part of me feels like she's doing this just to antagonize me. All I want is to do my job and not have to answer for both of their choices anymore. But here they are again, fucking everything up. Why can't they just stop?"

"I'm really sorry," Lucas says as he rolls to a stop at a stop sign. There's nothing in this world that I hate more than pity, but I tolerate it from him.

"Yeah, I know, thanks," I say, looking out the window. A mom is standing next to her toddler, who is throwing a fit on the sidewalk, arms flailing, legs kicking. The woman is patiently waiting, her arms crossed. It stings every time I see something like this, a mother with patience for their child, a father that stuck around, that wanted to see their daughter. I always wonder what my life would have been like if my childhood weren't built on the bones of my father's victims. What kind of life would I have lived? Who would I have become if I weren't shaped by trauma?

"What are you going to do?" he asks.

"I'm going to do what I always do. I'm going to pretend that none of it is happening."

.   .   .

A cool breeze whips past me as I emerge from the hotel. My stomach is growling and though I tried to tempt Lucas out with me, he's in for the night, trying to track down aerial footage of the farm since the New Paltz team hasn't been able to get us anything yet. I climb into my Jeep, relishing the cool cloth seats. I glance at my phone, taking in again the list of my food options that are still open at this time of night. With my windows open, the sound of the breeze rises around me. A scuff, like feet on concrete, draws my attention and my head snaps up. Out of habit, I hit the button on the side of my phone, killing the illuminated screen.

I scan the lot but can't find the source of the noise. My pulse quickens as the muscles in my neck tighten. Someone is watching me. I can feel it. I throw my car into drive and make sure that my doors are locked. I circle the parking lot, and I swear I see a figure slip between two cars. Throwing my Jeep into reverse, I spin around, flashing my high beams between the vehicles. The light gobbles up the darkness, but there's no one there.

My mind tells me I'm being paranoid, but Sergeant Dirby's warning echoes through my subconscious.

11

I'm in the office early. The only other person I've seen here is Sergeant Ortega, and she's been on the phone nonstop. Though I haven't heard enough of her conversation to pick up on what's being said or what brought her in so early, she's clearly trying to calm someone down. I pass by her desk with a cup of coffee and slide it to her, which earns me a warm and genuine smile. She's got her cellphone sandwiched between her shoulder and ear. I walk back to my desk and take a seat.

"So you think there's a chance that he'll come back here?" she asks. There's an edge to her voice, like she's irritated. For a moment, she's silent while she's listening to the person on the other end of the line. "Pretty much a certainty then? And you're sure he's going to be let out?"

She finishes up the call and I do my best not to eavesdrop. I watch as she disappears into her office. A few minutes later, she appears with her coffee mug in hand then walks over to my desk.

"You don't happen to know how to make someone disappear, do you?"

I swallow hard and I try to take her humor for what it is—

and not see it as an indication that she knows all my dark secrets. I laugh, careful that I don't let on how nervous her question makes me. "I wish. But why? What's up?"

"Vick. That motherfucker who I told you about. I verified he's out, and his parole officer has no idea where he's at. So he could have been here—he could have killed Mazie." Anger leaches into her words, clipping them.

"Do you have a description so we can keep an eye out?" I ask.

She nods. "I'll email his mugshot over. I know this guy is going to cause problems in this town until he's locked up again."

"You'll track him down again. And we'll do what we can to help," I promise.

"Thanks, I appreciate that," she says.

Lucas shows up a few minutes after I finish up my conversation with Ortega. We both got up early at the request of Sergeant Dirby. Last night he texted us both, asking for an hour. I motion for Lucas to head to the conference room, and after I grab my things I follow him. Anxiety has tightened around me since. I hate open-ended meetings like this. They're never good news. I'm half expecting he's going to take us off the case. We're down several detectives and I'm not sure this case will be priority if a body is found elsewhere.

I set up my laptop in the conference room, sipping my coffee as I open the lid. Though I know the caffeine isn't going to do anything to calm my anxiety, at least it keeps my hands busy. Lucas plops down next to me, and I swear his energy fills the room. Though he's said nothing, I already know he's had a bad morning. His pants are wrinkled, his hair disheveled—which isn't like him at all.

"What happened to you?" I ask as I give him the once-over.

"Why do you ask? Maybe because I look like a possum that rolled out of the wrong side of a dumpster?"

I press my lips together in an attempt not to laugh.

"But don't ask. It's been *a morning*."

"Oh?" I start to ask, but he shakes his head and clicks the link on my laptop to start the meeting.

The cursor spins for a minute, then Sergeant Dirby comes into view. His desk is stacked with folders, as per usual. He's squinting at the computer, his hand ruffling his gray hair. He looks paler than usual, making the dark circles beneath his eyes stand out. "This damn thing never works," he grumbles.

"Hey, Sergeant," I say.

"Oh. It's working. I can hear you, but I can't see you," he says before clicking a few times. "There's the window. Sorry for the technical issues," he says before shaking his head. He's always one to lament technology.

"No worries," Lucas says. "Good morning, Sergeant."

He nods and offers Lucas a tight smile. Sergeant Dirby is very hands-off when it comes to leadership, which I prefer. He's not overbearing and lets us do our work—which is rare.

"I wanted to talk to you both because there's a bit of a situation that I need you to be aware of." His words are more clipped than usual, and he's sitting up stick straight. Dirby is the kind of guy that usually hunches. I'm not sure if he's uncomfortable with the idea of a video meeting or if it's something else.

My stomach churns with anxiety, so I sip my drink, hoping to settle it a little.

"Officer Pike is dead," he explains. Pike was another officer we worked with back in Plattsburgh during our first case. He was an absolute asshole, and while I definitely wished karma would bite him in the ass, I didn't wish him dead.

"How?" I manage.

"Someone hid in his back seat and strangled him when he got into his car. It was clearly targeted, not a robbery."

That tells me that his wallet, phone, and other valuables were still in the car when he was found.

"After this, we're certain that there's a serial killer hunting law enforcement officers upstate. You're far enough south that you all are probably fine, but even so, I need you to be careful—extra vigilant." His mouth is a thin line when he stops speaking, and I can see the concern in his eyes.

"Of course we will," I say.

"Do you need our help on this?" Lucas asks.

He shakes his head. "No, not yet. I'm on it for now."

Lucas and I are silent when the meeting ends. I'm not sure what to say or what to think. We weren't exactly on great terms with Officer Pike but with another officer dead, I wonder what it means for our team—for our future.

12

The station is packed when we come back from lunch. Sergeant Ortega has several beat cops crowded around her as she gives them a briefing. From what I've heard so far, a teenage girl, Kaley Thompson, is missing. She never arrived home when walking back from high school. They're unsure if she ran away or if she's in danger. I wonder if it's connected to Mazie, if we're going to find another girl in this town dead. I can tell that Lucas is having a hard time not jumping into it, since his home base used to be missing persons. But so far, they don't want us involved—since there's no body. But Ortega is convinced it's connected to Vick, that he's hunting in this town again. As we enter the bullpen, she nods at us in greeting. So far, New Paltz is the most welcoming town that we've worked in. But considering how unwelcoming most other stations are, I don't think that I'm giving them quite the credit that they deserve.

I throw my things on my desk, while Lucas gives me some new details about the guy he's dating.

"He's watching my cat. How nice is that?"

I raise a brow. "Personally, I would never trust anyone in my apartment," I say, trying to ignore the fact that my apartment is barely more than a mattress and boxes that I've lugged all over the country but never unpacked. I have less than nothing to steal. But still, my space is *my space.*

"Well, you have trust issues," he says without skipping a beat.

"Thanks for that," I snap at him, but I know he's right.

Lucas laughs. "Trust issues and denial."

"Shut up," I say just as my cell starts to ring. Across the room, a desk phone rings at the same time. "Detective Durant."

"Detective, this is Max Brooks. I'm overseeing the construction at Ackert Farm. We were given the all-clear to start working on the edge of the property yesterday, and this morning we found something in the woods," he explains.

My thoughts skid to a halt. "What did you find?" I ask as my heart starts to pound. I've glanced at some of the aerial footage, so has Lucas, but we haven't found anything. Did they find another body out there?

"There's a cabin out here in the woods. It's so heavily wooded, we didn't know there were any structures. It didn't appear on any of the aerial footage or surveys that we have."

"Did anyone go inside?" I ask.

He clears his throat. "No, given what was found here previously, I stopped the construction."

"I'm sorry to shut you down again, but I'm going to need you to clear everyone off the scene so we can come and check it out. Could you also send me over the coordinates?"

"I assumed as much. I'll send everyone home for the day and text you the coordinates. How long do you think we'll be shut down?" he asks.

"Hard to say until we know what's there, but I'll have forensics give you a call with a timeline once we have one," I promise.

"Great, thank you."

I end the call with Max, then explain to Lucas what we've got waiting for us over at the scene. He nods and grabs his cell.

"I'll call Racq—" he starts. "Oh, she's out of jurisdiction for this."

That's the unfortunate part of being on loan down here, we can't work with any of our usual team.

"We've got to call Nadiya Ayad," I explain, remembering the list of contacts that Dirby gave both of us when we came to work on this case.

He nods and starts to make the call. I wave for him to follow me, and we head out of the station together. It's not a long drive to the farm, but it takes me about ten minutes to find the dirt road that leads us back to the corner of the property where they were clearing the trees.

A group of bulldozers and other yellow machinery is abandoned, blocking the road. I pull my Jeep alongside them, then yell at the last remaining crew members on the scene to clear a path for forensics. I'm not sure if we'll actually need forensics out here yet, but my gut tells me that we should plan for it—just in case.

The engines rumble as the guys clear a path, then disappear from the scene. I grab shoe covers and latex gloves, hand Lucas his, and walk down the dirt road. Ahead of us, the overturned dirt and decapitated trees stretch forward until finally they part, revealing what looks like a rough roofline. If I didn't know what was waiting for us on the other side of the trees, I'm not sure I'd even be able to guess that a structure was standing there.

I step forward, my boots sinking in the mud up to my ankles. It makes a sucking sound as I force myself to trudge toward the trees.

"Maybe try walking that way." I motion for Lucas to take the path closer to the fence, where the ground is less disturbed and seems far less muddy. I hear him shift to the right behind me, though I don't have to look at him. My phone chimes with a message, letting me know that the forensics team is en route, their ETA around thirty minutes.

I make it to the break in the trees, and the cabin really comes into view. It's about twenty feet long and fifteen feet wide. The roofline is lower than it should be, making the structure look stout. The walls are slick with green moss, as if this shack has never seen the sun. Boarded-over windows stand on either side of the door, with wrought-iron bars curling over them. It makes me wonder if the person who built this was trying to keep something out—or to keep someone in. The wood around the roofline is cracked, rotted through. And I wonder how long his house has been here. It must be at least ten years old—maybe more. A narrow chimney sticks out of the lichen-covered roof, pointing toward the canopy of trees that's woven above us.

Out here, the air is damp, earthy. And I'm not sure if it's the building in front of me, or if this is just how these woods smell. I pull on my shoe covers and latex gloves. When Lucas approaches, he does the same.

"This place is fucking creepy," Lucas says as he signals to the windows.

I nod. "We need to figure out who built this."

"We should call Asher and Marcus to see if they know anything about this cabin," Lucas says.

"I'll text Sergeant Ortega and see if someone on the team can give them a call while we're here," I say. I fire off the text quickly then step toward the door. The porch groans beneath my feet as I test a step onto the bowing wood.

The door is locked when I try the knob. I grab a lock-picking kit from my Jeep and in a few minutes, I've got the door open. It growls, then screeches as the rusted hinges protest against me opening it. The coppery smell of rust fills the air, drowning out the scent of rot and the musk of the forest. I click on my flashlight, trying to see into the darkened room. The air inside is stale and musty. The floor is littered with yellowed papers, boxes of cereal that look at least twenty years old based on the artwork.

Thick layers of dust and cobwebs cover every single surface I can see in the small slice of light cutting through the room.

As I push open the door more, I make out a small wobbly table that's covered in clutter. To the left of the table, there's a tall cabinet, and a counter with a hot plate atop it. I'm surprised that a cabin like this ever had electricity, but that's when I notice a propane tank next to the hot plate. I guess they didn't have electricity out here after all. I guide my beam to the ceiling. There isn't a bulb. Outside, the low drill of cicadas rises, setting my teeth on edge.

I take a step inside, trying to assess if this had just been a hunting cabin, or if someone actually lived here at some point. I'm careful of where my feet rest as I skirt past the half-opened door. The ceiling is so low we have to crouch. To my left, a worn floral couch with holes chewed through parts of it rests against the wall—several rusted springs have burst through the rotted upholstery. The boarded-up window allows shards of light to pierce the room from behind the couch. Another window sits across the room, the glass so crowded with grime that there isn't even a hint that daylight exists on the other side of the pane.

There are two doors that lead off from this small living room. Lucas slips in behind me, the beam of his flashlight creating a twin to my own as he surveys the room.

"This place has had a rough time," Lucas says.

"How long do you think it's sat empty?" I ask.

He picks up a box of cereal from the ground and examines it carefully. "The expiration date on this says 1998," he explains, then puts the box back where he found it.

I nod and make a mental note. "Want to check that door while I check this one?" I ask as I motion to the doors closest to each of us. I'm about three feet from the door on my left.

"Sure," he says as he approaches it. He's got the strap to his gun unsnapped on his holster, waiting, ready, just in case. I've done the same for mine.

My heart thuds loudly in my ears, the whooshing so loud, it drowns out the sound of the cicadas and the symphony of insects in the trees outside. At times like this, I wonder if this is how my dad felt. Before he killed, would his blood rush in his ears? Did adrenaline burn in his bloodstream? Sometimes, my body craves the rush of an active scene, the high of being up to my eyeballs in an investigation, a fresh body. And I wonder if some of that evil taints my DNA. Did he make me *need* this? During my first case with the NYBCI, I nearly killed a suspect. It would have been so easy to just snuff him out—to rid the world of that kind of evil, rather than waiting years for the justice system to make everything right. I knew that I was capable of killing in that moment. I knew I could have done it. And that makes me wonder if I'm too much like him, if at some point I'll go too far...

I shake off my questions and force myself forward. I can't linger anymore. I have to know what's waiting for us on the other side of these doors. Lucas reaches his door before I reach mine. It groans in protest as he opens it. I pause at my door, waiting for Lucas to tell me what he's found.

"Dirty bathroom," he finally calls back. "There's a bathtub that looks like a horse trough. And maybe a composting toilet or something. There's a bucket that looks like they had to lug water and bring it here," he explains.

"Really off the grid," I say. It seems like someone went through a lot of trouble to make sure that no one knew about this cabin. But why? What secrets were they hiding here? And how long has the forest kept them?

I reach for the closed door in front of me. As it slides open, a strange stale scent hits me, like decay and the smell of a room that's been closed up for years. In front of me, I find an old mattress atop a rusted metal frame. The mattress is worn, stained. But it takes me too long to process what I'm seeing.

"What have you got?" Lucas asks from behind me. His footfalls tell me that he's searching the rest of the cabin.

Atop the mattress, I make out a skeletal form, skin that's shrunken, like it's been shrink-wrapped around bones. The color of the leathery flesh is sallow, aged, dirt and grime clinging to it. A mummified body lies on its side, in the fetal position. As I step closer, I realize the victim isn't alone. The body is cradling a smaller skeleton, a baby or maybe a toddler that's also been mummified.

"We've got two bodies," I manage to get out, my training taking over.

I grab my phone and text the forensics team that we've got two bodies to recover. I take a step closer, and as my flashlight illuminates the left side of the room, I realize that it's not just two bodies—a third lies on the floor next to the wall, a bundle of dried dandelions resting on the chest. The body is wrapped in an old quilt, but from what I can see of the face, this one is mummified as well. I'm surprised that no insects or animals were able to get in here to get at the bodies. But I guess whoever sealed this place up did a good job. They turned this cabin into a crypt.

"Make that three," I call back.

Lucas approaches behind me, his flashlight illuminating the bed. The small dresser is shoved against the right wall, a boarded-up window above it. These walls are different than the living room. In there, the walls are two-by-fours. In here, they put up drywall and wallpaper. The floral paper is bubbling, some of it peeling close to the ceiling.

I take in the scene, trying to discern what happened here. "I'm guessing this woman died first," I say, motioning to the woman on the floor with the flowers. Someone had to have brought the flowers.

"How do you think they died?" he asks as he looks between the bodies.

I step closer to examine them. A swath of straight dark hair falls in the face of the larger body. The child has the same dark hair. There are no obvious signs of trauma on any of the victims that I can see, but bodies in this state can be incredibly deceptive. If these victims were strangled, we wouldn't see that at this point. They could have also been stabbed or shot in an area that I can't see based on the position of the remains. We really need the ME's expertise here to tell us what happened.

"I have no idea," I finally say. I take out my cell and snap a few pictures of the scene. Scenes like this break my heart. This woman died with her child—and for what? My gut tells me that someone did this to them. It's not like a mother and child died from natural causes. Lucas steps closer, squinting at something. After a moment I realize it's a necklace—maybe a locket— around the neck of one of the victims on the bed.

"What?" I ask.

"Nothing." He shakes his head. His words are off somehow, like he recognizes the necklace, but our attention is broken by the sounds of vehicles rolling up outside.

It takes twenty minutes for the forensics team to pull in. That's when the scene really comes alive—the people flooding in like this is a beehive. Lights go up in the corner of the room. Cameras flash. Markers are placed on the floor as the team finds evidence. This is when my blood really starts to rush, as we all start to piece everything together. The lead of the team, Nadiya Ayad, approaches. She's got her black hair pulled back. Brilliant blue eye shadow sparkles on her eyelids, accented by sweeping cat-eye liner. Her light brown skin shimmers with highlighter. I'm in awe of her makeup.

"Detectives?" she says as she glances between me and Lucas.

I nod, and she motions for us to step out onto the porch as more of her team floods inside. I give her a quick rundown of the scene, where we found the bodies, and anything we may have touched.

"Did anyone else enter the cabin?" she asks as she looks between us.

"No, none of the construction workers that cleared out the trees came in here. I did have to pick the lock to get in," I explain. There's no way the evidence could have been compromised by anything other than the elements.

"And you wore your gloves and shoe coverings the entire time?" she asks as she makes a few notes on a clipboard.

I nod. "Yes, we did."

"Thank you. It'll take us a few hours to process the scene. But we'll get the bodies over to the medical examiner's office as soon as we can. They should be there this afternoon," she explains. "If you two don't want to hang around, you can go ahead and clear out. It's really cramped in there as it is," she says as she motions toward the shack, clearly wanting us to go.

"We'll get out of here then. Call us if you need anything. Thank you for handling this," I say.

"Of course. I've got your cell if anything comes up." She offers me a kind smile before she heads back toward the cabin.

Lucas and I grab lunch while we speculate over the scene. The problem with lacking evidence is that your mind can come up with some really wild scenarios. After we finish up lunch, we finally get a call from the medical examiner's office, and head over to Poughkeepsie to talk to Dr. Dushku. It takes us about thirty minutes to arrive at the small office, and when we walk into the thick smell of antiseptic, the building is empty. Since the receptionist isn't in, I text Dr. Dushku to let her know about our arrival, and after a few minutes she comes back to retrieve us.

"Good afternoon," she says with a warm smile.

We offer our greetings and some small talk as we route our way through the sterile office. It feels oddly abandoned, like we're intruding on a holiday.

"It's quiet here today," I say.

She nods. "Yeah, a few people had to leave early. Someone called in sick. It was just one of those days. But I don't mind it. I'll enjoy the quiet before I have to get home to my kids," she adds with a wide smile.

We follow her back to the morgue, the cold air prickling against my skin as soon as we enter. She's got three metal tables set out in the middle of the room, a body on each one. White sheets cover the bodies, but from the way the shapes are arranged, I can tell which is which based on what I saw at the scene. From a table along the back wall, Dr. Dushku grabs a clipboard and joins us near the tables.

"So, we've got three females here. The youngest is approximately eighteen months old. The woman in the middle here, I'm estimating that she was around thirty-seven years old. And over here—" She motions to the last table, the woman I think that we found on the floor. "She is around seventy-five to eighty years old. Based on my initial inspections, I don't see any external wounds on the younger women. The older woman has a pretty severe head wound."

"Was the head wound severe enough that you think it caused the woman's death?" Lucas asks.

"I haven't determined cause of death yet, but it is possible. Once I know for certain and I've certified the cause, you'll be the first to know," she explains patiently, like she's said the same phrase a million times before.

"Why didn't these bodies decay?" Lucas asks.

"From what I can see on the report, they were inside of a cabin? If it was sealed up tight enough and it was dry inside, the bodies wouldn't have had the chance to decay. If a body is kept in the right circumstances, it'll dehydrate just like a mummy and end up like these women did," she explains.

"Are you able to get DNA from them?" I ask. I haven't encountered victims that were mummified before.

She nods and offers me a patient smile. "Yes, while it can be difficult to get DNA from ancient mummies that were kept in incredibly dry climates, this type of scenario is fine for DNA preservation from certain areas of the body. We'll be able to get what we need and get it into the system. The turn-around time right now is around three to five days." She takes a look at her clipboard as she's speaking, I'm guessing to verify the timeline.

"Thank you. How long ago do you think that these women died?" I ask. I take out my notebook and make a note about how long our wait for DNA will be.

"My guess right now is around ten to fifteen years. Maybe a little longer. I'll need to do some more work on the bodies to really get a solid timeline for you. But I would say the minimum time would be ten years."

"Will you be able to take fingerprints?" I ask.

"I'll do my best. But I won't make promises."

We finish up with Dr. Dushku, knowing that it'll take her some time to go over the bodies to determine cause of death, and to collect evidence.

When we arrive back in the office, Officer Nolan flags us down. The office is pretty empty, but he looks as though he's been sitting here, waiting for us.

"Hey, Harlow, we got a call into the tip line today," Nolan says.

"Oh?"

"Carly Abernathy called. She says she has some info for you in particular," he says.

"Okay, thanks. Can you text me her contact details? I'll call her in a few minutes."

"Yep, sending them over now," he says.

"Any luck with the list of vehicles that I asked for?" I press. I've followed up a few times, but there doesn't seem to be any urgency with this team to get me the list of trucks so I can try to track down who picked up Mazie from the party.

"Sorry, still working on it," he says before he walks back to his desk.

After I get Carly's phone number, I arrange for her to meet us at a local coffee shop. When we arrive, Lucas and I grab a couple lattes and take a seat. A few minutes later, a tall slender woman with light brown skin and sad eyes walks through the door. She plops down in front of us, like she knows exactly who we are, and in a town this small, I'm sure she does.

She introduces herself, though it's not necessary, and then knots her fingers together atop the table.

"I heard about the bodies found on the farm," she says.

I nod to keep her talking because I'm not sure where this is going.

She glances around the coffee shop, as if she's nervous that someone might be eavesdropping. Then she just stares at the table as she chews the inside of her cheek.

"It's okay. Whatever it is, I'll try to make sure it stays between us," I say.

She offers me a sharp nod, her pointed chin bobbing with the motion. She finally spits the words out. "When I was eleven, a man tried to kidnap me." Tears spring to her eyes, then she adds, "I've never told anyone before."

I pass her a tissue from my bag. "Why have you kept this a secret?" I ask as I try to do the mental math. This was likely in the late nineties or early 2000s, but I confirm the timeline with her.

"This was in 2001," she confirms. "And I thought that it

was my fault. I thought that they would blame me. Every time I saw something on TV about a kid getting kidnapped, all anyone ever talked about was what the kid probably did wrong, how they could have prevented it. I just couldn't stomach being told it was my fault."

"It was absolutely not your fault."

"What time of day was it?" Lucas asks.

"Right after school. My bus let me out on Mountain Rest Road. That's where I always walked home from. But I'd seen a stray cat run toward the farm, and I chased it. This man—I don't think I'd ever seen him before—offered to help me find the cat. Then he tried to force me into his truck. I ended up being able to get away, but God, what if I hadn't?" She wrings her hands as she talks.

"Can you give us a description of the man?" I ask. The idea of another pickup truck being involved—I make note of that. Though in a farming town like this, where pickups are plentiful, it may not mean much. But it really makes me wonder if this is connected to Mazie.

"Unfortunately, I'm face blind. I don't know that I could."

I nod. "Was there anything else that might have stuck out about him? Hair color? Tattoos?"

"White guy, older. His truck was dark blue," she offers.

"Okay, that's good," I say as I write it down.

"Oh, and he had a large scar on his arm."

"How large?" Lucas asks.

"About a foot long."

I flash a look at Lucas. A foot-long scar? That should be pretty easy to match up once we track this guy down. It's not often I see a scar that large on a perp. We ask Carly a few follow-up questions before we end the conversation. This is a good lead, but we need so much more to see if we can connect the dots between this man and the bodies we found at the farm.

13

As we're wrapping up at the coffee shop, my cellphone buzzes in my pocket. I retrieve it and find Nadiya's name on the screen. I throw the call on speaker as we cut across the parking lot back to my Jeep. Dark clouds crowd the sky above us, casting a shroud over the lot. The trees stretch toward the sky, their branches looking ominous against the backdrop.

"Detective, we're going to need you to head back over to the scene," Nadiya says as soon as I climb into the driver's seat.

Lucas closes his door and looks down at my phone as he buckles his seat belt.

"Sure, we can head over. We'll be there in about thirty minutes," I say and end the call with Nadiya. I'm unsure why exactly she needs us over at the scene.

My heart pounds and my mind races the entire drive. My thoughts swarm as I try to anticipate what's waiting for us. As we pull into the scene, it's swarming with activity. Did they find something else? Was there another body that we missed? For them to call us back out here, there had to be something big. We've already got the makings of a serial killer. The older victim with the head wound was clearly killed, and our two victims found previously—we know they were killed. But with new information, we could have over five victims or more.

As we jog up toward the scene—avoiding the mud this time —Nadiya meets us on the porch. She's got a large plastic evidence bag in her hands as she looks between the two of us.

"What have you got there?" I ask, trying to discern what's in the bag. It looks like papers to me.

"These look to be handwritten notes, possibly by one of the women that were living here," she says as she passes the plastic bag toward me.

Excitement flutters inside my stomach. Letters written by the victims. This could give us everything that we need for this case. How did one of these women even get the paper to write notes? The things inside the shack were incredibly limited, and I doubt that someone holding women captive—like we believe they were—would have given them the means to write down what exactly happened to them. It's going to be too difficult for me to review the pages here, as we could contaminate them. We need to get them back to the station and review them inside of a clean room.

"Can I take these?" I ask.

She nods. "I've cataloged them and taken pictures. Please take care of them, and then check them into evidence in New Paltz when you're finished reviewing them," she instructs.

"I will. I'll be making some copies, and I'll review those. All the originals will go into evidence," I promise. I understand how important these originals will be to the case. We will need them to tell the story of the victims about what happened to them firsthand when we hunt down whoever kidnapped and killed them.

She offers me a smile that shows she appreciates that I take the evidence seriously. Unfortunately, there are some officers that don't. Botched evidence means a botched case, and that means that killers go free. So I take this responsibility seriously.

We leave the scene and head back to the station. As I drive, Lucas reads the letter to me that he can see.

"Well, this bastard kidnapped this woman, and held her captive. She talks about how devastated she was to realize that her old life had been taken from her. But she was able to argue for the man who captured her to allow her mother to live." Lucas stops and swallows hard. He glances between me and the letter, and I can see him puzzling over something.

"What?" I ask.

"I didn't want to say anything at the scene originally, but the victim on the bed, she had a necklace that I recognize... and the fact that this woman was kidnapped with her mother... I don't want to jump to conclusions, but there are some ties here..." He trails off as his eyes continue to skim the page. I look at him as I roll to a stop at a stop sign. He's paler than usual, his eyes far off as he's lost in thought. "The timeline lines up too..."

"Lucas, I need you to give me more details. You're being too vague," I say. I hate when I feel like I have to drag the info out of him. But I will if I have to. I need to know what he's talking about.

"Harlow, I think that those victims could be my mom and my grandma," he explains.

It all finally snaps into place for me, and I realize what this case could mean to Lucas—how it could change his life. I reach over and squeeze his hand, offering what little comfort I can. But I'm not sure what to say, what to do.

I urge Lucas back into the ME's office with me, despite his protests. It takes me a few minutes to explain to Dr. Dushku that we need to expedite the DNA because it could have a connection to Lucas.

Though I know the chances are low, I don't tell Lucas my thoughts. I don't have the heart to tell him that may not be his missing mother and grandmother or maybe I just don't want them to be. My phone rings and I glance at it, seeing Carly's number. I accept the call and press the phone to my ear.

"Hi, Carly, what can I help you with?" I ask, throwing the call on speaker so Lucas can hear.

"I hope you don't mind, but I'm calling you on three-way," she says before clearing her throat. "I've got my friend Aggie on the call. She wanted to tell you about something that happened to her."

"Okay, sure. Hello, Aggie," I say before introducing myself and providing her with my credentials.

"Hi, Detective. So, when I was thirteen, I was pretty rebellious and stupid. I hitchhiked sometimes, hoping that word would get back to my mom and it would piss her off. Well, one day I got picked up by someone who wasn't local. That happened sometimes, but not often honestly. Anyway, I told this guy where to take me, and he completely ignored me and drove to the farm, like he'd been there before. Part of me wondered if I should get out of the car, but I talked myself into staying." She lets out a nervous laugh.

"We all did things like that when we were kids," I say, trying to make her feel better.

"Well, anyway. When we got to the farm, he tried to rape me. I bit him, got out of the truck, and ran into the woods. My heart was beating so fast, I thought I was going to pass out."

"That's awful. I'm so sorry that happened to you," I say, though I know exactly how useless those words are. "What kind of car did the man drive?"

"It was a blue truck, but I don't know what kind."

Another blue truck. I make a note of that.

"Do you think that you remember enough to work with a sketch artist to help us get the word out on this man?" I ask, hoping that she can give us something.

She clears her throat. "I'm not good with faces, and I don't think I can recall enough about his face to help. I'm sorry."

"It's okay, don't apologize. Did the man have any distinguishing marks?"

"Yes, he had a scar on his arm."

I gather a few more details from Aggie, then finish up the call. I need to figure out if the man who attacked these women was Vick Langley or if someone else was hunting in this town.

14

Back at the station after lunch, we need to start scouring the MP reports. I've left another message with Hershel in Florida. So far, we haven't heard back from him. Lucas seems distant, understandably—but despite my urging that he should take the afternoon off, he says that digging into work is the only thing that will keep him sane right now. I've been there myself, so I don't push him too hard on it. The conference room is quiet, the door shut, locking out the sound that I know is going on just outside in the bullpen.

Officer Nolan pops his head in and looks to me. "I just sent you an email with the list of all the pickup trucks in town," he says.

"Thanks," I say, and open my email as he leaves the room. For a minute, I scan through the list—it's so long I realize that there's no way it's going to help me track down Mazie's killer. We're going to have to hope that a tip comes in or that more evidence surfaces.

"How's the list?" Lucas asks.

"Useless," I say, as I turn my attention back to him.

"How many missing persons reports do we have?" Lucas asks as he opens up his laptop.

"I don't know yet. I was distracted with the list," I say as I glare at my computer.

It takes a few minutes for us to get our computers to cooperate, and for us to log in to the database containing the missing persons files. Once I finally log in and plug in the query, something seems *wrong*. I look over my screen to Lucas, who has his brows scrunched together.

"Nothing is coming up for me," I say as I glance down to my screen in disbelief.

"Same. I've tried several times. It's saying that there are no missing persons files from this area at all, ever, for any time," he says, frustration sharpening his words.

"This is ridiculous," I say as I pull out my cell, and scroll through my contacts to find the tech support contact for the NYBCI. I click to call them, then put my phone on speaker. After a few minutes on hold, a man named Cash takes my call.

"Thanks for calling the help desk. What can I help you with today?" he asks, his voice incredibly robotic, like he says this exact same phrase three hundred times a day.

I give him a quick rundown of the problem that Lucas and I are both encountering, along with the usernames that we're using to access the system. Though he's silent, I hear him typing in the background, and the clicking of a mouse, so I know he's still on the line, working on the problem.

"Huh, that's weird," he finally says.

"What's weird?" I ask, when he doesn't offer me any details.

"I'm not seeing any data on my side either. For the entire state, it's as if all the records aren't here. Give me a moment to see if there's a connection issue on the back end. Sometimes we have problems with this stack," he explains, then puts me on hold.

Lucas cocks his head to the side, his lips pursed. "That doesn't sound good."

"I've never had the database go down or had connection issues, have you?" I ask.

He shakes his head. "Nope, never. Sometimes it's slow, but it's never done anything like this before."

When Cash finally comes back on the line, I lean closer to the phone. "Thank you for waiting. We're having some issues with the back end of that database, so we're going to need to look into it a little further," he says, giving me an answer that's too political and doesn't have enough details.

"Back-end issues like...?" I ask, trying to get more out of him.

"Unfortunately I'm not able to give you any more details than that. If you want to have your commanding officer call in to get more details from the director of the department, that'd be fine, but I'm not at liberty to—" he explains, his words so rushed they practically run together. "Yes, sir, I know." Cash is clearly talking to someone else in the background. "Look, I have to go. I'll give you a call once the database has been restored." Before I can say anything else, he ends the call.

I'm not the type to settle for no answers, so as soon as the line goes dead, I call Sergeant Dirby and ask for him to intervene.

"All right, I've got good news and bad news," Dirby explains.

"Tell me the bad news first," I say. If given a choice, I always pick the bad news first. It's much easier to process it if you hear it early.

"The bad news is the database was hacked, and all of the missing persons files were erased," he says.

I look to Lucas, whose jaw is on the floor, and I feel like mine must be doing the same. Someone destroyed the entire missing persons database? What does this mean? Why would someone do that? A million questions rush through my mind as I try to figure out why this could be happening.

"Okay, but the good news is the IT team has regular back-ups, so they're going to shut down the access point for the hacker, then restore the last database that they have backed up. It'll take a day or two, but they'll be able to get everything restored for us."

While it's good that we're going to be able to get everything restored, it's still hard to wrap my head around this happening in the first place. "Are they going to be able to track down who did this?" I ask.

"They're going to try. They've at least figured out the access point. They've figured out how the hacker got in, and what they downloaded. So the next step would be them locking in an IP address or something—I think..." He rambles on for a bit. Technology isn't Dirby's strong suit.

We finish up with Dirby and I drag Lucas out of the station to grab some coffee with me. I can't imagine how hard this must all be for him. So, the least I can do is distract him. As we step outside, Lucas squints, then pulls on a pair of sunglasses.

"You're going to make me walk, aren't you?" he asks as he plants his feet in a wide stance.

"Sure am. You need to get in some steps," I say and he rolls his eyes at me. When his attention snaps back, I look him dead in the eye. "Are you hangry?"

He scoffs. "I don't get *hangry*. That's one of your character flaws."

I laugh because we both know that's not true. But instead of firing back, I just start walking. It takes a moment for Lucas to follow, but eventually he does.

"You doing okay?" I ask.

He's silent for a beat, then says, "I keep replaying the last day I ever saw them in my mind. I'd gotten into a fight with my mother. Usually, I went to the grocery store with them. But I wanted to stay home and watch a TV show. Eventually, they went without me, and I was so petty I didn't even say goodbye."

I slow my pace as he talks.

"I always wonder what would have happened if I went with them."

"You can't beat yourself up. You couldn't have done anything. You were a kid," I say.

"But maybe me just being there would have prevented it. Maybe whoever took them wouldn't have dared to take three."

I stop in front of the coffee shop and face him. "Do you think any of our vics are responsible for what happened to them?"

He crosses his arms and looks at me like he wants to argue with me. But instead, he says, "Well, no."

"You did not do this. You could not have fixed this," I say. Tears pool in his eyes and I pull him into a hug. He sighs and squirms away from me before he wipes his eyes.

"Okay, I need coffee," he says before he throws the door open and disappears inside.

15

It's taken three days for the database to be restored, for us to take any more steps in the case. I've gotten more context from Lucas—just in case our new victims are related to him—but other than that, we've had little to go on. I still can't get in contact with Hershel. I've gone over the loose diary entries from one of our victims a thousand times.

My cell rings, a number that's local but I don't recognize appearing on the screen. I accept the call and place it on speaker as I finish getting ready to leave my hotel room.

"Detective Durant," I say as the call connects.

"Hi, this is Alyssa Grant. I was at the party where Mazie was before she died," a girl says.

I scoop up the phone as I slide my feet into my boots. I don't remember an Alyssa being on the list. Did we miss her some-how? How did we miss Alyssa? I thought we'd called everyone who was at the party.

"Well, I wasn't really *at* the party, I was sitting outside most of the night. It felt too claustrophobic in the house, so I was hanging out in the back," she explains.

"So did you have something to tell me about Mazie?" I ask, hoping to get to the point.

"Yeah, while I was out there, I saw Mazie and Langdon outside. They were having some kind of fight, then Langdon grabbed her and forced her into his truck. She looked pretty upset," she explains.

It's always the boyfriend. "Did you get a sense of what the fight was about?" I ask.

"It sounded like he was mad that she was talking to another guy," she says.

"Is there anything else that you can think of?"

"No, that's it," she says.

I wrap up the call with Alyssa and text Lucas an update on what I heard. I tell him I'll catch him up on everything when he gets to the station. Now, we're going to have to take a much harder look at Langdon, and I know how well that's going to go over with Brett.

Back in the station, Sergeant Ortega flashes me a brilliant smile and offers me a little wave as I walk in. I nod to her. I know that her good mood is lighting up the room because the files got restored for her team too. To fix the database, they had to take several systems down, so for three days it's felt like we were all back in the stone ages. It's going to be nice to be a part of the twenty-first century again.

"How's it going?" I ask Ortega as I approach.

"This week has been rough, but this morning we're finally back up and running—so hopefully the guys will stop spending every moment they're clocked in complaining to me about the system as if I have control over it." She crosses her arms and rolls her eyes, then huffs a laugh. "Sometimes, I think I should have just become a kindergarten teacher. I think that'd probably be easier to manage, honestly." She glances to the conference room. "I'm sure you guys have a lot to catch up on."

I nod. "Yeah, this set us back a bit. But hopefully today we can make some real headway in this case."

"How do you feel about the investigation so far? How's the cold case?" She raises a brow.

"Honestly..." I lower my voice. "Working a cold case is just not as exciting as working an active case."

"I totally get it. You're also going to be dealing with evidence that's sat in these locations for years, that's been degraded, damaged. It's going to be so hard to connect a lot of those dots." She offers me a kind smile. "But if anyone can track down whoever did this out on Ackert Farm, I think it's you two."

"How's the search coming?" I ask. I know they're all hands on deck trying to find Kaley, the girl who went missing.

"It's strange. We know she didn't run away. There haven't been any logins on her social media. Her cellphone is off. The tip line is full of unhelpful bullshit. To be honest, I'm worried we're going to end up finding her body—that it may end up being like Mazie's death."

"Do you think someone took her?"

"Maybe. No one thinks a local would have... but I'm not so sure."

"Why's that?" I ask.

"She wouldn't have gone with someone she didn't know. I feel like there would have been signs of a struggle. Something."

She reaches across her desk to her coffee cup. While she's grabbing it, she points to the family picture of her with her wife and their daughter. The daughter can't be older than five. She's absolutely adorable. "Oh God, it feels like a million years." Her eyes go wide and she laughs. "I mean that in a good way. But we've been together about seven years now."

"Did she grow up here too?"

She nods. "Yep. We actually went to school together our

whole lives. The kind of bullshit you see in romcoms. We hated each other in kindergarten."

I laugh at that. "Did the two of you ever go out to Ackert Farm?" There seems to be so many stories about kids ending up out in those woods. It's odd though, none of the other farms have the same reputation or allure. What was it about this farm that drew people in? Why did everyone end up out there?

She shakes her head. "No, I was too chickenshit. I'd heard the stories about how it was haunted, that at night if you went into the woods, you could hear women talking, crying, screaming. Sometimes you'd hear a baby. I never witnessed it firsthand. I don't think Ashley did either. Not that she ever told me anyway. But feel free to ask some of the guys. They might have been out on the farm."

"I will, thank you."

"All right, I've gotta start actually working," she says as she motions to her computer.

"I probably should too. It was great chatting with you though," I say, and I head back to the conference room. As I throw my stuff down on the table, Lucas walks in behind me. I hadn't realized that he was even here yet.

He raises a brow to me as he passes me a coffee cup.

"Thank you," I say as I take the coffee, then eye him skeptically. I'm not sure why he's looking at me like this.

"Sure," he says. Then motions to the door. "What was that back there?"

"Oh, I was just asking Ortega about the farm, if she'd ever been out there. I wanted to get her take on it."

He lowers his brows. "From where I was standing, it looked like you were flirting with her."

I laugh and shake my head. "No, she's married."

He huffs out a skeptical laugh. "You realize that you *can* flirt with married people, right?"

"Yes, obviously I know you *can* flirt with married people,

but I wasn't flirting." What the hell has gotten into him this morning? Is he crabby because we've had three days of spinning our wheels—or is it the anticipation of waiting for the DNA to come back?

"I haven't seen you look at anyone like that since Bianca."

"Don't start with me."

He purses his lips. "I didn't start anything with Bianca." He looks me up and down. "But you on the other hand..."

"Shut up, I was just being friendly."

"Uh-huh," he says as he takes a seat at the table and pulls out his laptop.

I catch Lucas up on what Alyssa told me. We're going to have to tread carefully while questioning Langdon again. When Brett finally comes into the office, I signal for Lucas to come with me as I weave through the bullpen toward his office. Brett leans back in his office chair, swiveling back and forth slightly. The walls of his office are packed with family photos and New York Jets memorabilia.

"Hey, Sarge, do you have a minute?" I ask, hoping that Brett won't remember our first interaction. The look he gives me tells me that he hasn't forgotten it.

"What do you need?" He sits back in his chair and glowers at me.

Lucas shoves in through the door, and steps half in front of me—as if he's shielding me from Brett. I want to elbow him.

"We got word from a witness from the night of Mazie's death that she was last spotted getting into Langdon's pickup. We wanted to have a conversation with him about what happened after he picked her up," Lucas explains.

Brett crosses his arms across his broad chest. "Do you think my boy did something to that girl? Because there's no—"

Lucas shakes his head. "No, we don't. But Langdon might have information about who saw Mazie last, or where she might have gone after the party," he explains.

Brett's expression relaxes slightly. "You can talk to him. But I swear to God if it starts to look like you're going pin this on him..."

"We have no inclination to pin this on your son. We're just looking for the person that killed Mazie, and that's it," Lucas explains, holding his ground. I hate that in situations like this, chauvinism wins time and time again.

Brett nods, and that's all he gives us, silent permission.

Back at my desk, I grab my bag and pull out my computer as my cellphone starts to ring—Lucas is already on the phone trying to schedule time with Langdon. I pull out my cell, glance at the screen, and see Amelia's name. I accept the call as I slide the phone onto the table and click the speaker button.

"Hello, Doctor," I say as I scoot forward in my chair, then hit the power button on my laptop.

"Hi, Detective. Is Detective Park there with you as well?" she asks.

"Yes, I'm here," Lucas says as he leans over, closer to my phone.

My heart pounds. Did they finish matching the DNA? If we're able to find out whether or not those bodies are related to Lucas, that's going to change his entire life. On one hand, he may find out for certain that he can stop looking, that his mother and grandmother have been dead all this time. He can finally grieve and put them to rest. But on the other hand, I know some part of him hopes that one day he'll find them—that he'll track down his mother out there somewhere, that he'll find out that she's alive. If we find out that she's dead, that hope is extinguished forever. That's not closure. That's not the news that anyone wants to hear. That means that Lucas loses hope, and that might cut him to his core.

"We've matched the DNA for the first victim that was found out at Ackert Farm," she explains.

Lucas's face falls. He was hoping that the DNA had come back on the newer victims, not that we were finally finding out about our first victims. I reach across the table and squeeze his hand, then mouth the words *I'm sorry* at him. He shrugs, as if it's nothing, but I can see how he's deflated. His shoulders are slumped, the light in his eyes has dimmed. He's holding it together because he's at work, but I know how devastating this must be, waiting every single day for one answer.

"The victim's name is Keely Hanson," she explains. "We were able to find a match for her on a familial DNA database on the internet, but it's not a person that's in the system. I'm going to email you the information of the person who submitted their DNA to the system so that you can go talk to them."

"Thank you," I say. "Any word on the DNA for the two newer victims?"

She clears her throat. "We were down for a few days because of the database problems, so we haven't been able to process that DNA yet since we weren't able to access files or add any new files to the system. Then we had a harder time extracting good samples than I had expected for us to."

"Are you going to be able to retrieve any samples at all?" I ask.

"Honestly, I'm not sure yet. We're still trying, so I'm sorry but it could be another week or so before we know anything." I can hear the frustration in her voice, so I know that she's taking it just as seriously as we are. "Lucas, we're going to do every-thing that we can to get samples from these victims," she promises.

"Thank you, I know you'll do your best," he says.

We finish up the conversation with Dr. Dushku, and I end the call with her. I look at Lucas; his eyes are on the table, his gaze far off. He's obviously not seeing anything in the room, he's so lost in thought.

"Hey, you okay?"

He looks at me, his gaze sharpening. "No. I'm not okay. Do you want me to pretend to be okay so this is all easier for you?" he snaps at me, and I flinch back. While I fully understand him being upset, I don't know why he's taking it out on me right now. "It's so easy for you to just compartmentalize everything so you feel nothing, ever. You can just keep working, even though you've been stabbed, or you've got someone sending you threatening text messages. You just brush it off because—nothing affects Harlow." He's words are dagger sharp and incredibly condescending. "But sometimes, maybe you should stop and just feel something. Maybe you should stop pushing everything away—people, your feelings."

"This isn't about me. I wanted to know how you are," I say, trying not to let his words get to me. He's just lashing out because he's frustrated that he didn't get any answers—that's what I'm trying to tell myself anyway. But his words hurt because they're true. I push everyone and everything away because that's easier than ever stopping to deal with anything. That's exactly what my dad told me that I did as a child. Avoidance, that's my coping mechanism. But, you know what, it's served me this long, so maybe it's not so bad.

"It is about you though. Everything is about you."

I sigh. "Don't do that. Everything is not about me."

"Yes it is. Everything is about what was done to you, what happened to you. What poor little Harlow had to go through when she was a child. Boo fucking hoo, Harlow. So what, you ended up in foster care. At least your mother and grandmother weren't kidnapped and possibly held captive in a fucking cabin for who knows how long."

I press my lips together. He really shouldn't be trying to compare our traumas. They're not the same. We were both molded by what happened to us. But he really has no idea what it was like for me, what I went through. I won't say it's any worse than what he endured, what he lost.

"Maybe you should just take the day," I suggest, because I think Lucas really needs some time to process this and to work out his feelings.

"Would that be easier for you? I'm sure it would be. You can't deal with someone having emotions. So yeah"—he grabs his back and chucks his laptop into it—"I'll just go, and deal with my own shit, so you can be more comfortable. I know how hard it must be for *you* to deal with someone else having a crisis." He slings his bag over his shoulder.

"Lucas, please, just tell me what to do. I don't know how to help," I say, because I'm completely at a loss. I feel helpless, and I know that must be how he feels too, but there's nothing I can do. I don't want to make empty promises about how he'll eventually get answers or add mindless platitudes that really aren't going to help anything. I always feel so lost in situations like this, because I've never had anyone to comfort me, to tell me how to make someone feel better—these are the things that children learn by seeing someone else comfort them. So how am I supposed to connect these dots? How am I supposed to help him?

"Of course you don't." He walks toward the door and I'm so frustrated that tears prickle my eyes. I'm rarely the crying type, but Lucas is the closest I've ever let anyone get to me. He's the one person that I've got—the one person I don't want to lose. And if I lost Lucas, if after everything we've been through as partners he didn't want to work with me anymore, if he didn't want to stand by my side anymore—it would absolutely destroy me. I'd move on like I always do, go to a new city, join a new team. But I don't think I'd ever be the same again, because at the end of the day, I'd know that this fell apart because of me. It'd be hard for me to deny that maybe I'm just too broken.

He slams the door behind him without another word, and tears sting my cheeks. I wish I knew what to do, I wish that I had the mental playbook to fix this. But I don't. I wrack my mind and think about how my father might handle this with a client. And the only thing that keeps coming to me, is to give him a little space, to let him process his emotions on his own for a while.

While I know that I'm relying on old habits to move forward, I don't know any other way to function. So instead of dealing with my emotions, instead of worrying about Lucas, I shove it all to the back of my mind, wipe my cheeks, and open the missing persons database. Compartmentalization is the easiest way for me to function.

My phone rings, and I grab it. "Detective Durant."

"This is Langdon, you wanted to talk to me," Langdon says, his voice unsteady on the other end of the line.

"Yeah, I wanted to talk to you a little bit more about Mazie," I say. I was hoping that I could do this questioning with Lucas. But right now that's not going to be an option. I can't burden him with this.

"There's a burger place on Main Street. I was on my way there..."

"I'll meet you there in ten," I say.

When I pull up to the parking lot of the Burger Shack, the clouds are hanging low, blotting out the afternoon sun. A dark blue pickup is already waiting in the lot, and I pull in next to it, trying to determine if it's Langdon's truck or someone else's. But when I see the mop of blond hair in the driver's seat, I know I've got the right vehicle.

Langdon looks over and pops his door open when he sees me. I slide out of my Jeep and meet him at the back of his truck. He leans against it. He's got on a denim jacket over an old T-shirt. The color of the denim matches his jeans.

"So, why'd you lie to me about the party?" I ask Langdon.

His eyes bulge, then he swallows hard. "I didn't lie," he says a little too quickly, then crosses his arms.

"Well, we've got evidence that Maize didn't leave with a stranger, she left the party with you. After you two were arguing." I don't add any other information, instead I'm purposefully succinct. The best way to get a perp to talk is to be quiet. Guilt will push out the truth faster than questions will.

Langdon brushes the hair out of his eyes, then looks toward the street, where cars are passing by. His jaw is a little too tense, and I think he might be chewing the inside of his cheek. "Look, okay, so she didn't leave with a stranger."

I nod, but I stay silent, allowing him the space to speak.

"She left with me, and yeah, we got in a fight. But she was talking to some other guy, and maybe I got a little too jealous. So I picked a fight with her and we left. But on the way to my grandpa's house, she told me she wanted to get out. She was mad, she wanted to walk home. But—" He clenches his jaw and looks away. For a moment I think he's going to cry.

"It's okay. You can tell me what happened," I urge him when he's quiet for a few moments.

"She started yelling at me that I was super controlling and told me to pull the truck over. So I did." He looks down at his feet. "When I pulled over, she got out of the truck. We were just down the road from my grandpa's farm. So I thought she was going to walk the rest of the way. We were supposed to go over there for some cake with my grandparents."

I want him to cut to the chase. He's dancing around the truth. My pulse kicks up. "Langdon, what happened after Mazie got out of the pickup?"

"She stomped off and I left. I left her there." His voice cracks, and he won't look up. "I was at my grandparents' house for a couple hours, and I called her when she never showed up. I drove home and I didn't see her, so I thought she'd gone home."

"Did you drive by Ackert Farm?" I ask, wondering if he would have had the opportunity to see her body.

He shakes his head.

"What time was all this?"

He provides me with a general timeline of when they left the party, when he thinks he dropped off Mazie, and when he left his grandparents' house. He shows me the texts and calls to Mazie that went unanswered, but that's not enough. I'll have to verify his alibi. He had the opportunity to kill her—the motive is a little shaky, but it's there.

"Can I take a look in your truck?" I ask.

"Yeah, I'm gonna go get a burger. Go wild. It's unlocked," he says as he points to the vehicle.

I grab a kit from my glove compartment before I check the vehicle. With what he's told me, I technically have enough to get a search warrant—but this is much faster. Going through the courts always slows everything down. As Langdon disappears inside, I pop open his driver's-side door and glance inside. The old truck is a bit dirty, a couple old cups in the cupholder. The beige interior is dingy and smells vaguely of cigarette smoke. I glance under the seats, looking for anything that could be used as a ligature—we still don't know what Mazie was strangled with. But I find nothing.

On the passenger side, something on the seat catches my attention. There are drops of a deep brown substance that's freckled across the front half of the seat. It looks like blood. I grab a swab out of my kit and swab the substance and shove it into a vial. Though Mazie didn't have any blood on her when we found her, this may show evidence of previous abuse or violence in their relationship.

I finish up grabbing the evidence from Langdon's truck and drop it off with the forensics team. On my drive to the office, I confirm Langdon's timeline with his grandparents, and they confirm his alibi. Back at my desk, I plug Keely Hanson's name into the search, and my heart rate slows. Doing something so familiar, going through a routine that I've done a million times, that helps settle my mind even more. Somehow, policework can be a lot like meditation. The repetition, following the steps I've taken so many times before. I know other people like to walk the same path over and over because it's comforting. For me, this work is like that.

It takes me a few seconds to get Keely's file to load—the database is still slow, though I'm grateful that it's working at all. Once Keely's file finally loads, I start to look over the details. Keely was nineteen years old when she disappeared from Albany. That's quite a distance from Ackert Farm, so that makes me wonder if our killer had a reason to travel farther up north. Were they a trucker? Did they have family upstate? There has to be a reason to have a hunting ground that's farther from home. If our killer had been quite prolific, then it might make more sense for him to have gone shopping for victims in other cities.

Keely worked at a record store in Albany. Originally it was suspected that she left town because she was pregnant and her family wouldn't have approved of her being in the family way without being married. However, based on the accounts from her friends, she didn't have a boyfriend and none of them had any reason at all to suspect she was pregnant. So often in the seventies and eighties police liked to assume that women who disappeared ran off of their own accord. So many victims of serial killers were written off as runaways. It's tragic that killers were allowed to hunt for so long because the lives of women were cast aside when they didn't *behave*. That's still true now.

It took three months after Keely's disappearance for the police to realize that she might have been kidnapped, and that she didn't just leave town of her own volition—when they found her clothing in a ditch with her purse. The clothes looked like they'd been there awhile. Her purse had her identification in it, so they were able to match the clothes back to her. Imagine what they could have found out if they'd actually started investigating her disappearance in the beginning, rather than assuming that she'd just taken off.

After they started to investigate Keely's disappearance as an actual criminal investigation, they focused heavily on Albany, speaking to her friends, family, and an ex-boyfriend. But nothing led them anywhere. There were no other similar disappearances in the area, so the investigation went cold after two years. I scroll through the details, trying to see if there were any tips over the years, but there's nothing else on the file.

I pull up the records that Amelia sent over to me for the DNA match. I google the name, and after a few minutes I'm able to determine that the woman in the contact information is Keely's twin sister, Ella. I really wish that I could make this call with Lucas present. I don't want him to feel like he's missed out on a major part of this investigation, but I can't just sit around and wait for him to not be mad at me anymore.

"Hello?" Ella picks up the call on the first ring.

I explain to her quickly who I am and why I'm calling her. She's silent for a long moment, like she can't believe that I'm on the line.

"Oh, okay," she finally says.

"I'm sorry to inform you, but we matched your DNA to a victim that we recently recovered from a plot of land in New Paltz," I explain.

She takes in a sharp breath. "You found my sister?"

"Yes, I am so sorry for your loss," I say.

She sniffles and her breathing quickens. "I know some part of me should have expected this. I mean, I put my DNA in that database for a reason. I was hoping that one day I'd get answers —but this isn't the answer I wanted. God, I hoped that she was still alive out there somewhere." She chokes the words out. "But honestly I don't know if it'd be worse finding out that she was alive out there somewhere and she just didn't want to talk to me for forty years," she says.

"I know. I'm so sorry. Is there anyone else I can call?" I ask.

She sniffles again, then clears her throat. "No, our parents died a few years ago. So I'm all that's left, other than cousins that really weren't invested in the search for her. But I'll let them know eventually. Will I be able to get her body so I can bury her?"

"Yes, in a few weeks we should be able to get Keely's remains transferred to you so that you can do a proper burial for your sister."

"How did she die?" she asks, her question so rushed that she cuts me off.

"We believe that she was suffocated or strangled. There wasn't any major trauma to the body, but our medical examiner found indications that she was likely strangled based on some damage to the neck," I explain, simplifying the answer as much as possible for her. I'm not sure how much she knows about anatomy.

"What else do you know about what happened to her?"

"We believe that she was held captive. So I was hoping that I could ask you a few questions to see if we can fill in some details on who might have taken your sister, why they might have chosen her, things like that. Is it okay for me to ask you some questions?" I ask, needing to shift the conversation. I can't have her keep leading the call and asking me a million questions. I need to get through some basic questions for the investigation so that I have a good direction to move forward in, especially if Ella is the only real remaining relative of Keely. There won't be much else for me to go on. That's the difficulty of investigating a disappearance that happened around forty years ago. So much evidence is lost, so much is forgotten from that time. At the very least, since it was such an impactful thing on Ella, maybe she'll remember some details about the time before her sister's disappearance that can really help us with this investigation.

"Captive? Oh my God—" she starts, like she's going to ask another question, so I know I have to jump in now or she's just going to keep firing them off at me.

"What was Keely doing before she disappeared?" I ask.

She pauses for a moment, shifting gears I guess, thinking over the events that took place so many years ago. "Well, that day she was working at the record store. She always walked there and walked home. That night, she should have been home by eight, but when she still wasn't there around ten we got a little worried. She would show up late occasionally, but it wasn't until the next morning when she still hadn't come home that we realized something must be wrong."

"How far away was the record store?" I ask as I take a few notes.

"About thirty minutes," she explains.

"That's a very long walk," I say. I'm surprised that she would walk thirty minutes each way to get to work. That seems like an incredibly long way to go.

"She didn't have a car. Public transportation wasn't an option. So unless she was able to get a ride from someone, there weren't many options."

"Did she ever hitchhike?" I ask. While that's incredibly rare these days because people know the dangers, back in the eighties, unfortunately it was very common for people to take rides from strangers. There were several serial killers who found their victims that way.

"Sometimes. I always got onto her when she did, so did our mother. But she didn't listen. She didn't think that anyone in Albany would hurt anyone else, so despite our best efforts, she kept doing it."

"So that night, she could have possibly taken a ride from the wrong person?" I suggest.

She clears her throat. "Yeah, I guess she might have. I hate to think that's what happened."

"Do you know of anyone who might have wanted to hurt your sister or someone who was very fixated on her?" I ask.

"No, I don't think so. There isn't anyone that comes to mind anyway. My sister really kept to herself a lot. She liked music because it said things that she couldn't say. But she tended to hide behind things: music, me, whatever she could put between herself and another person. She was very introverted and incredibly shy. I was the extroverted twin. We were polar opposites in that way," she explains.

"Were you identical?" I ask.

"Yes, we were."

"Is it possible that someone took your sister and thought that Keely was *you*?" If she was more extroverted and had more relationships with people in town, it's always possible that someone mistook Keely for Ella.

She's silent for a bit. "I mean, I guess it would be possible."

"Okay, so did you have any enemies, anyone who might have wanted to target you?" I push because Ella is getting less responsive. I need her to dig deep and really think about who might have gone after her or her sister.

"I worked at the diner in town. I loved waiting tables because I interacted with everyone and chatted them up. I made really good tips. The couple weeks before Keely disappeared, there was a new guy who started coming into the diner. He was a little older than me, but cute. He was flirting with me a lot. He was coming in for every meal and asked for me to wait on him every time he came in," she explains. "I don't know that he would have targeted me. But he's the only person that sticks out to me, even after all this time."

"Did you see him again after your sister disappeared?"

"No."

"What was his name?" I ask.

"Oh God, I don't remember. It's been so long."

"Do you think you'd recognize him again if you saw a picture?" Though I don't have any images to send her now, hopefully at some point in this investigation I'll be able to track down a suspect to put in front of her.

"Most likely, yeah. I'm very good at remembering faces."

"Did you mention to this man that you had a twin sister?" I ask.

She's silent for a second. "No, I don't think there's any reason that I would have brought that up. When I was nineteen, I was very bothered by the constant focus on me being a twin rather than on me as an individual. That's when Keely and I started going in our own directions with interests, dressing very differently. Maybe that's why she started hitchhiking, so she could feel like she was doing something different than I was."

"Was Keely taking more risks in general?"

She clears her throat. "Yes, more than usual. I haven't thought about any of this in years." Her voice takes a sullen turn. "Does that make me a bad person? After she disappeared, I just tried to move on with my life. The police convinced us that she left, and that was easier to believe. She'd always talked about wanting to move to Manhattan, so I told myself that's what she did. When they told us that they thought she'd been kidnapped instead, I didn't believe them. I kept on telling myself that she was living her own life, she was better off." Her voice thickens, as if tears are streaming down her cheeks.

Times like this, I wish that I had Lucas with me. He has better soft skills. He knows how to handle people that are in crisis, that are saddened. For me, it's hard to figure out the right things to say. "That doesn't make you a bad person at all. That's very common for family members of people who disappear. And sometimes they're right. Please don't feel like you're a bad person here. There's really nothing that you could have done."

"She was taken all the way to New Paltz?" she asks.

"Yes, she was. We're not sure if she was always at this property. It is possible that she was held somewhere else and then eventually moved here." For now, I'm not going to mention that the ME thinks that Keely was alive long enough to have a baby, that we think she was held at the property for at least five years. All of that right now would just be salt in a wound, so I'll save that for a later conversation. But I need to flip this conversation back to the questioning. "Can you give me an idea of the other types of risks that your sister was taking before her disappearance?"

"She was going to a lot of parties, which was out of character for her. She also got a tattoo from a guy in town that she'd started talking to in the record store. Back then, you have to understand, tattoos were nowhere near as common as they are today. Usually men were the only people that had them, and that was because they were in the service. So, for her to come home with a tattoo—well, suffice to say our parents were absolutely livid."

"Did she say why she got the tattoo?" I ask, making a note about it. I'm really curious about why Keely had become such a risk-taker. Was she just ready to get out of Albany, or had something else happened to her? Was she acting out for some reason?

"She said she got it because she wanted to. Then she went on about how she was going to get more. She wanted people to know she was different when they looked at her. She was really wrapped up in the punk rock movement. Maybe it was so that she had something about her that was obviously different from me?" she offers, though her words waver. She sniffles a little, but overall it sounds like she's stopped crying. That's an improvement at least.

Though I doubt I can track down whoever gave her the tattoo, I'll at least keep that at the top of my mind. "You mentioned that Keely had a boyfriend. Can you tell me anything about him?"

"He was a guy that she met at the record store. He had a local band. They partied together a lot."

"Would you say that she started taking more risks when she started dating this guy? What was his name?"

"His name was Ian Shaw. He was the guitar player for a stupid band called Dumpster Divers," she says, vitriol dripping from her words. "He was an absolute asshole, but Keely fell head over heels in love with him the moment he first spoke to her. He was very much on the party scene, always doing drugs, always getting into some kind of trouble. So the moment they started dating, it was like she felt like she had to compete with him," she explains, her words rippling with annoyance.

"Do you think that Ian was capable of violence? Did he ever get into fights or anything like that?" I ask. Typically, guys with a violent streak tend to get into fights a lot, bar fights, street fights. Whatever excuse they can make to punch someone else in the face—they take it.

"Honestly, I don't remember him ever getting into any fights. That wasn't something that I heard about. Our mom was quite the town gossip, so if she knew that Ian was the fighting type, I'm sure I would have heard about it."

I write down a note about that. I'll need to see if Ian has any connections to New Paltz. "Did Ian and Keely ever have any fights or any problems?"

"Occasionally they fought. She'd get jealous if she thought that she saw Ian flirting with another girl at one of his shows, something like that. But overall, the fights really weren't that bad."

"So, it doesn't sound like Ian would have done anything to your sister then?" I know I'm leading her, but at first it sounded like she thought Ian was a piece of garbage, and now it doesn't sound like he did anything to Keely.

"It's not that I think Ian did anything to her himself. But I think his influence made her do things she shouldn't have. Does that make sense? Before him, I don't think she would have taken risks that made her end up getting kidnapped. I think he did that."

"Well, unfortunately I can't arrest someone for that. I can look into Ian to see if he has any connections anywhere that might make sense to this case. Is there anything else overall that you can think of? Anything about the guy from the diner?" I circle back to the guy from the diner, because that seems like a better lead than Ian. Especially since he was focused in on Ella and could have easily mistaken Keely for her.

"The guy from the diner said that he was going to be leaving town the day that Keely disappeared. He'd asked me if I wanted to go with him, and I'd laughed it off. I thought at the time it was flirting, so I'd joked back that I'd go with him. He'd pushed me a little bit, asking when I got off work." She pauses for a moment too long, so I push her to continue.

"And what did you tell him?"

"I got off work at the same time that Keely did... I also walked home. I told him when I would be leaving. But I didn't really think that he was going to show up. And when I left, he wasn't waiting outside or anything, so I didn't think anything of it. But oh God, maybe he picked up Keely because I told him when I was leaving and he really thought that it was me..."

She goes quiet. I know I've got to jump in.

"Ella, this isn't your fault. You had no way of knowing."

"I have to go," she says, and the line goes dead.

My heart races after the line goes dead, and I try to digest what happened on the call—I go over what I could have said, how I could have made it all go better. I wish that Lucas had been here. I feel like it would have ended different. Glancing at my phone, I realize it's been over an hour since Lucas left. Maybe that's been enough time for him to cool down. As it's nearing lunchtime, I grab my bag and head out of the bullpen. I text Ella, asking her for a list of friends that Keely had, and hope that she sends them over.

Outside the station, the sky is bright, almost obnoxiously blue. There isn't a single cloud in the sky, which is rare for New York. This is the type of summer day that most New Yorkers love, but it's not for me. I like clouds, rain. Probably because that's what I grew up with; a blanketed gray sky feels comforting to me. I climb into my Jeep, start the engine, and head to the small downtown of New Paltz. I stop at a couple places, grabbing a few sandwiches, cupcakes, and the barista at the coffee shop talks me into a couple tea lattes that I'm skeptical of.

The city is quiet as I weave my way through the streets toward the hotel. My guts are in knots and a cold sweat slicks my neck. I hate fighting, confrontation, which I guess is hilarious given my line of work, but the idea that something may have broken in my relationship with Lucas today that I won't be able to fix makes me absolutely sick to my stomach. I'm not sure what I'd do without him, if our partnership changed completely and I was stuck with someone who didn't see me in the same light.

I'd have to leave. I'd have to uproot myself again, which I've done so many times—that's what my brain is screaming for me to do now. It's easier to run than it is to face something. It's easier to pack my bags, shut off my emotions, and pretend that a new city will fix everything. But for the first time, I don't want to do that. I want to fix this. I want to stand beside Lucas as we hunt down the person who killed his mother. That's what I want.

My heart pounds when I pull into the parking lot of the hotel. In the back of my mind, I hear all of my father's psychobabble for how to handle fights, for how to be an active listener, for how to shift someone's thinking. But I don't want him or his experience to help me fix this. I want to trust my gut. Because if

I can't fix this myself, then maybe I don't deserve Lucas in my life.

I climb the stairs with my hands full and pause when I get to Lucas's door. I wait for a little too long, trying to figure out the perfect thing to say when he opens the door. Unable to knock, I kick the bottom of the door and wait. After a few seconds, Lucas opens it, his eyes red and puffy. His lips look swollen too, like he's been crying nonstop since he left the office. He looks at me, then the stuff in my arms, and grabs a bag to help me.

I follow him inside the hotel room as he heads inside. It smells like cologne in here, sweet and woody, much better than my room smells. I glance to the small table near the window in the room and find he's got a diffuser set up on the table. He's also changed out the hotel comforter for a down version that I'm sure he brought with him. I can't believe that I never thought to do that. Instead of having his luggage thrown on the floor, looking like it's vomiting clothes, he's got it stacked up in the closet. I'm sure he even put his clothes away in the drawers. Through the open closet, I can also see that he's hung up his jacket and button-up shirts.

"Let me call you back," he says as he ends a call. His phone was waiting for him in the small kitchenette in the back corner of the room.

I walk over to the counter, place down a bag, and offer Lucas his tea latte.

"I don't think I need the caffeine right now," he says as he glances at it. "Thanks though."

"There isn't much caffeine in it. The barista talked me into getting us tea lattes. She says that this is a calming blend, so it should just be refreshing," I explain. I'm not completely sold on the idea, but it tastes good, like velvety lemon and orange with a hint of Earl Grey tea.

He picks it up and tests a sip. "Not bad." Though I can tell that it's not his favorite thing in the world.

I open up one of the bags, and hand him a takeout container. "I brought you some lunch. You haven't eaten yet, have you?"

He shakes his head as he takes the container. "No, just been up here talking to Ethan."

I take my latte and go to sit by the window. The smell of the diffuser grows stronger when I sit next to it. "Look, I'm really sorry. I know that I'm not good at this"—I motion between us—"human shit. But I really do care, and I want to help track down the person who took your mother and grandmother. I know how important that is for you and I'm here to help however I can."

He hangs his head as he leans against the counter. Fresh tears spill down his cheeks. "I know. I overacted. I'm sorry—this is just all so..." He shakes his head. "My whole life, I've wanted to find out what happened to my mom, to my grandmother. But when you're on the cusp of it, and you realize that maybe you really don't want to know... Some part of you *needs* to know, so you're holding your breath knowing that the next words could change your life. It could change everything you've ever known and the future. But then that's ripped away. God, I just..." He stumbles over his words and stops. He sucks in a sharp breath and the tears flow anew. I put my latte down on the side table and cross the room to Lucas. I take his latte, put it down, then wrap my arms around him.

I've never been the hugging type. In fact, I typically avoid all touch if possible. It makes me so uncomfortable. But Lucas is touchy, and I know this is what he needs right now. So I hold him tight, I squeeze him, then pat his back slowly as he sobs.

"I know it's hard. But we're going to find whoever took your family. I promise you I will help you."

"I know, thank you. This is just so much harder than I ever expected this would be. I thought that after all this time, maybe it would be easier. But that kind of trauma, it never leaves you. But you know that," he says as he pulls away.

I walk back to the table and sit down. After a few seconds, Lucas joins me and sits on the other side. He swipes at his tears. His face looks so raw from all the crying. I shove up from the chair and walk to the bathroom, looking for a box of tissues. When I finally find one, I bring it back for him.

"Thank you," he says as he takes it and blots his nose. "God, I'm so gross right now."

"Don't FaceTime Ethan," I caution him. He does look absolutely awful, like a red snotty mess.

"Too late," he says with a sad laugh. "I was talking to him when you came in, and we'd been FaceTiming when I first got back."

"Everything okay with you two?" I ask.

He nods. "Yeah, he loves you. He said I needed to stop being such a dick to you because you were the best partner I'd ever have."

"He's sticking up for me already? Oh, I love him," I say with a grin.

He rolls his eyes. "If we work up there for a few weeks, I know the two of you are going to start ganging up on me. I can see it already." He sighs. "Look, I'm really sorry—" he starts again, and I hold up my hand.

"We're good. You don't need to do that." I look down at my latte and force myself to take a sip. I need to tell Lucas about the conversation that I had with Ella. But I'm afraid that it's going to make him upset with me again. He's going to be pissed that I did the interview without him.

"What's that face?" he asks, and he makes a circle in the air as he points toward me.

"I called Keely's twin sister, Ella, and interviewed her."

He looks at his phone. "I wasn't gone that long. How did

you already track her down and interview her?" His words are a little clipped, annoyance sharpening his words.

"Yeah, well. As you said, I do best with avoidance. So that's exactly what I did. She was available, so I asked her about Keely." I give him a rundown of everything that Ella told me, and that the leading theory for me is that the guy from the diner grabbed the wrong girl.

He nods, and the tension in his shoulders fades a little. I can tell he's not going to yell at me. The knots in my guts loosen a bit.

"So, what's next then?" he asks.

"I think we should track down anyone else that might have worked at that diner. I'm not sure we'll find anything, but it's worth checking. Then I want to see if we can talk to Keely's ex-boyfriend, or any of her friends from that time period."

He nods, then takes a sip of his drink. "Sounds like a plan."

"Unless you want to take the rest of the afternoon off?" Lucas has always been good about pushing me to take time off when I need to. I want to be sure that I'm giving him the same opportunity. He doesn't need to have the same unhealthy reliance on work that I do.

"Let's get back to it."

We set up shop in Lucas's hotel room and start doing our research. It's not easy to track down people that may or may not have worked in a small diner at the edge of Albany in the early eighties. For hours, I feel like we're running in circles, so I go in a different direction and look for the boyfriend—only to find out that he died of a drug overdose in the nineties. That rules him out. As the sun lingers on the horizon, my stomach growls.

"Want to take a break and grab some food?" I ask. It's been several hours since we both ate our sandwiches, and if I'm going to keep digging, I can't have my stomach distracting me.

"Can we go somewhere that doesn't just serve burgers and fries?"

I nod. "Yeah, if we have to. Back on a health kick?"

"I feel like my arteries are pushing around burger grease. I just can't eat any more red meat today. I need a salad or something."

"Fine, if we must," I say with a laugh, thankful that Lucas and I are back on good terms.

I throw my bag over my shoulder and we bound down the stairs toward the parking lot. As I shove through the door to the outside, an orange glow bathes everything. Tufts of clouds that dot the sky are highlighted in oranges, golds, and pinks. It looks beautiful. But as my eyes skim the lot and finally land on my Jeep, I feel like we're not alone out here.

16

NINETEEN YEARS AGO

The night is thick around me, the sky inky, only a smattering of stars winking in the heavens. I've got my jacket zipped up to my throat as the cold whips at me. I shouldn't be out this late, but I couldn't be trapped in that house with my mother anymore, bottled inside with her rage. I swear I could feel it vibrating in the walls. Every time she walked downstairs, she stomped her feet, making her rage echo through the entire house like a heartbeat. So, I slipped out my window, crept across the roof, and shimmied down the trellis until my feet hit the soft earth.

My father is late, again. He's late most nights now. Something my mother never lets him live down. Their constant fighting, their rage, it's become a static that I hear in my ears even when it's quiet—as if their words are imprinted on me. My breaths come quick as the thoughts pummel me, and it takes me too long to calm myself.

As I round the corner in my neighborhood, my head is swimming. I wish I could just be normal like everyone else, to not have to deal with the incessant thoughts that my father might be out killing someone *right now* or with my mother's abuse. Why did I end up with two parents that are so incredibly fucked up? It's hard to go to school, to listen to anyone else's problems. I don't talk to my friends anymore—I haven't since I found out what my dad was really doing. Because I can't tell any of them. I can't talk to my mom about it.

You should go to the police. The voice in the back of my mind says, again, like it does about twelve times a day. I should have gone to the police the day I found out. Sometimes I wonder how many lives I would have saved if I had. How much blood is on my hands now? The thought makes my guts threaten to turn to water, and my heart feels like it hiccups in my chest.

The wind whips at me again, making me pick up my pace. My fingers curl inside the loose sleeves that hang at my sides. I don't have gloves, so this is the best I can do to save the tips of my fingers from going numb. I've walked around the neighborhood twelve times now, and I know I'll have to sneak back inside soon. There's only so long that I can keep this up. My limbs are stiff as I loop back around toward my house. I search the street for my father's car, not sure if seeing it would make me decide to go back in or to hold off, to wait for the fight to die down. But when I don't see it, I deflate a little, my shoulders sagging. I should just go back inside, warm up, and go to sleep.

I walk up the street, my feet scuffing against the pavement as I drag them a little more than I should. When I'm about a hundred yards from my house, I look up and notice that there's a van parked outside my neighbor's house, for an electrician or a plumber. I've never seen a van like that here at night. Though I can see a logo sketched on the side from where I stand, it's too far to read it. It's weird, I hadn't noticed it on my previous passes around the neighborhood. Maybe I just wasn't paying attention.

I continue my trudge toward the house, my anxiety tightening around my chest, like I'm being squeezed by Godzilla's fist. When I finally reach the van, I pause beside it, a low beeping catching my attention. I pause, and widen my stance, waiting to hear the noise again. Then the van shifts, like something inside it moved. My heart skips a beat, and I freeze. The low murmur of voices catches my attention, like there's someone inside the van.

My mind roars with thoughts, as I realize that this must be a stakeout, one of those FBI vans that watches criminals. They're here to watch my dad.

17

I squint against the morning light, cursing under my breath that it's so damn bright. In a month, when it's cold and gray, I know I'll regret it. But for now, I wish the damn sun would just *calm down*. I shove my sunglasses on the bridge of my nose, and they pinch me a little too hard. But at least it's blotted out the light a bit. I walk down Main Street, the sun kissing my face as I stroll toward it. It's still early, but I swear the sun woke up early just to taunt me. The smell of coffee floods the street, luring me to the coffee shop—as if that wasn't the destination I had in mind in the first place.

The door chimes as I turn into the shop. Hissing fills the air as the barista works behind the counter making coffees. No one is in here yet, so I'm not sure if she's making the drinks for herself or for pickup orders. As I approach, she turns around and flashes me a smile. I place my order, getting Lucas a twin of my own order—I'm grateful that he's open to different flavors, just like I am.

Behind me, I hear someone else enter the shop, but I don't turn to look at them. But when I hear someone clear their throat behind me, I turn to see bright red hair. I know instantly that it's

Neal. I glower at him, hoping that my gaze will warn him off of fucking with me this morning. But he doesn't so much as flinch. In fact, a smarmy smile splits his thin lips, and he rocks back and forth on his heels—as if he loves nothing more than antagonizing me.

"I'm so glad I ran into you," he says with a grin, as if this were all a happy accident. I'm sure that he's been following me. There's zero chance that he just happened to run into me.

"Just get your coffee and leave me alone," I grumble as I grab my coffees from the counter and thank the barista.

As I turn to leave, Neal steps in front of me, blocking my path. If I wasn't in desperate need of the caffeine clutched in each of my hands, I'd throw one at his face just to knock the look off of it—but I won't sacrifice my drink or Lucas's. The way he grins at me, so pleased with himself that he's inconvenienced me, it needles me in the worst way—which I'm sure is exactly what he's trying to do. Angry people say more than they mean to, that's a fact that I know well from my own interrogations. If you piss someone off just enough, sometimes they'll tell you their life story.

"Look, Harlow, I just need a few minutes of your time," he says, his demeanor shifting.

"You don't deserve a second of my time," I say. "You're a vulture trying to profit off of my messed-up childhood. You don't deserve to hear all about my pain, my struggles. Just fuck off." This is what pisses me off the most about the journalists I've encountered in my life. They tell me that they're trying to find answers, that they're trying to tell the public the truth of what happened. But they don't deserve to know about my pain, about my struggle. That's irrelevant, that has nothing to do with what my father did to those women. These are separate things.

"The book is done. It's going to go to print whether or not I speak with you. But if you and I can talk for just a few minutes, I'll split my advance with you, along with ten percent of all my royalties. The publisher agreed to the split, and honestly, I may be able to get them to pony up a bit more—"

I shake my head and take a sip of my latte. "No, I'm not interested. You don't understand. There are some people in this world that aren't solely motivated by money. Blood money doesn't pay your bills. It takes your soul. And I don't want any part of that." I'm not trying to sound all high and mighty, because I'm not that person. But this money—money that is basically profiting off of my father's crimes—I don't want anything to do with that. I'd rather starve.

"You don't have any feelings on your mother and father reuniting or your father trying to get a new trial?"

Though I don't mean to, I raise a brow to that. My father is trying to get a new trial? Since when? How would that even work? Does my father really think that he's going to argue his innocence this time around? There was so much evidence for his crimes. The only connection between most of the women was him, and he had all their names written in a notebook. From each woman's house, when he killed them, he took a trophy and kept it in the den in our house. I don't know how you argue innocence after that.

The door chimes, and I see Lucas walk through. He looks between me and Neal before flashing me a questioning look. I wave my hand in dismissal, indicating to him that I can handle this. He doesn't need to jump in for me.

"Neal, I have no comment. I've made it clear that I'm not interested in being a part of your project. This is my last warning, please back off." I do my best to keep my tone even, but I say most of this through gritted teeth. There's a tightness in the pit of my stomach as anxiety coils inside me. This book is the last thing that I need. I've done my best to fly under the radar my whole life. It hasn't always worked out the way I've wanted, so I've had to jump from department to department as the dark history of my father's crimes has followed me. I've changed my name, dyed my hair, done everything in my power to pretend that I'm someone else. But no matter what I do, my past eventually finds me.

"You're going to change your mind. If you don't give at least a little statement, you're going to regret it. Give me your email, I'll send you the manuscript so you can at least review it," he urges me. I wonder if this guy used to sell used cars or something.

I shake my head. "No, I'm not going to change my mind." Curiosity nags at me. Part of me wants to read that manuscript, just to see what he said, to see what my parents said during their interviews. What did my mother say about me? What did she say she knew? I shake my head, as if it'll clear the curiosity that's digging its claws into me. But it's still there, whispering in the back of my mind.

Neal takes a step toward me, so close that I can smell his cologne. There's a sourness to it that makes my nostrils curl.

"You're going to regret it, Harlow. I'm warning you."

His tone makes me cock my head. There's a hint of something laced in his words that I don't like, and I'm not going to stand here and let him threaten me. Lucas inches forward behind Neal, his arms crossed as he appraises both of us. He's not even trying to camouflage his eavesdropping.

Anger rises up inside me at Neal's vague threat. I'm not going to let this smarmy journalist waltz in here and tell me what I'm going to regret this early in the goddamn morning. But before I can open my mouth to tell him to fuck off, Lucas closes the distance between himself and Neal, then steps between us.

"I suggest you get the fuck out of here before I take you in for threatening an officer," Lucas warns him.

Neal's eyes narrow as he looks Lucas up and down. "Maybe you should mind your own business."

Lucas points to me with his thumb, then back to himself. "This is my business."

"What, are you her boyfriend or something?" Neal sputters the question out, like it's the most hilarious thing he's ever thought of in his life. I'm tempted to roll my eyes at him.

"Oh fuck off," I say. I step around Lucas and Neal, then exit the coffee shop. The cool morning air hisses on the back of my neck. I'm not going to watch the two of them fight each other. There's nothing I hate more than Lucas trying to intervene on my behalf, as if I can't handle the situation myself.

I hear Lucas's feet scuffing on the sidewalk behind me as I walk past a tailor on the row of small businesses downtown. When Lucas finally catches up with me, he tugs on my shirt to slow me down, like a toddler would tug on their mother.

"What, Lucas?" I snap. Then I realize I'm still holding his coffee. I hand it to him.

He takes a step back, and surveys me from head to toe. "Are you mad at me now?" he asks as he presses his left hand to his chest.

"A little, yeah," I say, then take a sip of my coffee. I look around, noting that no one is near enough to us for them to over-hear our argument, so I don't hold back. "I really don't appre-ciate that you never think that I can handle anything myself. You're always interjecting on my behalf instead of letting me handle something."

He sighs and rolls his eyes at me. "Harlow, that's what people do when they care. It's not that I don't think you can handle it on your own, it's that you deserve to have someone else stand beside you and offer you support so you don't have to feel like you're alone in everything. I don't throw a bitch fit every time you intervene on my behalf when one of the guys at the station is talking shit to me," he says. "Do you think that I can't handle myself with them?"

I press my lips together. That's exactly why I intervene on his behalf, because I don't think that he'll stand up for himself when he should. But now I don't want to say that. I'm not trying to hurt his feelings.

"Oh, okay," he says, clearly slightly hurt.

"Okay, wait," I say, trying to figure out the right way to smooth this over. I don't want Lucas upset with me. "That's not what I was trying to say. It's not that I don't think that you *can* handle yourself. It's that I don't think you'll stand up for yourself when you should."

He raises a brow at me. "Yeah, same." He pauses, for the sake of impact, I'm sure. "I know you *can* handle yourself just fine. But you don't always push back when you should. Sometimes you start to cave a little, probably because women are trained to be nice and appeasing their entire lives. You don't need to do that. So when I see that you need a little strength, I'm going to be there to give it to you, and there's absolutely nothing you can do to stop me." The way he says it, there's a challenge in his words, as if he also added *I dare you to try and stop me* to the end.

I let his words roll around in my mind for a moment, thinking them over. I'm not sure what exactly to say. It's still such a foreign concept to have someone like Lucas in my life, someone I can count on, to help me. I've never had that before.

"I'm sorry," I finally say.

"You don't need to be sorry. I'm not trying to get an apology out of you. I know exactly how fucked up your life has been, so you don't need to start explaining yourself to me or anything like that. But if someone is coming for you, if someone is harassing you, you better get your ass used to me stepping in and *helping* you, because I am on your team."

Tears prickle my eyes, and I hate that he's making me feel like this. I've always been so good at compartmentalizing my feelings, at taking a step back and surrounding myself with an impenetrable wall. But somehow, Lucas knows exactly what to say to get through. The old Harlow, she would have pushed him away, she would have made Lucas hate her, just so she didn't have to let him in. But I'm not going to do that. I'm going to stop letting the desire to protect myself overrule everything else.

"Thanks," I finally say, then wipe my eyes on the back of my wrist. "I think we need to head up to Albany for a few days," I say.

He nods. "I think we do too. Let's see if we can find anyone who knew Keely, and what they remember about the time she disappeared. We should also ask around to see if any other women went missing around the time that Keely did. Maybe those two women were taken around the same time period. Though there's no way for us to know for sure, it's worth checking into."

The other thing I'm not saying out loud is that I think us getting out of town and digging into this case a bit more will keep Lucas's mind off of waiting for the DNA to come back on whether or not our second group of victims was his family.

It takes us about an hour to get ready and to pack our stuff into my Jeep. Albany is far enough that we'll need to stay up there for a few days, so I call Dirby to let him know our plans, then inform Ortega of the same. I've almost finished my coffee as I climb into the driver's seat. Lucas climbs in beside me, and I notice he's got a brown paper bag in his hands.

"What's that?" I ask, as I start the car and pull out of the parking spot. The hotel lot has filled up around us. It's the last chance of the season to get out here and enjoy the lake before it starts to get cold, so tourists have flooded into the city. On one hand, it's allowed us to not stand out so much. But on the other hand, it's so packed in town that there are lines everywhere and it's nearly impossible to park.

"I grabbed us a few donuts," he says as he shakes the bag in front of me.

"When did you even have time to do that?" I ask as I turn right out of the parking lot and onto the street.

"You took forever to pack," he says.

"I did not take forever. It took me like fifteen minutes," I say, a bit more defensive than I should be. Maybe I'm still annoyed by the interaction with Neal and that's weighing on my words.

"For someone who's moved four hundred times, I'd think that you could pick up the pace a little. I was ready in five minutes, so I took the liberty of getting us some breakfast," he says with a smug smile.

"Well, good for you." I roll my eyes at him then turn my attention back to the road. Lucas eats his glazed donut and I munch on a coffee roll. As we carve our way through a forest of pine trees northward, the sugar hits my bloodstream and I wish I had more to do than just drive.

The trees crowd around the road, and as we climb upward the hills grow into mountains, then finally give way. Above us, the blue sky is dotted with white clouds, and I'm glad that for now it's not raining. There's nothing I hate more than driving in the rain. It takes us a little over an hour to make it to Albany. Since Albany is a larger city than we usually stay in, we were able to get something a little nicer. And I'll relish it.

It takes us about ten minutes to find our hotel, check in, and settle into our rooms. I pull up Keely's file on my phone and look over it again. While we're here, I really want to talk to her sister again, see if she's come up with anything else. But I'm going to give her some breathing room first, since we didn't end our last call on the best terms. When Lucas finally knocks on my door, I know I'm done game-planning.

"What are we doing first?" Lucas asks.

"For now, we're going to the diner. While we're there grabbing some food, we're going to ask the staff there if anyone has worked there long enough to know Ella. I doubt we'll have that kind of luck, but it doesn't hurt to check. We can also see what we can do about the list of friends that Ella gave us." I wish the boyfriend was still alive. He would have been a great person to talk to about Keely, if only for a little while.

"We just need to be careful that we don't spook the sister," he says, and I nod.

My phone vibrates with a call from Dr. Dushku, and my stomach tightens. I'm not sure if this is the call for the identity of the remaining victim from the first set, or the second set that we believe could be related to Lucas. I place the call on speaker, thankful that we're still in the hotel room.

"Doctor, I've got Lucas here with me," I say.

"Afternoon, Detectives. We were able to find a familial DNA match in an online database for the second victim that was identified at the first scene. Her name was Davida Hall. It looks like she has a missing persons file that was entered into the database in eighty-six," she explains.

We chat with Dr. Dushku for a few more moments, and we find out that Lucas's results have been delayed because his original sample was lost. Frustration needles me, but I won't take it out on her—it's not her fault. But I know how much this has been eating Lucas inside. For us to face this kind of setback and all these delays, it must be so frustrating for him.

"I'll send a new sample over to the lab today," Lucas promises. Luckily, since all the state agencies are connected, he can provide his sample here in Albany and in a few days it'll arrive at her office.

"Great, thank you. Once I have it in my possession, it'll be two, maybe three days, tops, to process it," she promises and then ends the call.

"So, another week then... at least," Lucas says as he sighs.

"I'm sorry it's taking so long," I say. In situations like this, I'm never sure what to say. I know his training would be far more useful here for conversations like this. You'd think that as the daughter of a psychologist I would have picked up more, but unfortunately it didn't work out that way.

"Honestly, it's what I expected. DNA matching has been getting slower and slower as more departments lean on it. Keeping up with the demand, especially as they're trying to use the database to identify cold cases as well, putting in new samples every day—at some point it's going to strain the system. And you know... we're understaffed."

I don't mean to, but I laugh. "I've never been to a station that wasn't understaffed. It seems to me that they're designed like that on purpose."

He smirks, and it's as if he's shaken off all the disappointment from not getting any answers today. "It's almost like they need us to be this slow so we don't operate faster than the judicial system can."

I laugh a little at that, happy that for now, Lucas isn't too upset by the outcome here. I would have understood if he were. I'd be so pissed off if I kept facing the setbacks that he is, when he's been desperate for answers for years.

"My stomach is growling. Can we go get food now?" Lucas asks as he glances toward the door.

"Yeah, let's go," I say as I grab my bag.

It takes us about ten minutes as we carve through the city of Albany to make it to the diner where Ella used to work. On the outskirts of the city, stone buildings rise around me. In the distance I can see several towering buildings. This is one of the largest cities I've visited in New York. It's jarring how much traffic there is here versus what we've dealt with in the small towns in New York. We're stuck behind an old Buick driving about five miles per hour through downtown, so I'm able to get a good look at the city.

The diner sits on the edge of town, right off the highway. While most houses in Albany are large colonials, Victorians, these are more craftsman-style houses that are all one story. We pull into the parking lot of the diner, and I'm thankful that it looks pretty empty. I guess no one is trying to get food at two in the afternoon.

Everyone looks at us when we walk inside, and suddenly it feels like we've been transported back to one of the other towns we've worked in. Clearly, most of the people that come in here are regulars. A woman who's likely in her sixties greets us at the door, with two huge menus pressed to her chest. She offers us a thin smile that doesn't reach her cold eyes.

"You've got your pick of the place. Where do y'all want to sit?" she asks as she waves her hand in a sweeping motion to indicate how empty the diner is.

"Can we get that booth over there?" Lucas asks as he points to one in the corner that gives us the ability to see the entire restaurant,

She nods. Then raises her brow at Lucas. "You two cops?"

"We're detectives with the state," he says. "How'd you know?"

"That's the table the cops always pick," she says as she indicates for us to follow her. "I'd say that y'all are always cut from the same cloth." Her words don't make it clear if her statement is an insult or a compliment. She leads us to the table, offers us the menus, and introduces herself as Peggy, but before I can ask her a single question, she's disappeared.

She's moved on to the other side of the restaurant so quickly it's like she teleported. Maybe there's a secret passage or something because there's no way she managed to get there on foot. Lucas raises a brow at me as he shifts in the booth.

"What's your problem?" I ask.

"It's just kind of sticky. I wonder if they leave the booth like this because this is the *cop* booth and they hate cops." He picks up his menu and pulls the same face. "Ugh, this is sticky too."

"Have you never been to a diner before? It's a law that

everything in a diner must be sticky and smell like maple syrup. They're on brand."

He wrinkles his nose. "I feel like I'm in a daycare."

"I'll get you a hand wipe before we leave. We'll get you all cleaned up," I say in the most patronizing way that I can manage.

He pulls up his menu, creating a wall between us, so I can't see his reaction. But I'm sure he's making a face at me on the other side. I look over the options as Peggy reappears with water and coffee cups for us. I love that we didn't even have to ask for coffee. This woman is after my own heart.

"So, what are you all in town for?" she asks as she places our drinks down.

"We're trying to track down a few people connected to a missing persons cold case. Hoping that we can track down some friends and family," Lucas says, giving more information than I'd like him too. We always hold back some information from the public for a reason. Right now, we haven't released the names of the women found in New Paltz, their cause of death, nor that it was a suspected homicide. While it's clear we're investigating, we're keeping it quiet whether or not the bodies were buried on the property because they were connected to it somehow.

She nods slowly. "Any direction I can point you in?"

I wasn't expecting her to offer any help. "How long have you worked here, Peggy?" I ask, then I take a sip of my coffee. I hadn't expected much since restaurants typically don't put much effort into their brews, but this one is rich, dark, and flavorful.

She's quiet for a moment, and she looks like she's calculating the time in her head. "Probably forty years. I always meant to move on, to go do something else. But now I think I'll probably work here until I die and they'll just bury me out back." I expect her to laugh, but when she doesn't, I'm honestly not sure if she's joking.

"Did you work here with Ella Hanson?" I ask. It's likely going to be a stretch, but the timelines might match up.

She nods. "On and off for a long time. Ella tended to come and go when she felt like working. After Keely... well. Yeah." She shakes her head.

My heart skips in my chest at the mention of Keely's name. "Did you know Keely?" I ask.

A thin smile creases her lips. "Ah, so you're here about Keely then. That is a very cold case," she says. She signals for Lucas to move down. When he scoots over, Peggy takes a seat next to him. "I knew Keely pretty well. She came in here to get free French fries from Ella all the time. The two of them really didn't get along. So when she came in, they were always fighting about something. It got pretty exhausting. Ophelia, the owner, she had to ask Keely not to come back a few times because of their fighting." She shakes her head and pauses, as if she's trying to remember more.

"Do you remember anything in particular that happened up until Keely's disappearance?" I take another sip of my coffee, hoping it'll jump-start my brain a bit.

"They had been fighting a lot more than usual. I'm not sure why. Ella had been the type to overshare before then, but she hadn't given me any details about what was going on between the two of them. Ella started smoking, and she was taking a lot of smoke breaks. A few times, I found her making out with this older guy behind the diner while she was on her break." Peggy pauses and fluffs her curly gray hair.

"So, she'd never done anything like that?" Lucas asks.

I grab my notepad and make a few notes about what she's said so far. It's interesting that Ella didn't give us any of this information. I'm curious if after all this time, she forgot, or if she's lying by omission.

She shakes her head. "No, Ella had always been the reserved type. I'd say that Keely was the more *out there* sister when it came to men. Keely always had a boyfriend, Ella never did. Keely always wore makeup, wore shorter skirts. Ella covered up, was more conservative in how she dressed. They were just opposites that way."

"Who was the guy?" Lucas asks.

"Some guy who had been coming in here a lot. Ella had been flirting with him something crazy. I thought he was too old for her. He was in his thirties, I think, and she was about seventeen. It's not that you never see that age difference or anything, but it just seemed to be too much, especially since she wasn't ever dating anyone her own age. She shouldn't start dating a thirty-year-old, if you ask me."

I nod. "Do you know what happened with the guy? Do you happen to remember his name?" I ask, though I know it's a long shot.

She shakes her head and laces her fingers together on top of the table. Her skin is tight around her knuckles, as if someone sucked all the air out of her, like one of those vacuum-sealed packages of clothes you slide under your bed for the winter. Ropes of blue and purple veins bulge beneath her skin as she rubs her fingers together. I'm not sure if it's because of pain or nerves. Her face looks calm enough.

"No, that was too long ago. I'm not great with names anyway, unless it's someone I interact with a lot. This guy was in daily for a couple weeks, always sitting in her section, flirting with Ella a lot." Her nostrils flare and her lip curls. "I told her that I didn't like the look of the guy. Something about him just seemed off, you know?"

"Yep, I know what you mean," I say, when she pauses a bit too long, and I realize she's not going to continue until I acknowledge her statement. "So, when was the last time you saw him?"

"Right before Keely disappeared. She was in here before she went to work, arguing with Ella," she explains. "They were fighting in a way that I don't think I'd ever seen. They had spats now and then, like all sisters do. But they were screaming at each other across the restaurant. Ophelia owned the place at the time, and she had to drag them both out back."

I raise a brow at that. They were arguing? Ella hadn't mentioned that. That really makes me wonder what else Ella withheld from us. Not mentioning a blowout argument with her sister before she disappeared? That's a red flag. And a huge one at that.

"What were they fighting over?" Lucas asks, his eyes wide with curiosity.

"Keely was convinced that Ella had been flirting with her boyfriend. That she might have even slept with him. Keely was livid. I'm not sure where she got the information from—it was probably just a rumor. But she was trying to tear her sister's hair out she was so mad." She shakes her head and makes a clucking sound with her tongue. "To be honest, I wasn't sad to see Ella go when she stopped working here. Some employees just always attract drama, and Ella was one of those."

"Do you think that she could have been capable of hurting her sister?" I ask.

She ruminates on the question for a moment, her knobby knuckles tightening before she unknots them to scratch the back of her hand. "I don't like to talk bad about people. Really, I don't. I know you'd think that working in this diner, I'd be a bit of a gossip. But that's just not me."

It's clear that Peggy is holding something back from us, but I'm not sure what. I need to get the info out of her. This is the most we've been able to get on Keely thus far. "I know, you don't seem like the gossiping type at all. And we're not looking for gossip, we're looking for real information that could help with our case. So far, this is all incredibly helpful. Anything else you're able to tell us could help with an investigation—do you understand that?" I try to lay it on as thick as possible to keep her talking.

She purses her lips, but her eyes gleam. She's clearly pleased with herself. This is exactly what she wanted, exactly what she needed to hear from me. Peggy leans a little closer, her eyes sweeping the restaurant before she continues. Then she lowers her voice. "Shortly after Keely disappeared, Ella started putting on some weight."

I bite the inside of my cheek. There's nothing I hate more than women commenting on the weight of others. We should be lifting each other up, not focusing on whether or not someone has put on a few pounds. Who cares? I want to tell her that I'm not interested in Ella's weight, but Lucas flashes me a look that warns me to keep my mouth shut. Sometimes, I hate that he can read me so well.

"At first, I thought that she was just letting herself go a bit. I mean, I'd understand. I'd be depressed if my sister disappeared too. Or ran off. Whatever. But then it became clear that it wasn't just weight. She was pregnant. I pulled her aside and asked her about it. Well, I mean, I danced around it a bit but I tried to get her to tell me what was going on."

Ella was pregnant? Now I really need to speak to Keely's sister again.

"She wouldn't tell me a damn thing. She kept denying it, said that she was just a little out of shape and that she'd bounce back after the holidays. She ended up going *out of town* for four months, and came back looking just like she had before Keely disappeared."

"So, what happened to this alleged baby, then?" Lucas asks.

"I don't know. Never saw Ella with a baby. No one else in the family had a baby. It was as if the whole thing never happened. She didn't talk about her *vacation* or the weight gain. Nothing. She also wouldn't talk about the guy from the diner.

But I heard that she had a baby with Keely's boyfriend. That his family adopted the baby, and she went back to her old life."

"Did you ever see Ian with a baby?" Lucas asks.

She nods. "Yep, sure enough, Ian's sister, Veronica, she started walking around town with a baby right around the time that Ella came back."

I add Veronica to my list of people to speak to. This all isn't adding up for me though. While Keely might have been mad that Ella was sleeping with her sister, how does all of that play into her disappearance? Did she take some risks because she was mad at her sister? Did she hop in the car with the guy from the diner just to get back at Ella? I'm trying to go over all the variables in my mind, but there are just too many.

"Is there anything else that you can think of that might help?" I ask.

She purses her lips again. "That last night, or maybe one of their fights before that—I don't know, they all kind of blur together—Ella told Keely that she wished she'd never been born, that her life would be so much better if Keely didn't even exist."

While that isn't evidence of murder, it definitely doesn't look good for Ella. Though I didn't grow up with siblings, I know that saying awful things to one another during a fight is par for the course—so I'm not sure how seriously I should take the statement, but I write it down all the same.

We finish up with Peggy, though it's clear that she wants to keep talking. After we're done questioning her, I order a burger and Lucas orders a grilled-chicken sandwich. We spend about thirty minutes eating, as I look up the address for Veronica Shaw. When I finally find her, I realize that just like her brother, she's passed away. She died in a car crash in the late nineties. There's no mention of a baby. So I'm not sure if that's just gossip, or if the kid was passed on to another family member.

I catch Lucas up on what I've found.

"So, what are our options?" he asks as he quirks a brow.

"We can go scour her old neighborhood, see if anyone remembers her. Or we can just cut to the chase and talk to her sister." I offer both options as I pop a fry into my mouth. I don't give a shit about her old neighborhood; we need to talk to the sister again. She's going to be the only one with answers.

My phone rings with a call from the forensics team, so I grab it and throw the call on speaker.

"Hi, Detective?"

"Yes, what can I help you with?" I ask.

"We have test results back on the substance that you brought in on the swabs," a woman says on the other end of the line.

My heart pounds, and I'm anxious to hear what they found.

"There was blood on the swabs that we've matched to Mazie's samples," she explains.

I finish up the call with forensics then turn to Lucas. This is a major break for Mazie's case. There's blood in Langdon's truck. Though Mazie was strangled, he's going to have some major explaining to do. Was he abusing her?

"What are we going to do about that?" Lucas asks.

"There's nothing we can do about it until we get back. He still has a solid alibi, so it's unlikely he had time to kill Mazie. This just means we have more questions when we get back."

As we talk about the questions we have in mind for Ella and Langdon, my phone vibrates on the table. I glance down and see a text from Sergeant Dirby. There's an image captured from security footage, a man standing next to my Jeep in the parking lot of the New Paltz PD.

You seen this guy before?—the text reads.

The image is too small, too blurry for me to make out any of the details. Even if it were Lucas in the picture, I'm not sure I'd recognize him. But we saw a guy like this in the footage from

Plattsburgh, coming out of my old Jeep—now I make sure to keep mine locked—so is this the same guy? I squint harder at the image, as if that'll make the truth jump of the screen. When it doesn't, I text back.

I'm not sure. Why?

The bubble indicating that Sergeant Dirby is typing pops up on the screen, followed by the appearance of a message.

Long story. Have a min for call?

I cut to the chase and just call Dirby. I don't need to go back and forth over text messages. My stomach is in knots as I consider that there might be a man lurking around my Jeep. In Plattsburgh, while I was working that case, I got creepy text messages from a man who was clearly stalking me. On top of that, before we found our killer, I was attacked in my hotel room. I thought at the time it was the killer who did that—he admitted to it when we questioned him after all—but now, I'm starting to question if I just took his word for it. What if he wasn't the one in my hotel room at all?

18

My veins feel like they've been dipped in ice water as I wait for Dirby to tell me the story, the reason for the text, what he knows about the pictures. Dirby is a slow talker, his words coming out like molasses, thick and syrupy. I drum my fingers on the table, needing to do something while I wait for him to get to the point. Usually, I'd pace at a time like this, the physical actions helping to keep my mind occupied. But I can't do that inside a restaurant.

"We think this is the guy who's been killing law enforcement officers. Right now, it seems that he's following you, Harlow," Dirby explains.

"One picture doesn't mean that he's following me," I say, wanting it to be true. If the situation were reversed, and I was investigating those details for anyone else, I'd be alarmed. But I can't afford to let this shake me. I have a case to solve, I have work to do. I can't sit back being scared of a possible threat.

"I've been investigating this. They're trying to track down who killed Officer Green, Pike, and Chad Pearson. While they've been combing over the evidence in Plattsburgh and Saranac Lake, they found this guy on security footage quite a lot. And he always appears within ten to fifteen minutes of you arriving at a destination."

A brick settles in the pit of my stomach, pushing bile up my throat. I swallow it down with my coffee, which is now cold, it's been sitting too long. I'm not sure what to do here. My mind grinds to a halt as sweat prickles under my arms.

"So, what do I do?" I ask. This is the point I'd expect my training to kick in, but it doesn't. My mind is a void as I try to force myself to think of *something*.

"I need you to go check your Jeep, see if someone put a tracking device on it," he explains. "Based on the timing, it really makes me think this guy has a GPS tracker on you. Your movements aren't consistent enough on a case that he should know exactly where you're going so often," Dirby instructs, his voice dead serious.

The way that he says it, it sends a chill down my spine. He's genuinely worried. I'm not sure if he's just worried for me, or for both of us. But based on what he's said, it's clear he thinks I'm a target.

"I'll check my car. I'll let you know if I find anything," I promise. It feels like we've been in this diner for far too long anyway. I plop some cash on the table, and I head outside. Halfway across the parking lot, I end the call with Dirby. If I've got to crawl around on the ground checking my car for a tracking device, I'm not doing that while I'm still on the phone.

"You really think that someone is tracking you?" Lucas asks as we approach. He's half listened to enough of the conversation to know what's going on.

I can't deny the sinking feeling that's gripped me, like I know something bad is coming. For a while I've felt like someone was following me, ever since I got to New York, actually. But I kept telling myself that it was all in my head, that I was just being paranoid, a product of always running from my past. Why can't I just trust myself and my intuition?

"Anything is possible," I manage to say around the anxiety that's crowding my throat.

"I'll take this side," Lucas says as he points to the passenger side.

"We've got to check inside and outside. The guy managed to get inside my old Jeep, so I wouldn't put it past him to get inside this one too," I say.

Lucas nods before disappearing out of view on the other side of the vehicle. I drop to my hands and knees next to the front of my Jeep. I check under the engine, brushing my hand over all the metal edges. But nothing feels out of place. Grit and grime coats my hands, creating a disgusting film over my fingers. Next I check the wheel well for my driver's-side tire, and come up with nothing but a thicker layer of film on my fingers.

"Nothing yet," Lucas says on the other side of the car.

"Nothing here either," I echo as I start to check under the driver's-side door, then the rear door.

It isn't until I get to the rear of the car near the exhaust that I finally feel something unusual. My fingers graze something on top of the metal, something that feels slick, made of plastic. I wrap my hand around it and pull. A strong magnet holds the device in place, but when I pull harder, it releases from the metal. It's a little smaller than a hockey puck, but the same shape. As I roll the device over in my fingers, I can tell right away that it's a tracker.

"Got it," I say to Lucas. I hear his feet scuff on the ground before he appears beside me. I hand it to him as I shove up from the ground.

"Motherfucker, who put this on your car?" he grumbles as he looks at it.

"I don't know, but we're going to find out." Now I know why I've been feeling this way. So, I've got to take this to the technical team to see if they can track down who put this thing on my car. I grab an evidence bag out of my glove box, and

Lucas drops the device inside. Though it's already got my and Lucas's fingerprints all over it, we'll have to see if there's anything else they can lift off it.

I take a picture of the tracker and text it to Sergeant Dirby. He texts me back an address of where to take the device, the Albany tech team that can dig into it for us.

Just don't expect miracles. You can order these all over the internet. Not sure if we can track it back to the owner. He adds this after the address.

Lucas and I make it to the technical operations team headquarters. It's in a building across from the courthouse. On the fourth floor, I find the door to their office. The room smells like pizza when I open the door. Directly inside to the left, I find a young man sitting at a reception desk. He nods to me as we enter, and I flash my badge.

"Dirby's team members?" he asks me, ignoring Lucas.

I nod.

"Go on through. He called to let us know you were bringing in a device. Is it still active?" he asks me.

I hold it up. "Not sure, honestly."

"It's not ideal for an active device to come in here, but we can deactivate it, just go on back." He motions toward the door. "Quickly."

Lucas and I walk down the hall, past a few closed doors, and find one open door toward the end. I peek in to find a woman with a purple pixie cut in a room filled to the brim with devices. There are long tables along the walls that are stacked high with computer towers, hard drives, baggies filled with cell-phones, you name it. It looks like a Best Buy exploded in here.

"Hello, we're here about—"

"The GPS tracker?" She finishes my sentence as she turns around. She's got her fingers steepled in front of her chest, relaxing in her gaming chair the way a supervillain would in a comic book. She flashes me a smirk that tells me that's exactly what she was going for. She's got warm brown skin, and deep dimples when she smiles. "I'm Charlie Lynn. I'm the technical lead here."

I introduce myself, then Lucas. She motions toward the plastic bag in my hand, and I pass it over to her. From her desk, she grabs a pair of thick plastic-rim glasses with brilliant blue cat-eye frames, puts them on, and analyzes the device in the bag.

"This is a GPS tracking device from Amazon," she says before flipping it over. "It's currently still transmitting, so I'll need to take the battery out to disable it." She puts on some latex gloves, opens the bag, then unscrews the bottom of it. In a few seconds, she's got the battery extricated and it's lying on top of her desk.

"Is there any way to know how long it's been there for?" I ask.

"Well, I have some good news and some bad news," she says, her attention swiveling back to me. "The good news is these devices break rather quickly. They're not meant for PIs or anyone in law enforcement to use long term. These are usually bought by spouses trying to track down infidelity. They end up breaking around six months or sooner. Most people don't care because within a month they have the answer that they're looking for."

"So, it hasn't been tracking me for long, that's what you're saying?"

The edge of her mouth quirks upward. "That's the thing. The bad news is this device looks new, like came-out-of-a-package-two-weeks-ago kind of new. I'd say that if you think you've been followed prior to this, the person watching you has been updating devices as they die. There's no way for me to tell you how long they've been monitoring you, but this particular device hasn't been with you for long."

I look at the device, the battery. "So you're telling me this person swapped out tracking devices? Were they changing the batteries too?"

"Most of these devices require charging. This one has a rechargeable battery. Once a week or so these need to be charged so they can continue tracking you. The battery life really depends on many factors—how often the device is pinging the satellites, how often it's communicating back with the app about where you've moved to. But I'd say on average whoever is using this device would have to take it once a week to be charged."

Maybe that's why they've been able to keep getting this guy on surveillance footage near my Jeep. He's been babysitting his device. I try to suppress the creeping feeling that's working its way up the back of my neck. My mind goes over and over the possibilities of who it might be, then something clicks. Neal. The journalist. He keeps showing up everywhere that I am and has the uncanny ability to know my whereabouts. It must be him who put the device on my car.

"Is there any way for us to find out with certainty who owns that?" I ask.

"The only real way is to hack into their Amazon account and to verify the purchase, then you'd need to verify that the number of the device purchased is the number that was input into the app. The easiest way is to check someone's cellphone. That would give you all the info that you need," she explains. "But other than those methods, it'd be hard to track this down because there are so many ways to get these devices."

I nod. Something inside me wants to confront Neal, to track him down right now and make him tell me whether or not he's responsible for this. But the other part of me is curious if, now that the device is gone, I'll be able to shake him.

"Well, we need to get back on the road. If you find anything, please give me a call," I say as I pass her one of my cards.

She nods. "Got it. And please be careful. If I were you, I'd do a daily sweep of my vehicle at least for a while to make sure that no new devices are placed on it. Whoever is watching you, they're invested in this." She points toward the bag. "And if you start removing their devices, they'll realize that you know... That could make them escalate."

"Thanks," I say, but the truth is I know the danger here if it's not just journalistic curiosity that's driving Neal to watch me. If he's after more than a story, this could turn quickly.

As we leave the station, Lucas and I chat about whether or not Neal could be the culprit, and Lucas is very firmly on my side—that he seems like the most likely suspect. I haven't seen Neal around Albany. As far as we know he's still back in New Paltz. We'll have to see if that changes, but once I get back to New Paltz, I'm adding Neal to my shit list.

19

Ella Hanson lives in an old apartment building at the edge of town. The brick façade rises above me so high that I can't count how many levels it is as I squint against the afternoon sun. It's one of those brick buildings with detailing around the windows that screams *New York*. Outside, a few kids sit on the stoop playing Pokémon cards as I walk toward the door. They glance up at us as we walk past, but they don't stop their game.

Inside, we find a long hallway that cuts a path through the entire building, doors on either side. A central staircase climbs up ahead of us. To our right, we find the mailboxes and an old rusted elevator. Luckily, Ella lives on the second floor, so we don't need to chance it with the elevator. We climb the stairs, past some mail that's been abandoned on the floor. The sounds of the apartments' residents leach out into the common hallway. I hear arguing, a TV that's a little too loud, the gentle *thump, thump, thump* of trance music. It takes us a few minutes to find her door. But as we approach, the hallway goes eerily silent. I listen intently before I raise my hand to knock.

We wait for Ella to come to the door. When she finally appears, she's got on an oversized T-shirt and cheetah-print leggings. Her hair is bleached platinum blonde, teased out from her face. Remnants of yesterday's mascara clings to her eyes, creating a shadow around them. Her eyes narrow as she appraises me, so I introduce myself.

"You didn't get everything that you wanted on the phone?" She arches a thin brow.

"We've spoken to a few other people, so we had a few more questions for you," I explain.

"Do I have to let you in?" Her voice is deep, her words clipped.

"No, you don't have to. If you'd rather, you can come down to the station down the street and we can do a formal interview in one of the interrogation rooms. It's not the most comfortable. That's why I decided to just stop by here. But if you'd prefer something more *official*..."

She raises her hand, cutting me off. "No, fine. Just come in," she says, shifting away from her position blocking the door so we can pass her.

Though manipulating witnesses like this is typically frowned upon, I'm not doing anything that's explicitly illegal. We need to question her, and we can do that here or at the station—those are the facts. Sometimes it's just easier to make the station seem a bit more sinister than it really is. There's an innate anxiety that fills everyone when they enter a police station.

The air inside the apartment is thick with cigarette smoke. It hangs in the air, hazy. Directly in front of the door, we find a small living room filled with an oversized couch, a coffee table with an ashtray that's vomiting old cigarettes onto a stack of magazines, a TV on a cluttered entertainment center. To our left, there's a kitchen and a hallway that I'd guess leads to the bedroom. I glance around for pictures of kids, her sister, but there are none. She motions for us to take a seat on the couch, so we do. She pulls up a chair from a small table that sits off the living room and sits to the left of the couch, facing us.

"What else do you need to know about my sister?" She shakes a cigarette out of a soft pack and lights it.

My throat is already scratchy from all the smoke, and I wish she'd at least crack a window. "We were hoping that you could go over with us what happened the day that your sister disappeared," I say.

"Didn't I already tell you all that?" she asks after she takes a long drag.

"You mentioned that you went to work, but that's really all we know about your day," Lucas explains. He's got his notepad out, ready to take notes.

"Yeah, work was pretty much all I did at that point. I didn't really do anything else," she says, smoke trailing on her words.

"We spoke to Peggy," I explain, and at the name, her eyes bug a bit.

"Why would you speak to Peggy?"

"We just happened to stop in the diner, and she mentioned that she worked with you back in the day. She was able to give us some context that I think you may have forgotten about." I'm giving her the benefit of the doubt here, the opportunity to come clean. This is a tactic I use so I can determine how much I can trust anything else she says to us. If she has a story that aligns with Peggy's at this point, I'll give her a slight pass, since it was so long ago. If she tells me nothing about what Peggy mentioned, then I know she's a liar.

"And what did she tell you?" Her words and her eyes sharpen. They're dagger sharp.

"Quite a bit, honestly. So, I'd like it if you could give me your view of what happened shortly before your sister's disappearance."

"Peggy is a gossip. You have to take everything she says with a grain of salt. She hated me. From the first day that I started working there, she never liked me. She still hates me," she says, her words reflecting the girl she was back then, not the woman that she is now. I'd think that by now she would have moved past old drama, but it doesn't seem that she has.

"Fair enough. That's why we'd like for you to tell us what happened," Lucas urges.

"That morning, I woke up like I always did. My mom had made us breakfast. I don't remember what it was. As soon as Keely came downstairs, she started trying to pick a fight with me. She was on this tear that I was interested in her boyfriend," she explains, then pauses to take another puff off her cig. She rolls her eyes, as if even now after all these years Keely still annoys her. It strikes me that Ella isn't exactly acting like the grieving sister. It could be that Keely was missing for so long that Ella has run out of grief. Or it could be that the relationship with her sister was so strained that she genuinely didn't miss her.

"And were you?" Lucas jumps in.

She barks out a laugh. "No, I wasn't."

I let it rest for a moment, and flash Lucas a look. I want to hear what she thinks happened later in the day, when I know she and Keely fought in the diner.

"I went to work early. They were short staffed and I needed extra money. I was having problems with my car and needed to get it fixed. I got there, worked my shift. And then after that I went home."

Bingo. Lying to us it is.

"So, nothing happened while you were at the diner?"

She shakes her head. "Nope. Just my regulars. I worked my tables. I went home. It was a long day."

"That's interesting. Because Peggy mentioned that you and Keely had a big fight the day she disappeared, and that they'd also found you making out with someone behind the diner."

Ella adjusts her position in her seat, and her jaw tightens. I think she may be grinding her teeth. "I don't remember that," she says, her tone shifting.

"You don't remember being asked to go out back because you and Keely were fighting in the middle of the restaurant? Apparently it was a pretty bad fight. Did you fight so often in the restaurant that all the instances blur together?"

She purses her lips. I can see it written all over her face. She remembers. "I mean, it was so long ago. I don't remember every fight I had with my sister."

"Because you had so many?" Lucas asks, again.

"As if all siblings don't fight." She rolls her eyes and takes a long drag from her cigarette.

"It seems like it was more than just a regular fight," I add. I want to keep pushing her, trying to lead her to the truth. Behind her eyes, I can see it simmering there. Sometimes I swear I can scent the truth rising to the surface, as if it fills the air with a different energy. "Were you two in physical fights frequently?"

She coughs out a smoky laugh. "As if you were there. And what does it even matter?"

"We may not have been, but Peggy was there. We may be able to find others that were present as well. If there's something you're keeping from us, I promise you, we will find out what really happened." My words are harsher than I mean for them to be, my warning clear.

"And what exactly do you think you'll find?" She leans back and crosses her arms.

I go over all the scenarios in my mind. And I decide to recount the most absurd one. At least if I serve her up a ridiculous scenario on a silver platter, her reaction will tell us if we're going in the right direction or not. "I think that after your fight, you told the guy you were talking to in the diner to pick you up on your way home. I think that he picked up Keely, thinking that it was you. You wanted him to focus on your sister, not you. Because something nagged in the back of your mind, warning you about what type of man he really was."

Her face has gone pale, and I realize that I must have gotten something right.

"Then, after Keely disappeared, you went and comforted her boyfriend, had a baby with him. And tried to act like you weren't responsible for your sister's disappearance. I bet it ate away at you."

"Stop it," she finally snaps, her voice rising to an octave I wouldn't have thought possible. Her face has gone impossibly tight, as if someone has pulled all the skin back.

"Did I hit a little too close to the mark?" This isn't the first time I've had someone react this way while I was questioning them. But I didn't expect her to be quite so explosive.

"You don't know shit," she snaps, her voice venomous.

"Then tell us what happened," Lucas pushes. "If we've got it all wrong, you need to tell us what did happen."

She snuffs out her cigarette so forcefully it snaps in half. Then she lights a new one. The smoke is already so thick in here, I can feel its claws in my throat. There's a haze in the air between us, the air so thick it's like a foggy morning. I have to push through my discomfort. "I didn't tell him to go after Keely. I don't know what I was trying to do. I was just so mad at her. I'd already been seeing Ian for a while. He was actually my boyfriend before he dated Keely. They were fighting all the time, so he came to me complaining about her. One thing led to another. And we ended up having sex. I'm not sure if I got pregnant then... or one of the other times. But that's what the fight was about. Keely connected the dots. She realized what had happened."

She pauses, her eyes cast down to the carpet. Her shoulders slump, and maybe the guilt is finally getting to her. "I wasn't trying to do anything to her. Honestly, I was hoping that the guy might scare her a bit because he thought it was me that he was picking up. But that's obviously not what happened. I did something stupid that led to my sister being murdered." She doesn't look up as she takes another drag. "And there's nothing I can do to change that, or to fix it."

"You can help though," Lucas urges.

She looks to Lucas, tears pooling in her eyes. And though she's been a bitch up until now, my heart breaks for her. I can see the pain that I know was echoed through the hearts of the family members of my father's victims. I hold on to this, as if her pain, the look on her face, can keep me from becoming like him.

"How can I help?" Her voice breaks.

"We need to know as much as you can tell us about this man. The more that we know about him, the more it will help us. I know it's been a long time, but I really need you to think hard about anything he might have said, where he might have been going," Lucas says, his words so kind and patient. If he hadn't gone into missing persons, Lucas could have been a doctor, a teacher. He has such a good bedside manner, I know he could keep a rabid hyena calm.

"I don't remember much." She sniffles and wipes her nose on the back of her hand.

"Okay, let's start small. What kind of car did he drive?"

"He had a Buick, I think, or a Cadillac. It was a bigger car."

Lucas makes a note, and so do I. "Okay, that's good. Did he mention where he was from?"

"New Paltz," she says. "I think."

Lucas glances to me.

"Did he still live there?" Lucas asks. I'm glad that he's taken over the questioning as she's much more receptive to his questions than mine.

"I don't remember. I don't think so though. He didn't tell me where exactly he was living. But I think it was south of Albany. Oh, and I think he had a scar on his hand or arm."

A scar? That gets my attention. "And you're sure that you didn't see him again after Keely's disappearance?" I ask.

She nods. "I'm sure. He'd said that he was going to be in the next day to see me. He'd kissed me behind the diner that night. And I was kind of disappointed all day that he never showed." She crosses her arms, careful of her dangling cigarette. She's finally looking up again, her face not as drawn by sorrow. "I was so selfish, so self-centered. I didn't really even think about Keely for a couple weeks. That's when it really started to sink in that she was gone."

"Sometimes, it's easier to pretend that they didn't disappear, that they aren't really gone," Lucas says, and I know he's speaking from experience.

She sniffles and nods her head. "Oh, I think he was married," she adds.

I raise a brow at that. If he was flirting with her and making out with her behind the diner, I doubt he brought up a wife.

"He had a tan line where his wedding band had been. But he wasn't wearing it. I asked about it, and he said he was divorced. But something in his voice—" She stops for a moment, her brow furrowing. "I didn't believe him."

While she talks, I can tell that she's holding something back —that she's not telling us everything about what happened. I need to push her a little more to see what else I can get out of her.

"Ella, I want you to know how important it is that we have all the details. That's going to be the only way that we can track down who did this to your sister. You understand that, right? Everything matters, no matter how small the detail." I glance to Lucas when I finish talking, and he echoes my point.

She chews her lip for a moment, then grabs a cigarette. "I don't want to get into any trouble," she says.

"Look, unless you killed your sister or had her killed, the

statute of limitations has long since passed. So please just tell us what you know," Lucas urges.

She scoots back and recrosses her legs before lighting her cigarette. "I might have hinted to the guy that I'd be walking home on the road that I knew Keely would be on. I figured he'd drive by and confuse her... but I never imagined..."

I write that down. We need to track down the guy from the diner. It takes a long time for Ella to calm down, during which time we're not able to get anything else useful from her. We head out of her house with some leads, but we need something more tangible. We need to find our killer.

20

We've run out of leads in Albany—what Ella has told us has gone nowhere so far; we have no choice but to head back to New Paltz. The scar on the arm, the connection to New Paltz, it makes me wonder if this is all related to Vick. I wish that there were DNA to match against, so we'd have a clear path to follow. I've started looking into our next victim, Davida Hall, while Lucas drives. But unfortunately, the relative that submitted their DNA to the database for matching died in a car crash over three years ago. But based on the information that I've got on her missing persons file, she lived in Kingston, which is a city between Albany and New Paltz.

"She was working as a waitress in Kingston," I say to Lucas.

"At a diner near the interstate like Ella was?" he asks. Lucas is always so stiff when he drives, his hands firmly planted at ten and two, his shoulders locked, almost touching his ears. I'm not sure if he's just nervous because he's driving my car, or if he's always this tense.

I grab my phone and google the location of the diner. Sure enough, it's right off the interstate. More evidence that this guy may have been a traveler. Maybe our killer had a reason to drive from New Paltz to Albany frequently. But Lake Placid, where Lucas grew up, is so far north, so out of the way of that path. It's getting harder for me to connect the dots as to why our killer might have gone up there to take Lucas's mother and grandmother. Did our killer live near Lake Placid? Did he grow up there? If so, it would stand to reason that he may go back to visit. While he may have hunted these women along highway 32 for sport, maybe the crime in Lake Placid was a crime of opportunity.

"Yeah, this diner is along highway thirty-two. That may have been his hunting ground," I say. "I'll do a search to see if there are any other mentions of women who worked as waitresses disappearing along the same stretch of road."

Lucas nods, then flinches as his phone vibrates on the center console next to him. He glances at the phone, answers it, and puts it on speaker.

"This is Detective Park," he says in his authoritative tone that tells me he doesn't recognize the number.

"Hi, Lucas, this is Dr. Dushku over at the medical examiner's office," she says, her tone a bit sharper than usual.

"What can I help you with, Doctor?" he asks.

My stomach tightens. This is the call we've been waiting for, I know it. The next words out of her mouth will change the course of Lucas's life forever. Either the DNA is a match or it's not. If it's not a match, he'll have to keep searching, while feeling the sting of this loss—what could have been. But if this is a match, he finally has the answer he's been searching for for so long. Sweat blooms on my palms as I wait. I hold my breath, my heart pounding in my ears over the roar of the tires on the road.

"We have the results back on the DNA of the victims and your DNA sample. And we were able to match all three victims to your sample."

Lucas sucks in a sharp breath, and I reach over to grab his hand. Just so he knows he's not alone in this.

"All three? What does that mean?" He stumbles over the words as his eyes bug.

"Based on the results, I'd say that victim one was likely a grandparent or great aunt. Victim two, you share half of the DNA with, so I would say that's likely your mother. And the other victim you share slightly less than half of your DNA with, so I would say that's your half-sibling."

"I had a..." He trails off.

"A sister. You had a sister," she clarifies.

Tears roll down Lucas's cheeks, and I signal for him to pull over. His breaths are coming faster, and I think he may hyperventilate. I take his phone, thank Dr. Dushku for the information, and end the call. Once his phone is back in the center console, the tires skid against the loose gravel of the shoulder. He throws open the driver's-side door and gets out without even checking for traffic. My stomach creeps into my throat as I check the road. I'm relieved to find it empty.

He walks around the rear of the Jeep, pacing in a way that makes me want to grab him, hold him still. I'm terrible in situations like this. I have no idea what he needs, what I can do to make it better. So now, I stand, lost, unsure what to do for Lucas.

I open the back of my Jeep so there's a shelf for Lucas and I to sit on. I pat the seat, and motion for him to come sit. The emotions wearing on his face kill me, because I'm so helpless. There's nothing I can do to fix this, to help Lucas with this.

Tears stream down his face as he finally paces over and plops down next to me. His body is shaking, practically vibrating with a mixture of rage and sorrow. I put my arm around him, and pull him into me. I feel like he needs this, even though I don't like it

"Do you want me to call Ethan?"

He shakes his head. "I haven't told him."

I'm taken aback that he didn't tell his new boyfriend about one of the most impactful moments of his life. But I'm going to let that sit for another time.

"How about your dad? Would you like me to call him?"

He shakes his head. "We can't tell him this over the phone." His voice breaks and new tears spill down his cheeks. He hunches over, his elbows on his knees, and hides his face in his hands. His body shakes as he sobs, so I rub soft circles on his back with my hand.

"Let's drive up there. I'll tell him."

"It's a three-hour drive," he finally says.

"Then we should get going. We can be there before dark," I say. We're halfway between Albany and New Paltz, so it'll be less than three hours to make it up there. I know that this is what Lucas needs. He and his father can grieve together. If I have to, I'll leave him up there. He can take a week or more to sort this all out. It kills me to set aside hunting the killer, digging up more information about Keely and Davida, but Lucas comes first. He's a victim too.

"You can't be serious," he says, his mask of sadness slipping for a moment. His eyes are red when he turns to look at me.

"I'm absolutely serious. Get in the passenger seat. Put your dad's address in the GPS. Let's go."

For a moment he just stares at me. Then he narrows his eyes. "This is the only way you know how to help."

I nod. "Yep, you got me there. Now get in the goddamn car," I say, pointing toward the front of the car with my thumb. He sniffles, stands up, and takes a few steps before turning back toward me.

"Thank you," he says.

"Of course," I say. As he walks toward the passenger door, I text Sergeant Dirby what's going on, so he doesn't have any surprises. Though he doesn't keep close tabs on us like some of my other sergeants have, I don't want to take advantage of his hands-off approach.

When I climb into the driver's seat, I look to Lucas. He's staring straight ahead, his lips swollen from crying, his eyes red and raw. His jaw is slack, a far-off look in his eyes. Seeing him like this breaks my heart. This is what every victim of my father's crimes went through. This is how they felt. Some of them wondered for years what happened to their loved ones. Some of them waited over ten years for closure. Then, when they finally got it, this was the fallout. When you get the confirmation, when you stop searching, that's when the grief collapses around you like a dying star. It sucks you in, the sorrow, the overwhelming grief that has been in your orbit for years.

"Can we drive up highway thirty-two for as long as possible? I want to note the diners," Lucas says. I don't think he should. I think right now he shouldn't be focusing so much on work. But if I were in his shoes, I'd throw myself into work so I wouldn't have to feel anything.

"Yeah, sure we can," I say. Honestly, at this point I'd probably agree to pretty much anything to make him feel better.

I update the GPS so that it steers us toward that highway, and then we head north. The road is crowded with trees; small houses appear occasionally. Their appearance is so sudden it's as if the forest were sheered out with a pair of scissors. Small towns crop up until finally we pass back through Albany. After we leave the city, we watch the same scenery rise and fall on repeat. Then mountains and hills bloom in the distance, and we veer west, toward Lake Placid. As we approach the city, the sun is dying on the horizon.

"Do you want me to come in with you or do you want me to go get a hotel room and let you and your dad talk?" I ask as we round the last mile to his father's house.

"I want you to come in with me. I need you there," he says. I wasn't prepared for him to request that. I really thought that he'd want some privacy, to deal with this with his father. As good as I may be at my job, I'm not good with emotions. If Lucas thinks I'll be able to comfort them, I'm not sure I'm going to be any help.

The town itself is small, with a few more squat modern buildings than I'd been expecting. Most of the small towns we've driven through in upstate New York look so similar it's as if the same architect designed them all. They've all got identical houses and a strip of downtown that's lined with stone buildings, and Lake Placid is no different. The population of the town is incredibly small, not quite 3,000. As we drive through the patch of downtown, several people wave to us—recognizing Lucas, I'd suspect. Though he no longer lives here—he lives in Monroe near the state office—he comes back every few months to see his father.

Lucas turns off my GPS and starts directing me where to turn. There's a shift in him now that we're back, as if the light inside him got just a little brighter. If I were him, I'd be dreading the conversation with his dad, but it seems like there's an edge of excitement to his voice. As we turn down a residential road, I'm surprised that it's not lined with colonials or Victorian houses, like you find all over upstate. Instead, the houses are newer, raised ranches. We turn into the driveway of a pale yellow house. The flowerbeds are filled with bushy flowers, small plants that I can't identify, and something with leaves that are bigger than my head. Though it all looks pretty, I don't have even a mild green thumb, and I know under my care all of this would die in about a week.

"How are you feeling?" I ask Lucas as I throw the car in park.

He's still staring wide-eyed out the windshield, as if he isn't really seeing anything at all. His pallor, the way his jaw hangs slightly, it looks to me like he's still in shock. I'm not surprised.

It's just when it's someone so close to me, I wish that there was more that I could do.

He shrugs. "I don't feel anything right now. It just..."

"It doesn't feel real?" I ask. It's something that so many family members of victims have said to me. Many times, it isn't until they see a body that it feels real, because it's so easy to tell yourself that it didn't happen, that we mistook identities. Everyone wants nothing more than for their loved ones to come through the door safe and sound, but that's not reality. And eventually, it does all hit them. That's what I'm worried about for him. Though he already got a lot of tears out, I know he's not past it. I know there's more to come.

"Yeah," he says, but still doesn't look at me.

"Do you want me to do the talking?" I motion toward the house. I'm not sure how long he wants to sit out here, but night is slowly blanketing the city. We need to get in there before his father starts getting ready for bed.

"No, I don't think that would be a good idea." He opens the passenger door, his movements stiff and robotic.

I kill the engine, pop open the door, and slide out of the car. My feet hit the driveway, and I turn back toward the house. Lucas is already at the front door, so I jog a bit to meet him there. He doesn't bother knocking, or announcing his presence, instead he just slides a key into the door and opens it. It baffles me. I don't think I'd feel comfortable just walking into my mother's house, even if I had a key.

The house smells a bit stale when we enter, as if it's been sealed up tight for a while. And I wonder how often his dad gets out into the world. The foyer is lined with a maple syrup–color wood floor, beyond that a marigold carpet takes over and stretches down a small hallway and fills the living room. To our right, the stairs lead down to a lower level, but Lucas walks forward, toward the living room. I follow right behind him, taking in a small room with a plush sofa, a large flat-screen TV mounted on the wall, ornate wooden end tables, and a coffee table with a few too many coffee cups abandoned atop it. The living room connects to the kitchen, which looks like it was plucked directly from the early nineties. To our right, there's a door that leads out onto a screened-in porch, and out there is where I see Lucas's father for the first time.

Lucas opens the door, and the man turns. "Appa," he says to the man, and he smiles.

Lucas's father stands up and throws his arms around his son. They embrace for a long moment, and I skirt them as I walk out onto the porch. Under the shade, the air is cool, and the sound of the crickets swells in the trees that circle the property.

"Who's this?" Lucas's father asks when he pulls away and finally notices me. It's awkward being here during their reunion, and though I want to support my partner, I wish he'd just let me book a hotel room.

"This is Detective Durant. She's my partner in the NYBCI," he explains.

"So nice to meet you," he says as he extends his hand to me. "I'm Joon."

"Very nice to meet you. I'm Harlow," I say.

Joon motions for us to sit, and I take a seat next to Lucas at the small rattan table. The seats are plush, and the chairs are not quite as stiff as I expected them to be. Mine flexes a bit beneath my weight, and it makes me nervous. There's a bit of anxiety swelling inside me about how the conversation is going to go, how Joon will take the news. I know he's going to be devastated.

"Would you two like anything to drink?" he asks.

"Tea for both of us," Lucas says and his father nods. He disappears into the kitchen, and I give Lucas a look. "What?" he asks, as he motions toward my face.

"You really needed to give him something to do? We don't need tea. You're just trying to avoid having the conversation with him," I say, and though they're my words, they sound like I plucked them directly from my father's mouth. I want to take them back, to swipe them out of the air before Lucas hears them. But it's too late.

He rolls his eyes at me. "Oh, so you're a therapist now. I'm sorry, I hadn't realized that I scheduled an appointment, but if we're really going to dig into my problems, maybe we should talk about my codependency because of my fear of abandonment since my mother disappear—"

I hold my hand up, cutting him off. "I'm sorry, I didn't mean it that way."

"Mmhmm," he says as he crosses his arms.

Part of me loves that Lucas isn't afraid to call me out on my shit. He's always there to point out when I'm being an asshole, which sometimes I appreciate and sometimes I hate. Right now though, I'm just glad he didn't get mad at me. I know I shouldn't feel this way, but with the death of his mother still heavy in the air, I feel like I need to be careful with him.

His father returns and places two coffee mugs filled with steaming tea in front of us. Though I've never really been a tea person, the scent is enticing.

"Thank you," I say as I pull the mug a little closer to me.

"You're very welcome," he says as he takes a seat next to Lucas, after retrieving his own cup of tea. "Were you two in the area? Are you going to stay the night? Oh, I hope you are. I could make you breakfast in the morning. That would be nice, to have you here for a few days," Joon says, his eyes shining. He lights up when he looks at his son, and it nearly brings tears to my eyes. Neither of my parents have ever looked at me that way. I wonder what it was like for him, to grow up with parents that loved him.

"Do you mind if we stay the night here?" Lucas asks me.

I shake my head. "No, that's fine. But if you're more comfortable, I can absolutely get a hotel room," I say to Joon. I'm not sure that he's going to feel comfortable having a stranger sleeping in his home.

"No, you must stay here. I won't let you stay at that hotel. It's for the tourists. They will not treat you well. I've got plenty of bedrooms. It would be wonderful to have some life in the house again," Joon says. Sadness swims in his eyes, and I can tell how lonely he is.

"We'll stay then," Lucas says. "But we came by because I need to talk to you about something..." He trails off as he looks to me. I'm not sure if he needs strength or if he wants me to take over. But when he's silent for a long time, I decide to step in carefully, keeping my words measured enough that Lucas can take over at any time. I explain to Joon the reason for our visit, what we found in New Paltz, that we have a confirmation that the DNA on the bodies matches Lucas.

He's quiet for a long time, his eyes searching my face, then Lucas's. As if he isn't sure what to believe. I know he wants it to not be true. I'm sure some part of him was holding out hope that one day his wife would be found, that she would be returned to him. The house looks like it hasn't changed since Lucas was a child, except for the TV. Did he keep this as a shrine for her, so that everything would be the way she left it when she came back? My heart squeezes with pain as I think about that loss, what it must have been like for him.

"No." He shakes his head. His shoulders have gone tight, and I realize that he's clenching his hands together under the table. "It can't be her. She would have never gone down to New Paltz. She didn't even leave the town."

"We don't think that she went willingly," I explain, and I notice that fresh tears are streaming down Lucas's cheeks. Joon looks to his son, and maybe it's the tears that make him realize that this is real, that she really is dead. "We have reason to believe that she was held captive with her mother. She was likely taken while she was out running errands, then kept in New Paltz until her death."

"How did she die?" he asks.

"The medical examiner believes that she likely died of natural causes, given the state the body was in. There was no obvious trauma," I explain. I don't go into details, that we think she may have starved to death with her daughter in her arms. I'm not even sure that I want to bring up the child—that would be up to Lucas.

"How long has she been dead?"

"There's no way of knowing for sure. But we think at least ten years," Lucas says. And I'm surprised that he's jumped back in.

"Can I bury her here? In town?" Joon asks.

I nod. "Of course. I believe the medical examiner is done with her portion of the investigation, so we should be able to bring her up here in a week or so."

Lucas shifts in his chair, then glances at his father. Joon is cupping his mug, his fingers interlaced around it. He looks down at the pool of liquid, as if scrying in it for the right words. His eyes are rimmed with tears, threatening to spill onto his cheeks. But somehow, they don't.

"There are some things that I never told you about your mother," he says. Still not meeting Lucas's gaze. Lucas has gone stiff, his mouth a grim line.

"Like what?" he finally asks when his father doesn't continue. I feel so out of place here I'm tempted to slink out the back door, but I know Lucas would see me and he wouldn't appreciate me abandoning him during a time like this. But I can't understand why he even wants me here for this.

"Before your mother disappeared, she told me that she had some concerns at work. She was working as a waitress at that diner by the interstate. I always hated that she worked there, but she liked it."

Joon's words strike a chord with me. Another woman working at a diner near an interstate. This officially connects the dots for me. This is how he found his victims. This was their profile. Though the women all come from different backgrounds, different ethnicities, that doesn't seem to matter. Instead, he focused on where they worked, how easily he could get back to the highway. He must have hunted at these highway diners for ease of transport, since he took these women back to New Paltz.

"What kind of concerns?" Lucas asks, and I resist my urge to take notes. I need to be here for emotional support, not to take notes on the case. I'll write everything down as soon as we wrap up here.

"The last few weeks, before she disappeared, she was complaining about this man who kept coming into the diner. He insisted on sitting in her section, asked her way too many questions. He made her very uncomfortable. But she put up with it because he tipped really well—and we needed the money. Despite her gut telling her to stay away from him, she kept doing her job."

"You let her keep doing that?" Lucas says, his words hitching up a few octaves.

His eyes tighten at Lucas's outburst. "You know very well that there was no *letting* your mother do anything. She made up her own mind about what she was going to do."

"You know what I mean." Lucas's tone is dismissive, and I squirm in my seat at the tension blooming between them.

"She wanted to keep doing her job, making the best money that she could to support the family. When it became clear that the guy was stalking her, that's when I tried to step in. I told her to take some time off work, to put some distance between herself and this man..."

"He was stalking her? Why didn't you tell me any of this?" Lucas asks, his fists clenching under the table.

"What good would it have done to tell you?" He releases his cup and waves his hands through the air with dismissal.

"I could have—"

"You could have done nothing." Joon slams his fist on the table, sloshing tea from the cup. I flinch at the sound and curl my hands around the edge of my chair, the wood cutting into my palms. "There's nothing that anyone could have done. By the time you were old enough to understand, she was probably already dead," he says, his words heavy with the weight of loss.

"I've been looking for answers for years. I've asked you hundreds of times—"

"Yes, you've been obsessing. I didn't think that your mother would ever be found. I didn't want you wasting your life just to prove that your mother's life ended. At some point, you have to let go."

"Like you have? Living in this time capsule as if you've been preserving it for her, living in a museum dedicated to her memory." Lucas points toward the walls, the sagging sofa, the kitchen.

"That's different. Your mother was my life. I'm not keeping it as a museum. I'm keeping it this way because it reminds me of her. I can close my eyes and pretend that she's still next to me, the warmth of her arm brushing mine when we sat on the sofa. Sure, she'd hate the TV. But everything else I've left just the way she liked it so I could savor those memories. You have a lifetime of memories to make for yourself. You don't need to build a museum in your mind for her. You need to build your life, not live in the life that could have been."

Lucas lets out a humorless laugh, his eyes brimming with tears again. "But that's exactly what you're doing. Don't you realize how ridiculous this is?"

"Exactly. I don't want you living like this. I don't want you living with the shadow of loss mirroring every move you make. I don't want your entire life to be defined by losing your mother."

I know Joon's thoughts are in the right place, but there's no way Lucas can just move on after his mother and grandmother were killed like it was nothing. To have unanswered questions that large your entire life, there's no way he could just brush that off.

"Joon, I'm sorry to interrupt. But Lucas needs closure here. It's not about carrying loss for the rest of his life; it's about carrying the questions. If he can't get the answers about what happened to his mother and grandmother, he will never be able to move past it," I explain, and immediately regret it. I should have just kept my mouth shut. They don't look angry, but they're looking at me as if they'd forgotten my presence entirely.

"But do you not understand why I kept these things from you? There was nothing to be done," Joon says, his eyes on Lucas.

"Fine. But there's something to be done now, so I need to know everything. Why did she think she was being stalked?" Lucas asks.

"One night, when she was leaving the diner, she said that it looked like items in her car had been moved. She'd left something on the seat, she swore. But when she got back into her car it had been moved to the back seat," Joon explains, then pauses to take a sip of his tea. "She told me about it, but shrugged it off. She thought maybe there was a chance that she put it in the back seat. But obviously it bothered her enough to talk to me about it. I told her to be more mindful of locking the door to the car. She told me that she would."

"Did she say who she thought was stalking her?" Lucas asks, clearly impatient that his father is taking too long to get to the point.

"Yes and no. Later that week, there was a car in the parking lot still when she left the night shift. That didn't happen often, so it stuck out to her. And shortly after she pulled out of the diner on her way home, a car started following her. She wasn't certain it was the same vehicle, but she told me it could have been. It followed her for miles, until she finally lost it before making it home. That day, she said that the man in the diner had been particularly pushy, trying to get her to sit and eat lunch with him. He asked a lot of questions about her life, where she lived, if she lived alone. It started to make her very uncomfortable, so she had another waitress take over and she took her lunch break."

It sounds slightly familiar to the guy who was in the diner in Albany, though Ella was obviously more receptive to the man. So, it didn't matter to our killer whether or not the woman was interested. I was curious if he only took women that showed some sort of interest, that may have come with him willingly. But clearly Lucas's mother would never have gone with him, unless she was forced. It sounds like she tried to rebuff him at every opportunity.

"When she went on her lunch break, it seemed like it really angered him. He ended up coming outside and found your mother while she was sitting in her car. He started pounding on her window, and tried to open the door."

"What the fuck?" Lucas spits the words out, venom lacing every syllable. But then his eyes bug, like he regrets cursing in front of his father.

"She ended up coming home early. She was too shaken up about the incident after that. I told her to take some time off of work, but she didn't think we could afford it. I begged her to switch her shift, take some time, or even find another job if she had to. But she didn't want to. She swore to me that she could handle herself, and that it wouldn't be a problem." He shakes his head, his hands curling back around his mug. Tears finally spill down his cheeks, and he wipes his nose on the back of his hand. "I wish I'd forced her to quit, to stay home. I kick myself every day that I didn't put my foot down and take her out of harm's way."

"I know that's a tough feeling to shake, but I really don't

think that it would have done any good," I say. This is a common feeling, survivor's guilt. Everyone feels like they could control the outcome, fix it if they could only go back and do things differently. But it doesn't work that way. Especially not when we're talking about a serial killer. Chances are, if the killer couldn't get Jae when he wanted her originally, he would have waited around until the perfect time. Once a killer has their desired target, it takes a lot to shake them off, to change their focus.

"You have no idea what this is like," he says, his eyes narrowing on me. "I know you work with people every single day, people facing circumstances just like ours. But those words are not helpful. I could have kept her home. I could have kept her safe. But I decided not to do it. I decided to let her make the decision instead of protecting her. Excuse me." He rises from his seat at the table and disappears from the room. A few moments later, Lucas follows.

I stand up, stretching my legs. My knees ache from all the sitting I've done today. I cross my arms as I stare out the back window. It's late August, and some of the trees have started to change colors. It's happening earlier this year, which makes me wonder if we're in for an early winter. My mind drifts back to my first snow here in New York, and the bodies that we found in the snowbanks that followed the snow. A chill tickles my spine. That was my first case in New York, a serial killer that hid bodies in the snow. After that, I hunted a depraved killer, who tortured their victims and set them on fire. And now, here I am, hunting a phantom that killed along highway 32 over thirty years ago. It strikes me that our killer may not even still be alive. We may actually be hunting a ghost.

From down the hall, I can hear Lucas's and his father's hushed words, their edges softened by the walls between us. They're too hard to make out, but at least they're not screaming at each other. I wonder what it would do to them if the killer was dead. Would they see that as justice served already or would they be crushed that they couldn't bring him to justice?

I scroll through the missing persons database on my phone. I'm trying to identify other women who went missing from diners along the interstate, but so far I haven't found anything else. I know they're there though. A killer that held women captive on his property, who hunted up and down the highway, he didn't stop at four victims. I know that much for sure.

21

I've been staring at a wall for two hours. Though the sun isn't up yet, my mind has been firing on all cylinders since the moment I woke up at 4 a.m. Lucas and Joon are still asleep, so I've been lying in the stiff guest bed, alternating between staring at the wall and going through the missing persons database on my phone. Though I know sometimes I should just let myself unplug, my mind *needs* to be doing something right now, so I turn back to the glowing screen and start scrolling.

At 6 a.m. my phone rings. Sergeant Ortega's number flashes on the screen. I tug on my shoes and step outside the house into the backyard to take the call to avoid waking anyone up.

"Good morning," I say as I accept the call and press it to my ear.

"Hey, Durant. Sorry to call so early, but I wanted to give you a heads-up," she says, somewhat out of breath, like she's in a rush.

"No problem. What's up? I was already awake."

"Vick Langley has been spotted in town. And I got a call that a fifteen-year-old, Abigail Anderson, never came home last night."

My pulse kicks up a notch. "He didn't even take a night off," I say through my gritted teeth. But in the back of my mind, I can't help but wonder, was it Vick or is this related to Mazie or Kaley?

"Do you think Lucas would be open to pitching in on this since his expertise is in missing persons?" she asks.

"We're in Lake Placid right now, but I'll text you when I have a timeline for us heading back." For a second, the line goes quiet, then I remember the blood we got back from Langdon's truck. "Hey, unrelated but possibly related—we found evidence of blood in Langdon's truck. It was Mazie's. Got any thoughts on that?"

"She was strangled, so there would have been no blood. But she also had really bad nosebleeds. So, I wouldn't be surprised if we found her blood all over the town," she says without skipping a beat.

My heart sinks a little. But that at least clears it up. "Okay, thanks. We'll reach out when we're back in town."

"Thanks," she says before ending the call.

I don't want to commit Lucas to working on the case, especially with everything going on. But I'll bring it up to him when the time is right.

From my position in the backyard, I hear signs of life in the kitchen. I slip in through the back door. I'm thankful to find Lucas at the coffee pot. I wouldn't know what to say to his dad, and I feel like I pissed him off yesterday.

"How'd you sleep?" Lucas asks as he shovels coffee grounds into the filter until it's nearly overflowing. "What were you doing out there?"

"Honestly, not great." I sigh. "Ortega called, problems back in New Paltz. We can talk about it later."

He raises a brow. "I never sleep well here anymore," he says before pressing his lips together. "Though I come back a few times a year, it always feels strange. Like I'm not supposed to be here. I've never been able to pinpoint if it's because I've outgrown this town, this house, my place here—or if it's because it just doesn't feel like home without my mom."

"Maybe it's both," I offer. Though I only tried to go back to Washington once, it felt the same way. It was the same place I'd lived in for eighteen years, but it didn't feel the same. It didn't make anxiety bloom inside me the way that it always had. Instead, I felt nothing. And I think that was the most jarring part. As if I had expected going back to awaken something inside me. It left me wondering if there was something wrong with me, if I could feel anything at all anymore. I've always felt like maybe I didn't have the same emotional range as everyone else around me. I'm not sure if that's a product of my father's psychobabble or the rest of my fucked-up childhood.

He nods slowly. "I suppose it could be."

"Everything end up okay with you both?" I say as I motion toward the back bedrooms down the hall. I keep my words quiet. I don't want to wake his dad. I make the decision not to tell him the details of Ortega's call until Lucas decides he's ready to head back to New Paltz on his own. I'm not going to rush him here.

"As good as it can be, I guess." He shrugs. "I just can't believe that he kept all this from me. My mom had a stalker. The guy was trying to follow her home. He told me that she and my grandmother had gone out to grab groceries together, because she thought she'd be safer that way—then they both just ended up being taken."

"Are you going to tell him about your sister?" I ask, dropping my words to a whisper.

He shakes his head. "Absolutely not. That would kill him. I'm going to bury her separately. But he doesn't need to know. I'll take that secret to my grave."

I know that's probably for the best. And we should be able to keep the information from getting out to the media. I'll have to make sure that none of it will be released in the case files. Luckily, cold cases aren't as sexy to the news as other homicides, so the chances of this getting picked up and talked about are pretty low. Though the more bodies we find on that plot of land, the more likely it is that it'll gain some traction.

"How long do you want to stay?" I ask. I'm itching to get out of this city, to get back on the case. But if Lucas wants to stay here for a day or two, I'll stick around. I'll just work on my laptop from the guest room. I've got to see what else I can find out about Davida, and see if we can track down any other possible victims at other diners.

"Just long enough for this to brew." He motions to the coffee pot. "It's good seeing my dad, but if I stay, we're both just going to spiral into depression together. I've got to get out of this city, to get back to work, get my mind on something else."

"You know it's not healthy to suppress all your emotions and just focus on work," I say, parroting the exact words that he's said to me before.

He rolls his eyes at me. "Oh, so I guess you do listen when I talk—sometimes."

"Shut up. Where are the coffee mugs?" I ask as I motion to the cabinets.

"Over there," he says as he points to a set next to the sink. I grab two mugs and hand them over to him. Though the pot isn't done brewing, he fills both of our mugs and passes one back to me.

"This is so strong it looks like gravy," I say.

"Well, chew fast. We need to get on the road."

Within thirty minutes, we say our goodbyes to Joon and climb back into my Jeep. On our way back, I tell Lucas about what's waiting for us back in New Paltz and to my surprise he isn't annoyed that I kept it from him. Before noon, we make it back to New Paltz, and I finally let out a stale breath. Now that we're back, we can keep this case moving. We swing by the farm to check out the status there. On the outskirts, there's a grave-yard of bulldozers, tractors, and other heavy machinery that's been abandoned since the cabin was discovered. Our speed is slow as the forest flickers by. A creeping feeling snakes up my neck, and I swear that there's someone in there watching us. I don't know if it's the stories getting to me or if there's really someone out there. The GPS device we found on my car sounds an alarm in my mind. We need to check it again.

"Looks like the developer has given up," Lucas says, and I can only see the back of his head as he stares out the window.

"They don't give up. They're just taking a break because the crime scenes are making it impossible for them to really break ground the way they need to."

"Do you think there are more bodies out there? Do you think there were more than the four women?" He doesn't look at me, and I wonder how he feels about this now, the shift that's happened. The air in my Jeep is thick with tension. This place was just a crime scene before, but now it's more than that. Instead, this is the place where his mother was trapped for years, where she lived, where she died. How does he see it all now? How does he feel?

"Honestly, I think it's incredibly unlikely that there were only four victims. While I know he probably took only enough women at a time to appease his urges, I think it's unlikely that four women were able to do that. I think chances are that we will find a woman elsewhere that he tried to kidnap, but it didn't work out the way that he expected. There's no way to know how many victims there are in all, unless we use GPR on the entire plot of land, but there's no way that with so many acres they're going to approve that," I say.

He nods. "That would take weeks." He's quiet for a long moment, then he adds, "I want to read the pages that we found in there. I want to know what she went through, what it was like for her," he says.

"We can arrange that, but are you sure you want to read that? It's not going to say that she had an easy life. She had a daughter... I seriously doubt that she willingly had sex with her captor," I say, not wanting to be too harsh. But I also want Lucas to understand what he's really signing up for. Reading that journal, the real accounts of what his mother went through, it's going to be absolutely heartbreaking. I hate that he wants to put himself through that. But as someone who dug through all of my father's client records to try and understand the women that he killed, I get the compulsion.

"I have to read it. I have to know what she went through. Otherwise, it's just going to keep eating me alive." He looks back at me, and the pain in his eyes splinters me. I can't imagine what it would be like to lose someone like this.

My cellphone rings, the noise cutting through the tension in the Jeep. I accept the call and throw it on speaker.

"Detective Durant," I say as I answer the call.

"Hi, Detective. My name is Ezra Glass. I heard that you're working out at Ackert Farm, investigating some terrible things that happened there." The man's voice is deep.

"Yes, that's correct. What can I help you with, Ezra?"

"I owned the farm for a little while in the early 2000s, so I wanted to see if there was anything you needed from me, if I could help at all," he says.

This farm seems to have changed hands a lot. I don't remember seeing Ezra's name in any of the files. Something strikes me as odd here, so I can't help but wonder if Ezra really owned the farm or if he's just calling to try and poke around what we know.

"That's interesting, I didn't see your name at city hall when I was pulling some of the property records," I explain.

He clears his throat. "Oh, yeah. You aren't a local. In 2011, there was a really bad storm. There was some flooding, and the basement of city hall flooded. A lot of the records were destroyed, and up until that point there hadn't really been a push to digitize the records. A lot of historical information about the town was lost," he explains.

Why didn't the workers warn us about this? Because we didn't have the full picture all along, we have missed out on questioning a crucial witness in this case. Anger crackles inside me, like lightning.

"How long did you own the property?" I ask as I pull my Jeep over to the side of the dirt road and grab a notebook. We're still on the outskirts of the farm, the forest looming to our right. The pine trees sway in the afternoon breeze, their ends bleached by the bright sunlight.

"For about eight months, maybe a little longer," he explains.

"That's a really short time," I say. "Why even bother buying the farm?"

"I'd really hoped that I could turn things around. My goal had been to clear out some of the trees and to try planting some other crops. No one else had ever had any real luck with anything other than apples on this land. But the farmland in New Paltz is usually very rich, great for growing apples. I wanted to try expanding a bit. I cleared behind the house, had about an acre of test land before I invested in clearing the rest. But I swear that land is cursed. Not a single thing sprouted."

That seems to be the story for most of the owners of the farm. But I'm surprised he cleared out some of the forest to try planting there.

"So, since nothing grew for you, you ended up selling it?" I ask.

"Well, there were some other things. Something about the property always felt off to me. I had thought about fixing up the house, getting it in good shape so that my wife and I could live there. But it gave me the creeps when I walked through it. There was bad energy in that house."

"Did you ever hear anything in the woods?" I ask, and I realize I'm leading him. I shouldn't have asked it so directly.

"Frequently, but I always thought it was the kids. I could always feel someone watching me when I was at the property. Every time I was out there, I'd catch Calvin on the property and I'd have to ask him to go home."

That information strikes a chord with me and I note it down. We spoke to Calvin early in our investigation. He was the farmhand for this property for years. But I don't understand why he'd come back here if Ezra hadn't hired him.

"You'd catch him at the farm? Why? What was he doing there?" I ask.

"Usually, he was stalking around the woods. I'd catch him walking out of it, toward the house. Sometimes I'd catch him on the porch looking into the windows of the farmhouse."

"Did he ever tell you what he was doing?" I jot this information down. This is a lead we definitely need to follow up on. There's no reason that Calvin should have been trespassing. Was he going into the woods to check on the women that were trapped there? Did he put them there?

"Whenever I asked him in the beginning, he said that he was just checking on things. He worked at the farm his entire life, so he said this was like a second home for him. And for a while, I understood. I cut him some slack. But he didn't stop. If anything, I felt like it became more frequent. I'd catch him there several times a week. I think he was at the property more often than I was. I had a stern talk with him and asked him to stop, but he didn't listen to me. He got very upset and tried to punch me. He said that this was meant to be his farm, not mine."

That's not an escalation that I would have expected. I guess I can understand Calvin's attachment to the land, but wanting to attack Ezra over it? That makes me think he had more at stake here than memories.

He continues, "I told him if he loved the farm so much, he

should buy it from me. It wasn't growing anything. What did I need it for anyway? He took another swing at me, missed, and stormed off the property. After that I didn't see him again for a couple weeks. And when I did, he was carrying something into the woods. I tried to go after him, to follow him, to see where he was going, but he disappeared."

What would he have been carrying into the woods? This strikes me as very odd, especially since Calvin had gone out of his way to tell me how much the woods creeped him out so he stayed away from them.

"Did you stick around to see when he came out?"

"I was there for hours and I never saw him come back out."

"Did he have a car there or anything?" I ask as I try to piece together where he could have gone. Lucas raises an eyebrow as well. There's nowhere to go in the woods. It goes on for acres and acres. If he came out the other side, he'd have to walk down the dirt road to loop back around to the city. The only place he could have been headed in the woods is the cabin.

"No, not that I saw. Sometimes he parked his truck near the orchard. Sometimes he didn't bring it at all."

"How did you end up getting rid of him?" I ask.

He clears his throat. "I didn't. I sold the damn farm at a loss. I didn't want it bleeding me dry, so I passed it on to Asher, then he sold it to Marcus, I think."

We haven't spoken to Marcus yet. "Did you ever spend much time in the woods?"

He laughs. "No, why would I have spent any time in the woods?"

"From the others we've spoken to, it seems like teenagers liked to hang out in the woods. I didn't know if you'd ever explored them."

"I walked into them a few times, but I don't think I'd say that I explored them. There was too much land for that, the trees are pretty thick. I was afraid I'd get lost in there. It gets a bit disorienting."

I don't want to lead him again, but I don't see any other way around asking him about the cabin. But I need to keep it as vague as possible. "Did you ever notice any other structures on the property other than the house and the barn?"

He's quiet for a moment. "Structures? What do you mean?"

"Did you ever see anything in the woods? A structure that you were never told was there." That's as specific as I want to get. I don't want to tell him directly about the cabin. I'm trying to keep too much from getting leaked to the media.

"No. Did the teens build something out there? I could see them creating a better spot for them to hang out. I'd heard stories about them taking a couch out into the woods. But I'd never seen it myself."

"Is there anything else that you can think of that might be helpful?"

"I think that's all I've got. But if I remember anything else, I'll give you a call back," he promises.

22

The ride back to New Paltz is mostly quiet. Road noise, the sound of my tires hissing against the pavement as I drive, fills the car. My mind is going a mile a minute, wishing we had more to go on with Mazie, and wondering how this all tracks back to the farm—because I know it's connected. On either side of us, pine trees tower, their feathery branches brushing the sky. Thick gray clouds are crowding the horizon, warning that rain might be coming our way. Beside me, I can feel Lucas's presence, though he doesn't speak. I know that Lucas is still processing, dealing with the weight of the news about his mother, grandmother, and sister. He's been unusually silent, his eyes glued out the window.

When the trees scatter and the road opens up, the town of New Paltz comes into view. Something feels like it's shifted since we left. Along the side of the two-lane highway there are cars parked, at least twelve of them, with their drivers nowhere to be seen. There's nothing near this stretch of highway, so I can't figure out why anyone would have parked here.

The station is packed when we pull up; civilian cars fill almost every single space. I carve around the rows, finding one of the few free spaces. As we climb out, I overhear a woman speaking.

"Okay, we've already got a group searching off the highway. I need the rest of the groups to fan out here, here, and here," she says, and though I can't see her, my guess is that she's pointing at a map of the town, indicating where the searches should happen.

"Abigail Anderson, that's the new missing girl," I say. It's only been a few hours since Ortega called to tell us that she went missing. They've organized the searches much faster than I would have expected.

As we walk into the station there's a chaotic energy in the air. I walk through the bullpen with Lucas on my heels. Before we're even ten feet into the room, Ortega flags us down.

"Hey, you got a minute?" she asks.

"Of course," I say before we both change course and follow her. Ortega's office is on the larger side for what I've seen sergeants get in small towns like this. On her walls hang pictures of her, her wife, and their daughter. She's also got several pictures hung up that her daughter must have drawn for her.

"Take a seat," she says as she points to the two squat chairs in front of her desk.

We follow her directions but I can't help but notice how tense she is. This plus the stress of the other disappearance must be getting to her.

"Thanks for getting back here so quickly," she says, then turns her attention to Lucas.

"We really need your help finding these girls. But something just as pressing has come up," she says, then looks to me.

"Oh?" I ask after sneaking a glance at Lucas.

"Officer Nolan Dunn has gone missing as well. We just realized, as he didn't show up for his shift this morning. I called his wife and she hasn't seen or heard from him since last night."

"Do you think this is related to Abigail's and Kaley's disappearances?" Lucas asks.

She straightens and crosses her arms. "Unlikely, but maybe not impossible. Nolan had it out for Vick, because he'd tried shit with his sister before he was locked up. I was thinking maybe he went over there when he heard that Vick came back into town, but no one has seen him." There's a deep crease between her brows as she looks down at her desk. This is weighing on her.

I make note of that.

"Were there any other connections between the two of them?" Lucas asks, and though he doesn't spell it out, I know the subtext in the silence. Would he or could he have run off with one of the girls? Could they be together and it's all unrelated to Vick? I didn't get any weird vibes from Nolan, but that's not saying much. I barely knew the guy.

Ortega shakes her head. "Not that we know of."

"Can we get a copy of what you have on file so far for Vick, Abigail, and Kaley? I assume your team already did some interviews?" Lucas asks. It's so clear in the confidence in his voice and his posture that he's totally comfortable navigating all of this.

She nods. "I'll email it over to both of you."

"Where do you have your team searching right now?" I ask.

She turns around and grabs a map of the city, then holds it up for us to see. The image has blue, red, and green circles on it. "Red are the first places we checked, blue is going on now, green will be our targets tomorrow if we don't find anything today," she explains as she points at the map.

I notice that Ackert Farm isn't part of the search area. Neither are a few wooded stretches of land on the outskirts of town.

"We're going to take the farm," I say. I don't want to overlap with the team and I want a little time to game-plan with Lucas.

She nods. "We also have two units in the area of where we believe that Vick has been staying."

We catch up on a few more items then head out of the station. Lucas and I grab a coffee and once we're back in the seclusion of my Jeep, I say, "It's odd to me that they're doing a foot search. It's like they expect to find a body."

"It is. Typically, at this point I'd be tracking her cellphone, other devices, social media account usage. And unless there's any real reason to believe she's dead, run away, or lost, the search is just spinning its wheels at this point—some place to burn off nervous energy."

I take a swig of my coffee. "So, what's our best move?" I ask.

"We should go back to the farm for now. I need to review the interview notes from the family and friends interviews for Abigail," he explains.

I nod and start my Jeep. It takes ten minutes to drive through town, past groups getting ready to start their searches, until we finally reach the farm. I do my best to let Lucas read and not interrupt him as she scrolls through the details on his phone.

"So, what have we got?" I ask as my car starts to rock back and forth on the dirt road that leads up to the farm.

"A girl that could be a good target for kidnapping. She didn't get into much trouble, but the little that she did was for sneaking out of the house. If she did that often enough, it could have drawn attention from the wrong person," he says.

I nod. "Any other red flags?"

"Just normal teenager stuff, nothing that really sticks out."

"Anything about Nolan?"

"Haven't seen anything come through on him yet." He offers a shrug then looks up to the farmhouse that's looming ahead of us.

The house towers above us, casting a long shadow onto the car. As we slip out, the sunlight dims as a thick cloud rolls in front of the sun. To the right of the barn, the construction equipment still sits abandoned, a veritable graveyard of bulldozers and machinery. As I walk toward the barn, the doors yawning open, I realize there's something inside I haven't noticed before. My pulse quickens as I walk closer and swallow hard as I realize—it's a body.

23

I keep a wide birth from the body. Though gauzy light pours in from the open doors, I flick on the flashlight on my phone to be sure I don't walk too close to the body or disturb any existing footprints on the dirt floor. All the prints near the body are smeared, like our perp knew what they were doing, that they needed to conceal the path they walked.

The form is tall with broad shoulders and close-cropped hair. I realize immediately that it's Nolan. I unlock my phone and start dialing for a bus, and when I look back to Lucas, he's got his phone in his hand as well.

"Calling Ortega," he shouts from the door of the barn, then walks back to the car.

Within thirty minutes the scene is swarming. Officers from New Paltz pull up, forming a strobing half circle. EMTs confirm that Nolan is dead, with a stab wound and a deep purple bruise on his neck showing me just how hard he was to take down. My mind makes a mental checklist of what has to happen next; the body must be collected by the coroner, taken to the ME, cause of death then gets determined. I know, unfortunately, that his wife has already been notified.

My cellphone rings and I notice it's Sergeant Dirby. I step away from the scene, and with each step between me and the markers, the noise quiets. Lucas is on the other side of the barn, talking to Ortega, but I signal to him that I'm taking the call.

"Sergeant," I say.

"I heard about the officer there," he says, and I'm somewhat surprised that news reached him so fast. "I need to pull you and Lucas in on this serial killer. He's in your neck of the woods."

My stomach twists. He cannot pull us off our current investigation, it would crush Lucas. "We can take it on, but we can't step back from our current case," I say. "I won't do that to my partner." This is the first time I've really pushed back on Dirby, so I'm not sure how he'll take this. But I'll stay firm regardless.

"You think you can manage all of this?" he asks.

"We'll have to," I say. In my gut, I know this is all connected. We just need to piece it all together.

As Lucas lingers near my Jeep, still clearly talking on the phone, I circle around the back of the farmhouse. Though the front porch looks perilous, back here it's not so bad. The back door is yawning open, half-rotted steps leading up to it. Curiosity gets the best of me, and I creep closer toward the house. Leaves, twigs, dirt, and trash are littered along the floor. My pulse kicks up a notch as I slip into the house. The wooden boards bow and groan beneath my feet.

You shouldn't be in here. My mind and heart seem to scream in unison. But I've never been good at listening to my own intuition.

I creep past a small galley kitchen, the cabinets all open, the insides barren except for abandoned bird's nests. The entire first floor is littered with leaves and dirt. Thick cobwebs are in every corner. Several small nests that look like they belong to animals are in the corners of a few rooms. Though there are stairs that lead to a second floor, they look too risky to scale. Instead, I switch on the flashlight of my cellphone and descend the stairs to the basement. The air down here is thick, heavy with moisture and the smell of moss. I glance around the darkened corners, finding nothing.

"Harlow! Are you in there? We don't have permission to enter the house," Lucas calls. His voice startles me, nearly making me drop my phone. I straighten and suck in a sharp breath.

"Yeah, I'm coming back up. There's nothing in here anyway," I call back as I climb the stairs.

Once I finally emerge out the back of the house, my heart rate has returned to normal. Lucas scowls at me, so I roll my eyes.

"We don't have permission—" he starts, but I hold my hand up, cutting him off.

"I heard you the first time. There's nothing in there. I was just checking it out," I say.

"The team will be here in twenty minutes," he says.

I nod to him, and look out toward the dirt road that leads to the farm, as if I'll already be able to see them coming. I steel myself for what's to come—finding the body of a fellow officer, that's one of the worst things a team can experience. We need to figure out fast who's haunting this farm before more people disappear—or worse, we end up with another body on our hands.

24

NINETEEN YEARS AGO

Under my bed, I swear I can hear the book. I'm sitting atop it, my legs crossed and it's as if the voices of the women are whispering to me, retelling me the stories from my childhood from their points of view. Bile claws at my throat, as it has since I found the book. Every single story he told me was about killing. How many women are dead because of my father? How many has he *saved*?

I've been weighing what to do, what I can do with this book. Worry nags at me, because I'm terrified that my father will figure out that I have it. But now that I know the cops are watching us... and the news keeps talking about the cops closing in on the Seattle Sleeper, I don't know that I can hold this all inside. The guilt has been dragging me down, making me question what kind of person I want to be. If I don't tell anyone what he's done, I'm just as bad as he is. That's what I'm slowly realizing.

The anger that I know I'll face from my mother without the buffer of him being here, that's what's stopped me cold. Facing her full rage—I'm not sure I'll survive it. But I'm also not sure I can survive knowing that women are dying because I didn't speak up for them. My father has been convincing himself that he's not killing women, he's saving them. After reading his journal, I realize just how far gone he really is. He's convinced that there are some patients that can't be saved through therapy, through psychiatric drugs. And once he's decided that there's only one way to save them from themselves, he kills them.

I want to gag, but I push it down. I swear I can feel a heartbeat coming from beneath the bed, but maybe it's because I read "The Tell-Tale Heart" last week in class and now it's getting to me. The bed shudders beneath me, and the whole thing shakes, propelling me off the bed so quick it may as well have electrocuted me. My heart pounds and my breaths are ragged, but I realize it wasn't the bed, it was my mother slamming a door downstairs. Though I try to calm myself down, I can't slow my pulse or my breathing.

Do it now, or you never will.

I clench my fists at my sides and force myself toward the door. Part of me wants to take the journal to show my mom, but the other part of me knows that she's turbulent. She could destroy the accounts of my father's crimes, then the police would never believe me. I have to keep that journal safe so that I can make my father stop killing. My palms sweat as I turn down the hallway and walk toward the stairs.

Another door slams and I stop, my whole body tensing. My mother is pissed. My dad hasn't been home in three days. I read a book on serial killers in the library, and it said that before they get caught they reach a berserker state where they become unhinged. They stop hiding their crimes as well as they once did because they just continue escalating. Sometimes it's because the killers are angry that they're not getting the credit or attention they think they deserve. Sometimes it's because they think they can't get caught no matter what they do, because they're just *too good* at what they do.

In the kitchen, something is rattling, glasses. She's probably pouring herself another drink so she's nice and drunk by the time my dad gets home. That'll either make her fall asleep early or it'll throw her into a rage that forces me onto the roof just to put some space between us. My whole body is rigid as I walk to the kitchen. I've learned that this is the time to avoid her, to let her rage simmer and burn itself out. But then again, she's always teetering on the edge, always about to boil over. I can't keep putting this off because she's in a bad mood, because when I think really hard about it—I can't remember the last time my mother was happy. Maybe she's just not capable of it.

As I turn into the living room, I keep my steps silent. I'm always careful of my movements. Any noise I make can set her off. I feel like a gazelle picking my way through a field as I avoid a cheetah. Finally, I see her, in the kitchen with a glass of amber liquid in her hand. She's not drunk yet. I can see that on her face. Her dark brown hair sticks out from her head, like she's been pulling on it. Dark bags hang under her eyes, her lips are pale and cracked. She offers me what I'm guessing is an attempt at a sneer or maybe a smile as I approach.

"Why are you still awake?" she asks.

I look at the clock on the microwave behind her. "It's eight thirty." I try to keep my voice as even as possible, so she doesn't come after me. But I know why she thinks I might be asleep now. Usually I lock my door at seven and pretend I'm asleep to avoid them both, to avoid their fighting, their rage. "I guess I'm just not tired yet."

She nods slowly then takes a sip of her drink. She flinches, and I wonder if the alcohol burns her lips.

"What do you want?" she finally asks when I don't speak.

My mind is a blur of thoughts, and I don't know what to say or how to say it. How do you tell your mother that you think your dad is killing women? There's nothing about that in my textbooks at school.

"You and dad are fighting a lot about why he's staying out so late," I say, feeling like this is probably the best place to start.

Her eyes tighten and her knuckles flash white as she grips her glass harder. "Ah, so you're not minding your own business again. Why is it any of your concern that your father and I are fighting?"

"I'm just—"

"Are you worried that we're going to get a divorce? Because that's not what's happening." Her words are oddly comforting, something I didn't think that she was capable of. But somehow her tone doesn't contain the normal disdain for me it usually has.

I shake my head. "No, that's not what I'm worried about. I think... well..." I try again to get a grip on the right words to say. How do you tell your mom that your dad is a serial killer? How do I spell that out? Do I present her the evidence and let her draw her own conclusions? Do I just spit it all out? I look at the counter as I try to piece it all together. But I can feel her staring at me, her eyes unkind.

"Just spit it out already. I don't have all night," she says, her words returning to their usual venomous slant.

"I know you wonder a lot where dad is." That's all I can manage to get out. As I try to form the rest of the words, I swear they crowd in my throat, cutting my sentence off.

"Of course I do. He's always gone. He's been gone for three fucking days." She rages and slams her empty fist on the counter. "Do you know how many times I've called his cellphone? About three hundred. Where is he!?" Her voice raises in octaves until she's screaming.

I want to shrink away, to go back up to my room as her anger floods the room like a toxic fog. Standing in front of her like this, I feel like nothing but a target. She's going to take out everything she's feeling on me. It's only a matter of time. But even if I do feel her wrath from this, I at least have to try to get it out. I can't hold it all inside forever. It will poison me. It'll grip me just like this madness grips my father. I can't live with it anymore.

"I think I know where he is."

Her eyes narrow. She sets her glass on the counter and moves around it to face me so smoothly I'd swear she actually slithered like a cobra. Her eyes are sharp as she approaches me, getting so close that my body screams at me to take a step back. More. There's never a time that my mother is this close to me that it ends well. Warning nags at the back of my mind, and I know already how this will end. At least one bruise, maybe a scar. We will both come out of this changed, but for different reasons.

"Spit it out, girl," she growls at me. The smell of liquor is sharp on her breath. It floods my nostrils.

"Dad's patients have been dying. I've seen a few of them on the news. I'd heard him mention their names, but I connected the dots," I lie. I didn't just connect the dots on my own. The book helped me do that, along with a few internet searches. But I can't tell her about the book. I can't let her know that I have solid evidence. That evidence has to go to the police.

"Of course they've been dying. He works with women that are suicidal. There will be a certain number of them that end up killing themselves. He can't fix everyone," she says with frustration rippling her words. She rolls her eyes at me and stalks back to her drink.

"No, it's more than that, Mom. Please listen to me. I think that he's out because he's killing them. There's too much of a coincidence. So many of his patients have died, at least ten of them. You really think that ten women killed themselves after working with Dad? I read their files. They were doing better—"

She whips around, her eyes narrowing on me again. "You read their files?" The question comes out punctuated with anger, each of the words so sharp I take a step back.

I nod slowly. I'm never supposed to touch my dad's files.

But when he and my mom leave together, I sneak down to his office. I peek at them. There's no reason for me to tell her that though. It's just going to make her angrier. He never takes her to his office. I think if it were up to him, she wouldn't even know where it was. She's always had a problem with showing up at his work and accusing him of sleeping with all of his staff and patients. She won't believe he's capable of murder, but if I would have told her that he was sleeping with a patient, she would have believed me in a second.

My dad told me about this. That my mom is similar to some of his patients in that way. She's built a scenario in her mind, something that she's absolutely certain has happened. And even despite evidence to the contrary, it's unlikely she will ever snap out of the delusion because she's convinced herself of it so thoroughly. For a while, I wondered if that's what I was doing. That maybe the same delusion she has ran through our genes and settled in me. Maybe my dad never killed, maybe I imagined it all.

"You know that you're never supposed to read those files. Those are private. You cannot invade the privacy of your father's patients that way."

"I know. I'm sorry." I spit the words out, hoping that she won't come after me. That this won't incite her rage. I back up, my foot sliding against the carpet.

She moves forward, but the counter is still between us, like she's caged behind it. There's a ferocity in her eyes that reminds me of facing the tigers at the zoo. But then again, she's always looked at me like this, like she is just dying for me to give her an excuse to come after me. Sometimes I wonder why she had me at all if she was just going to hate me.

"But I had to read them. I realized that the news was talking about one of his patients. She was found dead in her apartment." I step back again as I talk, my tailbone hitting the dining room table. It digs into me there, the pain somehow making me feel more present.

"Why are you always trying to start trouble? Nothing is ever good enough for you. The moment things are calm around here, you have to swoop in and try to destroy everything." Rage is woven into every syllable as she speaks to me. It always crackles beneath, the static undercurrent to any interaction that she has with me. She's dynamite that's always primed to blow, no matter what I do. A few years ago, when I was a bit younger, I would have believed her. I would have thought that I was the problem, that maybe I did always cause trouble. But now, I know it's not me. None of this is my fault.

I want to stand up to her. To shout at her everything that I've been feeling. But the idea of standing up for myself, facing her full rage alone, that terrifies me. My hands shake at my sides, so I reach out for the table, gripping the sides.

"I'm not," I say meekly.

"What was that?" she growls.

"I'm not starting anything." The words come out of my mouth, though I don't mean for them to. My tone is all wrong. It's going to set her off. But once the words are out, hanging in the air between us, I can't stop. "You want so badly to believe that dad is out there cheating on you because what he's doing needs to be a betrayal to you. But it's a betrayal toward both of us. He's not cheating. He's killing women. In his twisted mind he thinks that he's saving his patients, but Mom, I swear he's killing them."

"You stupid little girl," she says, an unhinged laugh slipping between her thin lips. She moves around the counter again, slinks into the dining room, like a snake. Her eyes are sharp, her mouth a thin line that warns me of what's to come. But it's too late. I can't take it back. I have to face it head-on.

All the words I've wanted to say for weeks rise to the surface. "You're the stupid one. You've listened to him for years, listened to his excuses. You let him do whatever he wanted, and with a leash that long, he chose to kill. This is your fault," I say. And it feels so good to unburden my soul. "Maybe that's why he chose you, because he knew how easy you would be to fool."

Her fist moves so fast through the air I barely have time to register that it's coming straight for my face. I don't have time to get my hands up to block her attack, so instead I move to the left, trying to dodge the punch. Her knuckles slam into the farthest edge of my cheekbone, then hit my ear. Pain radiates from my cheek all the way through the side of my head.

I grit my teeth, trying to push past the ache that awakens in my face. This is nothing new. It seems like it's always a matter of time until she hits me again, one of those markers that shows that it's been three days without an incident. Before I came downstairs, I could feel the storm brewing. It would have boiled over whether I started this or not. I just sped up the timeline.

"I hate that you're my mother. You don't deserve to have a child," I say.

She grits her teeth as a vein bulges in her neck. There's another snaking through her temple. It pulses with warning. But I don't back off. I don't rub my cheek. I don't let tears fill my eyes. Instead, I face her head-on. I'm so sick and tired of cowering. I'm sick of being scared.

"What the fuck did you just say to me?"

"You heard me. You don't deserve to be a mother. You're stupid. You've got your head in the sand. And when the news breaks that dad was killing people, don't come fucking crying to me because you didn't listen." I've never spoken to her like this. And for a moment, her eyes are wide but she doesn't move. Like she's in shock that I stood up for myself.

Finally, I see it all click into place on her face. She raises her hand again and slaps me. But an openhanded slap is nothing. I've had a million of these. It's a closed fist that does more damage. So while I grit my teeth at the sting, that's all there is.

But she doesn't stop. She raises her hand again, her fingers curling, and she punches me. Again, and again, and again. The pain pummels me just like she does, blooming on my cheek, my jaw, my eye.

"You're a fucking coward. You two deserve each other." I spit the words at her. She grabs me by the throat, a sour taste filling my mouth as she squeezes. Then she throws me into the wall. My head hits it hard, making bright spots explode in my vision.

My heart pounds and my breaths come quick as she launches herself at me. Her fingers thread through my shirt. Her eyes are wide, feral. I can see it now in the way she looks at me. My dad isn't the only killer here. She would kill me. She slams me again, the back of my head knocking so hard against the frame of the window that my teeth slam together and bile burns my throat.

Everything goes so white, until black edges my vision, my face goes cold and the world fades.

There's a low beeping far off, like my alarm clock was shoved beneath my pillow. It lulls me to the surface, as if I've been trapped beneath miles of cold dark water. My throat is on fire, aching as I come to. The smells, the sounds of my room are off. It's too bright. It smells like a bathroom.

Light pours into my eyes so brightly that I blink over and over against it. The sunlight needles my eyes, sending a shooting pain into my head. It spreads through my brain, then stabs the back of my skull over and over again. As I blink, the room starts to come into focus, the white walls, a small window that's letting the sunlight in, metal poles beside me. It all clicks together as my brain processes the images. I'm in the hospital.

"You're finally awake," a woman says to me as she walks

toward the bed and tucks in my sheets around me. She looks at my IV, then back to me. "How are you feeling?"

"My head really hurts. Who are you? Where am I?" My mouth feels like it's on fire as I talk, as if it's been dry for too long. I lick my lips. They're cracked and swollen—so chapped that it hurts to move them.

She hands me a cup of water, as if she was expecting this. "Drink it slowly. It'll help," she says.

I take a slow sip, and the cold water feels like it's stabbing its way down my throat. Though it helps to have liquid in my mouth again, when it settles in my stomach for a few moments it feels like I've swallowed a block of ice.

"It'll get easier. You've been out for a few days, so the IV has been keeping you hydrated." She brushes my hair back, and I flinch from her touch. She appraises me, sadness in her eyes as she pulls her hand away. "I'm Melinda. I'm a nurse. You're in the pediatric ward. Your father had you brought in."

"My father..." I manage. The night all clicks back into my memory. My mother hitting me, her slamming me against a wall over and over until she knocked me out. I wish I could say it's the first time she's put me in the hospital, but it's not.

"Yeah, he dropped you off, but he hasn't come back. Do you have anyone else that we could call?"

"The police." The words come out strangled. But I know it's what I have to do. I have to tell them what my parents did, both of them. I've always covered for my mother before, agreed with her accounts of my injuries being caused by accidents. But I can't do it anymore. I can't cover up both of their crimes.

She looks at me like she's not surprised that I asked to talk to them. "They're actually already here. I looked at the number of injuries in your file... It stood out to me. I'm going to send the officers in if you're ready to talk to them."

I can't say yes, so I just nod. I want to save my words for the police. I need to be strong, to give them all the information that they need to know.

It takes a few minutes after the nurse disappears for two officers to come into the room. A man and a woman approach. Though I expect for them to be in uniforms, they're not. Each is dressed in slacks and a dress shirt, the kind of outfits that my dad wears to work. The woman has dark skin, short black hair that's flecked with gray. She's taller than the man, and I wonder if I'll be as tall as she is. The man is short, with a little bit of a belly that pokes over the top of his pants. He's got a thick mustache and wide-set eyes.

"I'm Detective Marshall, and this is Detective Weiss," he says as he motions toward the woman.

"I only want to talk to her," I say, sitting up a little straighter in my bed.

He looks from me to the woman, and she nods, obviously giving him permission to leave. He motions toward the door. "I'm going to be right outside if you need me." I'm not sure if he says it for my sake or for hers. But I don't say anything else until he leaves the room.

Detective Weiss grabs a chair from the side of my room near the window and takes a seat. She pulls out a notebook and crosses one leg over the other.

"What's your name?" she asks.

"Harley," I say.

"Nice to meet you, Harley. What did you want to talk to me about?"

"There's something that I need to tell you about my parents," I say.

She nods. "You can tell me anything that you'd like."

I know I can't just jump in and tell her about my dad. I'm worried that she won't believe me as it is. So, I start with my mother. It takes me a long time to find the words to explain the abuse that I've suffered at the hands of my mother. I recount it all. The times that she's made me kneel on rice, when she whipped me with wood she made me find in the backyard, then when it escalated, she stopped using items and started using her hands—her fists. She started throwing me at walls, punching me, a few times she choked me until I blacked out.

The whole time, Detective Weiss writes down the points that I tell her. She doesn't look at me while I talk, and honestly it helps so much. She doesn't ask any questions. She just lets me get it all out, to pour the years of abuse out into the air between us. Tears spill down my cheeks, and I feel lighter. As if getting the truth out has unburdened me somehow.

"The nurse let me know that in your records you had a broken arm about six months ago. How did that happen?" she asks.

I had actually forgotten about that. It happened shortly after we moved into the new house. My mom got so angry with me because I'd left my shoes near the front door that she pushed me down the stairs. She'd screamed at me the entire drive that it was my fault that I'd fallen, that she yelled at all. And honestly, I'd believed her. For years, I've tried to do better, to not make her so mad. I tell the detective all of this.

She looks up from her notebook, her eyes meeting mine. "None of this, absolutely none of it, is your fault. If someone hits you, if someone raises their voice at you, that's a choice that they are making. It has nothing to do with you. So please, I know that she's tried to convince you that this is all your fault, but it's not."

I nod slowly, and I think that maybe I can trust her with the information about my dad. I think that she'll listen to me.

"There's more," I manage. "I need to tell you about my father."

She nods. "Of course, anything you need to tell me, I'm here."

It takes me a long time to find the words, the right way to

say them. I test them out in my mind first, to figure out the best way to put it. "A little over a year ago, I saw my father murder a woman."

She raises a brow at me, and I can see the surprise lighting up her eyes. Her mouth goes slack, and for a moment she just stares at me. This is obviously not what she was expecting me to say at all.

"I'm sorry, what was that?"

"I think my father is the Seattle Sleeper," I say. Then it all just comes spilling out. I tell her about the woman in the house, the address, how he tried to make me kill a woman, that I found his book, his records, about the patients he had that went missing. When it all is finally out, I look back up, scared to death that she's going to look at me like I'm crazy. But she doesn't. She's still furiously writing the details down. "There's a book," I add. "It's hidden under my bed. I wedged it between the mattress and the slats. It's my dad's journal where he detailed what he did to these women, why, when. It has all their names, the dates."

"So, you've known for a year..."

I bite my lip as guilt wells up inside me. This is what I was afraid of, how bad it would look that I've kept this a secret for so long. How many more women have died because I didn't come forward? Because I didn't tell the police.

"I have, but I didn't think anyone would believe me. I tried to tell my mom, and she did this." I point to my head. "It was really hard. I don't want to lose my dad and I guess I kept trying to convince myself that it wasn't true, that none of it was really happening. But then I found the journal, then I stared researching and..."

"I'm not blaming you. This isn't your fault. I just want to be sure that I have the timeline right," she says.

My heart is pounding as my palms slick with sweat. I don't know what to do, what will happen. Fight or flight is taking over and it's telling me to run. I'm so scared of what will happen when all the truth comes out. I can't be alone with my mother. She'll kill me. And I can't be with my father—he'll be in jail. Where does that leave me? What happens now?

"It's going to be okay," she says as she stands up and walks toward me. She puts her hand over mine and offers it a light squeeze. "You are so brave for coming forward. Do you mind if I ask you a few more questions?"

I shake my head and she goes to sit back down. "The police were watching him already, I think. I think I saw cops staking out the outside of our house in an electrician van."

"That may have been the FBI. I don't think our team has the resources to do something like that. But I will be sure to share that information with the team. You said that your father killed a woman in front of you. That sounds awful and I'm very sorry that you had to witness it. But how exactly did he kill her?"

"He strangled her. In the journal, most of the time he suffocated the women or strangled them. He thought that he was hurting them less when he did it that way. But he also mentioned that he wanted to be as careful as possible to not have the exact same MO each time so he could continue to do his work. He thought that he was helping these women that couldn't be helped in any other way. He thought that killing them was the only way to help."

She nods and presses her lips together as she jots down notes. "Do you know what her name was?"

"I don't remember, but I think it's in the journal." I should know all of their names by now. I should carve them all onto my skin so that I never forget them, especially the women who are dead because of me.

The questioning goes on for a long time. I answer questions about what I saw the night my father killed someone—what I was doing out there, how long I've suspected he was up to some-thing—and then her questions shift. Her eyes move to the door.

"Do you have any reason to believe that your mother may be involved?"

"No, I don't see how. She's always so mad when he's late coming home," I explain. "That's when I know he must be following women, plotting out how he'll do it. If she were up to something, she'd be out there with him. But she rarely leaves the house. My dad says she may have mild agoraphobia, but I don't think she does. She just doesn't want to go out."

"I'm going to talk to my partner about all of this. In the meantime, we're going to call a guard to come out and watch your room." She sends a text message then stands up and folds her notebook up before shoving it in her pocket.

"Why do I need a guard to watch my room?" I ask, as anxiety tightens my throat. Am I going to be trapped in here? Did I say something wrong? All at once, I start to wonder what I've done. Maybe I shouldn't have pressed my mother, maybe I should have just kept it all to myself.

"Everything is going to be okay. I just think with what you've told me and what the nurse mentioned about your head, it's probably best if you had an officer close if you need us. I'm going to instruct that neither of your parents should come in here without an officer present," she says. Her confidence makes me feel a bit better. But I still don't know what's going to happen, what the future holds.

The woman's phone rings, and she grabs it. She stands near the door to my room, but I can still hear her as she talks.

"A body? Already? We're on our way." Those are the last words I hear before she opens the door and slams it behind her.

25

I've got the names of three property owners that we've never had on our list before. After our talk with Ezra, I feel like we've got a real direction to go in. I keep checking on Lucas, as if I'm expecting him to crumble—to break down entirely. But he's holding everything in just like I do. I want to shake his shoulders, to tell him that it's okay to let it out, that he doesn't need to bottle it all up inside and focus on work to cope. But then my father's words ring in my mind, that I should tell myself those things when I compartmentalize.

"Who do we need to call?" Lucas asks as he glances at me across the table. He's got his laptop open, and we're camped out in the coffee shop.

This morning, the New Paltz team needed to have a meeting and I figured it was best to just give them their space. While they've been far more accommodating than any other department we've had to set up shop inside, I don't want to wear out our welcome. With this cold case and Mazie's homicide feeling so far from completion, I know they'll get sick of us eventually—we need to make nice with them for as long as possible.

I slide my notebook over to him, showing off the names that I've written down.

He picks it up with a flourish, glowers at the page as he squints, then looks back at me. "Your handwriting is awful." He slaps the notebook back down and slides it toward me with one finger. "If you don't work on your penmanship, someone is going to find your lost notebooks and think the Zodiac Killer is active again."

I roll my eyes at him. "Want to just start taking my notes for me?"

"Only if you buy me some pretty calligraphy pens."

I grab my phone, Lucas and I both connect to it on Bluetooth, and then I dial the number for our first previous owner. Though we ask the guy all the same usual questions, he doesn't have much to offer. He's well into his nineties and owned the farm before it's likely that any of the women were on the property. He sold it off in the early seventies. We thank him for his time, then call the next person on the list, the person who owned the farm later in the seventies. Again, this man doesn't have anything real to offer us, but the one thing that does stick out to me is that neither man mentions seeing people in the woods, hearing voices, or the phantom cries of women. They also never refer to the land as cursed.

After I hang up with that owner, we've got one name left, Hershel. He owned the property from the late seventies until the early nineties. The timeline could line up for us, but the one question that I have lingering is, why would the women have still been on the property well into the early 2000s? This detail makes me wonder if the person who was keeping these women on the farm didn't live here at all. During the questionings, we've learned the last person to really live at the farm stopped doing so in 1971. It occurs to me again that we're not necessarily looking for a property owner at all, maybe we're just looking for someone in town who had access to the property, someone who lived nearby. It's been so hard to get a read on who we're looking for though, since everyone in town could access the farm—hell, we know kids partied in the woods frequently. My mind keeps drifting back to Calvin.

"Are you liking anyone for this?" I ask Lucas. I want his take on it, but I don't want to tell him my theory and have him just agree with me.

"No, but I can tell by the look on your face that you are. I thought I smelled rubber burning. Those gears are spinning too fast."

I glare at him. But I don't say anything, despite my burning desire to punch him in the arm.

"If you keep making that face, you're going to get wrinkles."

"And you're going to—"

He holds his hand up. "Oh my God, Harlow. Take a joke. Do you need a coffee or a Midol?"

I do the quick math in my head. Maybe he's right, maybe I am a little moody. But I still want to punch him.

"Anyway, I don't think we have enough evidence to tie this to anyone yet. Hell, the only evidence we really have is the journal, which doesn't tell us any names, and the people we know owned the property. But since we have no timeline for when the cabin was built, who it was built by, it's going to be difficult to tie that to a specific person. There's so much land it could have been built by someone who didn't own the land."

"That's what I'm thinking. We're not looking for an owner at all," I say.

He nods. "So, who do you like for this?"

"I'm not sure that I'm ready to bring anyone in yet. But I think we should keep an eye on Calvin. The fact that he's had the kind of access to the property that he's got for so many years, he would have had more of an ability to do this than an owner. Especially since none of these people lived in the vicinity." Our killer needed to have quick, frequent access to keep these women alive while they were being held captive. "We've got one person left to call," I say.

I dial Hershel's number and it rings several times before an older man answers. The tone of his voice makes me think he was just laughing. I introduce myself and Lucas, then explain the reason for our call.

"Oh, hello, Detectives. I hadn't heard about what was going on back in New Paltz. I would have chatted with you already if I had known," he says.

"I moved to Florida in the nineties," he explains. "I've lived in the Villages since then. Have you ever been? It's so nice out here. I got so sick of the weather in New York."

"I can't say that I've ever been down there, but I imagine that the weather is nice. Do you mind if we ask you a few questions about the farm?"

"Of course not!" His tone makes me think that he doesn't talk with people often. He's very excited at the prospect of having a conversation with us. I imagine that maybe he's older, living without any of his family around.

"Could you tell me what dates you owned the farm?"

"From seventy-two until about ninety-one."

"And why did you purchase the land?" I ask, as I make notes about the timeline. I need to map out all these dates, who owned it and when.

"It was a very profitable orchard when I bought it originally. It was making over a hundred thousand dollars a year, and considering the size of the land, that was pretty incredible. It seemed worth it. So, I went ahead and pulled the trigger, so to speak."

"We've heard from some of the other owners that the land stopped producing. Was that the case for you?"

He chuckles. "Not at all, both times I owned the land I made plenty off of it. I didn't have any problems at all."

"Why did you sell it each time?" I ask.

"Well, the first time, I had decided to move to Florida. I had the farm up there for a while after I moved. Calvin took care of it for me. I paid him. It seemed like a good enough arrangement. Then as I was just trying to relax, enjoy my retirement, it felt like everything just started going wrong. The tractor broke, then the city wanted to raise my taxes, then Calvin got hurt, so he couldn't man the farm, and I'd just had enough. So, I decided to put it up for sale. I sold it for less than I probably should have, just because I wanted to get it off my plate."

"And who bought the farm from you?" Lucas asks.

"Ben Fennick, he bought it in ninety-one."

"And then why did you purchase the property again?" It seems odd to me that after all that trouble that he'd bother buying the farm again.

"It was years later. I was thinking that if I didn't start making some more money, my retirement may not make it as long as I had expected it too. Ben called me. He told me that he was having trouble with the farm. He wasn't able to have it output the way that he wanted. So, he told me that he'd give me the deal of a lifetime if I'd take it off of his hands. It really felt like things were aligning the way that I needed them to, to get some income flowing in again. So, I went ahead and jumped in. I figured if it wasn't working out the way I expected, I could just sell it off again."

"Did you travel to the property at all after the second time that you purchased it?" I ask.

He lets out a slow breath that whistles out of his nostrils. "You know, I'm honestly not too sure. I don't think that I did. But it was so long ago," he says.

"And did Calvin take care of the property for the entire time that you owned it both times?" I ask.

"Yes, he did. He was out at the property every day. He took care of all the operations at the farm. He'd call me about once a week to tell me what was going on, if there were any problems, if there was anything that needed to be purchased or sold. We would also talk about what we expected the income to be for the next planting season," he explains. "There's a lot that goes into running a farm, and he always did it so well. I don't know why he didn't just buy it. He loved that property."

"Did you ever offer to sell it to him?" I ask.

"Oh, only every single time something went wrong. I thought that he'd end up owning it eventually, but he never took the chance when it went up for sale. Now that those property developers have bought it, I wish I'd held on to it for a few more years. I would have walked away with a million dollars. Though, at my age, it's not like I have time to spend a million dollars. So I guess it all worked out the way that it was supposed to."

"Did you ever hear about anyone being on your property that shouldn't have been?" Lucas asks as he leans a little closer to the phone.

Hershel laughs again. "Oh, only all the time. I'm sure you've heard about the teenagers that come and go constantly. I heard all the stories about women laughing in the woods, babies crying, that the land was cursed. None of that ever happened while I was out there. I think they were all just urban legends, something the kids needed to keep themselves occupied."

"Did you ever see any structures in the woods?"

"What kind of structures?" he asks after a pause.

"Any structures at all? Did you ever explore all of the forest around the farm?"

"Not really, no. I didn't have any reason to. I know there was the farmhouse, the barn, the root cellar."

"Did you ever live in the farmhouse?"

"No, when I owned the land, Calvin was living in the farmhouse."

I look to Lucas. That surprises me. I've never heard of Calvin living in the farmhouse. Why didn't he mention that to us? That really stands out to me and makes me wonder what else Calvin didn't tell us.

"He lived in the house?" Lucas asks.

"Yes, he'd lived there for a long time. I think for at least five years when I bought the land for the first time," he explains.

"According to our records, no one had lived in that house since the seventies," Lucas explains as he looks at his notebook to check the date.

"That's incorrect. Calvin lived on the property. That was one of the tradeoffs of having him work at the farm. He got free lodging, was always available to take care of anything that came up. As far as I know, when he turned eighteen he left his family home and moved to the farm to live there."

Why did Calvin lie to us about living on the property? And for how long did he live there? And is he still living there now? This information is raising some major red flags for me. Now we're going to have to call Calvin down to the station for official questioning. But first, I'm going to go out to the old farmhouse to see if we can find any evidence that he lived there. I like to be as prepared for lies as possible.

I glance at Lucas, and I'm sure the skeptical look on his face mirrors my own. "Did you ever see anything suspicious when you were on the property?"

"Like what?" Hershel asks.

"Did you notice Calvin coming out of the woods often? Did you see him taking things into the woods that he shouldn't have been?"

He's silent for a long moment, and I imagine that he's thinking. "It was so long ago," he finally says. "And I wasn't on the property often, but I'm sure I saw him in the woods occasionally. But it's not all that surprising. It was his responsibility to monitor the entire property, not just the farm," he explains.

"He told us that he didn't ever venture into the woods when we spoke to him," Lucas chimes in.

"Really? He was supposed to check at least the permitter of the farm at least once per week to make sure that all the fencing looked good. He had an ATV to make it easier on him for the places his truck couldn't easily get into."

That's another red flag. He's specifically told us that he wasn't able to use the ATV. It was something that stuck out to me at the time—it seemed odd that the farm would have an ATV that he wasn't allowed to use.

The wind whips at my Jeep as we pull into the farm. It rocks us from side to side as it swirls around. Fluffy white clouds skitter across the sky, so low they nearly touch the tops of the towering evergreen trees. I slide out of my Jeep, with Lucas following suit. In my pocket, I've got some shoe covers, latex gloves, a flashlight, some evidence bags, anything that we may need to collect evidence inside the farmhouse. We didn't have permission to enter the house previously, but now the developer has finally relented. If we'd collected evidence without permission or a warrant, none of it would be admissible in court.

As we approach, it looks so decrepit that I'm not certain that someone has actually lived here anytime recently. The front porch bows, sagging in the middle, as if a great weight was left sitting on it for a long time. The wood is peeling, bubbling, parts of it already torn away, revealing splintered wood beneath. I look up at the windows, crowded with grime, some of the panes broken. The roof is actually in better shape than I would have expected, only a few shingles have flown off in storms.

"You ready?" I ask as I glance at Lucas.

He nods. "As ready as I'm going to be."

As we approach the house, the porch groans beneath our feet. The way it groans, I'm worried that it'll collapse under us. Dark clouds have started to roll in around us, shrouding the trees. It always amazes me how quickly the weather can turn here, one moment it'll be sunny, the next it looks like the sky is about to open up.

I pull open the front door, my hand looping through a hole where the handle used to be. The wood on it is frayed, decaying in the brutal winters. As soon as we step inside the house, the air shifts. The smell of dust, old leather, stale air curls into my nostrils. In here, at least, the floors don't shift beneath my feet. Instead I feel steady as I walk to the right through what looks like a small sitting room. A couch is shoved against the wall, the fabric frayed. It looks like at some point an animal nested in here. There's fluff, dead grass, papers strewn all over the floor. A bundle of papers huddles near the window, and I can imagine a cat or a racoon keeping its babies there.

"It doesn't look like anyone has lived here in years," Lucas says as we creep around the debris on the floor.

"I have to wonder though, how long it took to get like this. While the outside is rough, there's no real damage in here. Really think about it. There's no water damage, no mold, it doesn't smell musty. It seems like someone is still checking on it," I say.

Lucas sweeps the room again, taking it all in. We step through to the kitchen. I would expect the cabinets to be empty, for animals to have ransacked anything that might have been left here. There are still a few boxes of cereal in the cabinets, and they don't look as old as I would have expected. It's clear to me based on some of the items still in the pantry that someone has been here—recently. These boxes aren't ten years old. Some of them look brand new.

My pulse quickens and a muscle in my neck tightens as anxiety and awareness take over. Adrenaline floods my bloodstream, and I wonder if there might be someone in this house right now. We need to search it carefully, quietly. It's possible that a squatter could be living here, someone from the town, teenagers. But again, that would lead me to believe the house wouldn't feel quite so... taken care of. There's no graffiti, no broken windows. There's still a perfect oval mirror hanging on the wall in the hallway. This isn't the kind of scene that screams *abandoned* to me.

I motion to Lucas for us to continue our round of the downstairs, then to head upstairs. I'm not sure if there's a basement, but if there is, that'll be our last stop. We loop through several more rooms, a library with books still filling the shelves, a dining room with a table that doesn't have a single speck of dust on it. We should have come in here sooner. I feel like such an idiot for letting the façade fool me into thinking this place wasn't something we should explore.

As we head up the stairs, it's clear that someone has been maintaining them, swapping out aging boards, fixing broken steps.

"Look at the stairs," I say to him, pointing to one of the boards that's brand new. "Someone replaced this recently. It doesn't match the others." Though I can tell that someone has been here, it doesn't feel like there's anyone else in the house but us right now. There's no vibration of energy here, no hints that someone is waiting for us in a hidden corridor. But I'm still ready, just in case.

We turn left at the landing, finding a bedroom and a bathroom. Like the other rooms we've been in, it's in staged disarray. In the corner, a pillow has been sliced open, some of the feathers pouring onto the floor. But they're localized, not spreading across the floor with stray winds. The curved metal bedframe holds no dust, no rust. It looks as if it were plucked from an antique shop earlier this week. My eyes scour the ceiling, looking again for any indication that there have been leaks, but there are none. There's no chance that a house abandoned for this long wouldn't have at least one leak, some yellow and brown pooling on the ceiling indicating the old water damage.

"This feels wrong," I say to Lucas as I head to the next bedroom.

"It does. It feels like a museum, not an abandoned house."

"Yes, exactly," I say. "It feels curated."

In the next bedroom, we find some women's clothing shoved beneath the bed. I pull on my gloves and pick it up carefully, placing it in an evidence bag. As I'm sealing it, I notice a brown stain on the pale blue fabric. Blood.

I hand the bag to Lucas, and make sure that he notices the stain as well. We move to the next bedroom, and I find more clothing. This time it looks like a men's undershirt. I shove that in another evidence bag. We work our way through the rest of the house, gathering small pieces of evidence here and there. But in the bathroom, I find several used tissues discarded on the floor. They're new, not yellowed with age, so I shove them into the bag. A smile curls my lips because I know what we have here. At the very least, we have some DNA.

We sweep the rest of the second floor, then the attic. The attic is clearly somewhere that hasn't been touched for years. Everything is coated in a thick film of dust, cobwebs hanging from the ceiling like stalactites. We find food wrappers, clothing, toothpaste, things scattered around the upper floors of the house more casually, as if whoever curated the first floor knew that no one would venture this far.

As we walk around the first floor again, I notice a door I hadn't seen previously. I point it out to Lucas, then open the door. A musty scent floods into the room, damp earth, mildew, something vaguely rotten. I click on my flashlight, and shine the beam into the pooling, inky darkness. Dust drifts in and out of the beam as I take the stairs to the basement slowly. If the porch outside was decaying, what state are these stairs in? I force myself down as quickly as possible.

Lucas's feet thud loudly behind me, sounding hollow on the ancient wood. But as my feet finally hit the bottom, I glance back toward him, finally looking at the stairs—and I notice something odd. They're brand new. Someone has replaced the stairs recently, just like upstairs. Whoever has been staying at this property isn't a squatter. They're taking care of it. Keeping it up.

"Look at that." I point it out to him.

"Are we looking for a carpenter?" he asks.

"I'm not sure that we're looking for the owner of the property. Matilda Thurston knew that this property was about to be sold. She'd been negotiating with the property developer for years. These stairs can't be more than three months old. No one was allegedly living here, so there's no reason they should have built new stairs in a crumbling farmhouse that was about to be torn down."

Light from my flashlight illuminates Lucas's face enough for me to see him nod. He clicks on his own light and begins to look around the basement. The floor is littered with small rocks, debris, stray clothing that's yellowed. Nearest the stairs, everything looks aged, but as I work my way around to the back, my blood runs cold. Along the back wall, Lucas's light meets mine on an old mattress shoved up against the wall. On the sagging bed, chains are coiled up like metal snakes, shackles open. Food packages are littered on the floor, potato chips, cheese crackers, cookies, several gallon jugs of water, nonperishables that would have been easy to provide so that someone could survive here for weeks at a time. There's a metal toilet, like the kind you'd see in a cell, set up against the wall next to the bed.

"God, this is where he kept them," Lucas says.

I can't imagine how this must feel for Lucas. Were his mother and grandmother held here before they were moved to the cabin? I hope for their sakes that they were never shackled to this wall. That they were never kept in darkness in a basement, until a killer came down the stairs for them. I imagine the fear that must have coiled inside them each time a footstep echoed on those stairs.

This is a crime scene that we need to process. I wish that we'd searched this sooner. I wonder if we'd have found the woman that was being held here. It can't imagine it was long ago that she was here, still chained to that wall. But that begs the question—where is she now?

26

It was a long day, surveying the scene as the forensics team collected evidence. I handed over the tissues that I found upstairs, so we can get them processed for DNA as soon as possible. The great thing about DNA is that if there's a match in our database, we'll have an answer soon. The bad thing about DNA is we'd need our suspect to have had their DNA processed at some point in the past to have something to match against.

Long past midnight, I head back to the hotel. I sent Lucas back hours ago, when he was yawning so frequently it was making me more tired. It's a waste of both of our time to just stand around anyway. Technically, I probably should have left as well, but I'm too much of a control freak.

As I pull into the hotel and climb out of my Jeep, my body is so tired I feel like gravity is working double-time, dragging me toward the concrete beneath my boots. I sling my bag over my shoulder and head toward the stairs, but the scuff of feet on the pavement behind me makes me whip around. The warnings from Sergeant Dirby, the GPS device I found on my car, they are fresh in my mind. But as I turn, it's Neal that I see.

Over his arm, he's got a bag that's so packed with notes, papers, whatever else he may have in there, it's bulging at the seams, threatening to rip open. Though the worn leather swells with ease, it looks like he's pushed it past its breaking point.

"Detective, so good to see you," he purrs, as if he isn't here to rile me up, to try and get some kind of info on me to put in his fucking book.

"Can't say the same," I say as I cross my arms. While my anger rises inside me, for now at least, my anxiety is slowly ebbing away.

"I wanted to see if you'd had some time to process the news about your parents' engagement, their upcoming nuptials. Are you going to be attending? That'd be such a nice little reunion." His words are dripping with sarcasm, and I want to punch him in the teeth. This is just a story to him, but this is my life. He wants to sell books. He wants the *hot take* from the daughter of a serial killer because how scandalous would my quote be on the front cover? But he doesn't realize that every word he writes about me is a nail in my coffin.

That's the problem in situations like this. Neal doesn't realize the danger that he's putting me in. There's a cop-hunting serial killer already active in upstate New York. Someone put a tracking device on my car. Someone killed a woman right here in New Paltz. A little more media coverage could make the killer's attention turn to me. And then what? It wouldn't be the first time I've had to fight for my life. But I don't want to do it again. I don't want to face death.

"I'm not sure how many times I'm going to have to say the words *no comment* to you before it finally sticks," I say, my words razor sharp.

"Probably a thousand more times," he says with a smarmy smile. I'm sure he thinks that it's filled with charm, but all I see is a weasel with a leather messenger bag standing in front of me.

"All right, well, good luck with that," I say before I turn

toward the hotel. But Neal grabs my arm, stopping me. Rage flares inside me at his touch, his assumption that he has the right to place a hand on me at all. "Do not fucking touch me," I seethe.

I turn around to face him, but it takes me shaking him off before he drops his hand.

"Come on, Harlow. Let me come up. We can have a chat. I can help you work out some of that anger," he says as he steps toward me.

My lip curls involuntarily as I retreat just a little. Is he serious right now? He's writing a book about my family, and he thinks that he can turn on the charm and get into my pants? What the fuck is wrong with this guy?

"Are you kidding me right now? What is your problem?"

"You just don't realize how beautiful you are. And when your anger starts coming to the surface like that, it's so hard to hold myself back." He steps forward again, his arms outstretched like he's going to grab me. I shove him, hard. His body slams into the door of my Jeep with a hollow thud before he falls to the ground. His bag slips off his shoulder and falls at my feet. Without thinking, I grab the bag, sling it over my shoulder, and jog toward the hotel.

My heart is pounding when my feet hit the patterned carpet. I check behind me every three seconds as I work my way through the lobby toward the elevator. Neal runs in after me, his feet pounding on the carpet, but I don't slow. My heart threatens to burst from my chest with each furious beat. I slam my hand on the elevator button, my flesh stinging from the impact. A door opens and I throw myself in, then I press the door-close button over and over again.

Though I can't see him, I hear his feet, his approach. The doors inch closed, so slow, as if their gears have been dipped in molasses. I didn't have much ground on Neal. He's going to catch me. He's going to try to get this bag back. But I'm not going to let him. He wants me to read his work so bad, I will. I'll dig through this whole fucking bag.

I see his face through the metal slit as the door finally shuts. He slams his palm against the doors, and I stumble back. The cold metal walls bite into my shoulder blades, but I lean into it as I try to steady my breathing. What are the chances he finds my room? I debate filing a complaint against him as I finally reach my floor, and head to my room. My pulse has almost returned to a normal pace when I throw open my door, but somewhere on the floor, I hear the door of the stairwell fly open and feet pounding on the carpet.

27

To say that Neal is obsessed with me would be the understatement of the century. As I dig through his bag, I'm absolutely disgusted with what I find. He has pictures from my childhood, notes about my life, where I went to school, the few friends I made over the years, each of my foster homes. It's all enough to make bile climb my throat. Why is Neal so obsessed with me? It doesn't seem that he is writing a book about my father at all, it seems like the book is about *me*. As I dig through everything, I'm filled with regret. I wish I hadn't looked through all of this. I wish I had just turned Neal away and never spoken to him again. The idea that he's gone this deep collecting information, it doesn't show a good work ethic, that he's trying to write a good book—this is stalking.

There are recent pictures of me. Some taken from far away while I'm at a crime scene, others taken candidly while I'm eating dinner with Lucas. In the notes, there's speculation about whether or not Lucas and I have a relationship, who else on the team I might have had a relationship with. What the hell is this?

As the sun peeks in through my window, I realize that I've been up all night going over these files.

"Shit," I mutter under my breath. I didn't get any sleep at all. My day is going to be miserable. I call Lucas and ask him to come over to my room just as I find the notes from the interviews with my mother. It's going to take me months to read through all of this.

A few minutes after I call him, Lucas knocks on my door. I open it and he sweeps inside. He's dressed in gym clothes, like I just dragged him off a treadmill when I called.

"I'm so glad that you're up early," he says in a rush. "I was watching the news this morning, and something's happened."

I raise a brow, and gesture for him to keep going.

"That journalist that's been hounding you, they found him dead this morning. He was found in his hotel room. Someone hung him from the ceiling, cut him open, and used his blood to write a message on the wall."

My mouth goes dry. "What?" is all I can manage to say. How can he be dead? I know some part of me should feel relieved. But I was probably the last person to see him... I have his notes in my hotel room. Fuck, this doesn't look good.

"Apparently he's ex-law enforcement. He was a beat cop, then made it to sergeant before quitting the force to become a journalist. They actually think that the entire time that he was working he was selling tips to journalists, and he just decided to start collecting the money himself rather than taking small handouts."

"Wait so... You're going too fast." My cellphone rings, and I grab it. Dirby's number flashes on the screen. I answer it and let him know that I've got Lucas here with me.

"Put me on speaker," he says, and I follow his instructions. "You two need to wrap up this cold case. I don't have enough agents and I need to put someone on this cop killer," he says.

"We need four more days," I say.

"I can give you two."

"Fine, two," I agree. It's better than being ripped off of this case now. We're so close to solving this, to tracking down our killer, we can't abandon it now. There could still be a woman being held captive at this moment.

"What did you guys know about this journalist?" he asks.

"Sergeant, let me call you back," I say before ending the call. I'd never cut off a sergeant like that in normal circumstances, but I've got to talk to Lucas. He's already looking at the papers that are scattered around the room.

"What is all this, Harlow?" he asks, looking at a picture of me that was taken while we were at the farm.

"Neal and I got into a fight last night. He tried to grab me, I pushed him, and when I did he dropped his bag. I wasn't thinking. I just grabbed it and ran into the hotel," I say. "He chased me. I wasn't sure I was going to get away from him, but I did... and I started going through it. He was stalking me."

"I can see that..." he says, tentatively. "But Harlow, this doesn't look good. Did you run by the security cameras?"

"You mean the ones in the lobby? I think so. I ran through there with the bag to get to the elevator. He ran after me. If they review the footage that'll be clear."

He nods. "Do you want to come forward with this or..." He motions to the piles of papers and notebooks that are scattered all over the room.

"I need to go through all of it first. He has so much here. There are interviews with my parents. He took pictures of me. I think he was the one who put the GPS on my car," I say. "I'm looking for evidence of that in here."

He nods slowly. "Then we shouldn't tell anyone about the encounter until you've taken pictures of everything that you need, cataloged it all. But you're going to have to turn this in. You're going to have to make a statement," he says.

"Or I could destroy it all," I say. I don't want anyone to have all of this information about me. None of this should exist. I especially do not want my colleagues digging through all of the details of my entire life. I may as well just lay my entire life bare for the entire bureau. The idea of all this being out here, the slideshow of my life being so accessible, it makes me want to vomit. I've spent so much time and energy trying to leave my past behind me, but no matter what I do, someone has to dig it up, someone has to chase me down.

He nods slowly. "You could. But you might get suspended for that. You'd be destroying evidence."

"This is my life, Lucas. My entire fucking life laid out here. And I'm supposed to just turn this over so that everyone in the department can rifle through it? I cannot do that," I say, my voice breaking.

"I can't imagine what that'd be like, but I can't help you get rid of it. If it happens while I'm not here, then I'm not involved. But I can't help you destroy evidence," he says.

His words hurt, because if the tables were turned, if this was information about his life that he didn't want to share, I'd destroy it. I'd tell them that we never found anything.

"Fine, go then," I say, and I can't help the hurt that leaches into my voice. Part of me knows that I'm asking too much of him, more than I should. But the other part of me thought that Lucas might stand by me no matter what. At the end of the day, I guess we're just partners.

"Promise me that you didn—"

"I can't believe you'd even ask me that." My whole body feels weighed down even though the accusation didn't leave his lips. I can see it on his face though, what he expects of me, what he thinks I'm capable of. I think that's the part that hurts the most. That's how most people look at me once they find out about my history—as if they're waiting for something inside me to break.

"I didn't ask…"

I shake my head, disappointment clenching around my heart. "You were going to. I would never. *Never.*"

He turns and leaves the room without another word. I get to work, taking pictures of all of the evidence, everything in Neal's bag. It takes me hours, but finally, once I've got it all cataloged, I shove it back in the bag. I head to my Jeep, with a lighter in my pocket.

28

The scent of smoke is heavy in the air as I emerge from the woods. I found a campsite where I could burn the evidence without sparking any concerns about a fire or drawing attention. In a secluded part of the forest, I burned every last trace of the notes that Neal took on my life. The details about how my mother blamed me for my father's murders. The pictures of him holding me when I was little. Notes that I wrote in foster care when I begged for my mother to take me back.

I thought I might get some joy from watching it burn, from watching the fire devour my secrets. As the smoke curls into the ether, I feel nothing. No relief. No unknotting of my anxiety. Instead, it feels like a thread left unfinished. This is not the end.

My phone vibrates in my pocket, and I grab it, noting Sergeant Dirby's name on the screen. I accept the call, then cradle the phone between my ear and my shoulder.

"Is Lucas there with you?" he asks.

"No, I was running an errand." The lie comes out too easily, and I almost feel bad about it. Almost.

"You need to grab him and head over to Calvin's house. We just got word that the search warrant was granted. You both need to get over to the house ASAP. Some of the New Paltz officers are on the way to assist along with the forensics team."

I swear I can still feel the tension in the air between Lucas and me, even though he's not here. "How much time do I have?"

"Thirty minutes, likely," he says.

"I'll be there, thanks."

"Wait, Harlow. Is everything okay? You sound... on edge," he says, his words careful, like he's afraid to set me off. I've always been careful with my tone with my sergeant. Maybe I'm just too frustrated about Neal and it's coming through.

"Yeah, I'm fine," I say, though even I can hear how hollow my words sound.

"I need you and Lucas to be careful right now. If you can help it, try not to run any errands alone. There's a killer out there right now hunting cops. They were tracking your vehicle. I think you need to take this more seriously."

My eyes scan the woods as his words needle me. Am I being too reckless? Maybe I shouldn't be out here on my own after everything that's happened. But I did try to bring Lucas. My goal hadn't been to be here alone. Lucas didn't want to be involved.

"I know," I say, wanting to stave off the lecture. I know I'll either get it now or later, but I'd rather not deal with it at the moment.

"We're at five victims now. Five cops that have been killed. And I hate to point it out, but so far the crimes have all been committed very close to you and Lucas. This killer might be stalking the two of you. You might be the real target here," he explains. "With all the media attention on your last two cases, I just—please be careful."

His words strike a chord inside me. He's right, obviously. My concern though is that the attention is going to turn to Lucas and me in a different way, that we're going to become suspects in these crimes.

After I finish up my call with Sergeant Dirby, I head back to the hotel to grab Lucas. I call him on the way, and when I pull up outside, he gets in the passenger seat. Though I glance at him, he keeps his eyes forward, like he's pretending that I don't exist. I didn't think that destroying the evidence would create a wedge between us. And I hate the idea that my trying to protect myself, to protect my secrets, could drive the two of us apart. Doesn't he understand what that information could do to my life if it got out?

I try to ignore the tension between us as I drive to Calvin's house, but it's so hard to stew in silence. We pass a few stray cars lining the streets downtown as we carve our way toward the farm. I hadn't realized just how close Calvin lived to it. He probably could have walked if he wanted to. We pull in front of the small house. Sergeant Ortega is already on site and it appears that she's served the warrant already. Though it should have been Lucas and me that served it, since it was requested by our team, she wanted to serve it since this is her community, her town. So I'd let her.

I notice someone in the back of a squad car as I climb out of my Jeep. We walk up the driveway and meet Ortega halfway. Her team is swarming the house, the forensics team already at work inside. I motion to the squad car.

"What's going on with that?" I ask Ortega.

A smile quirks her full lips. "He didn't like the idea of us searching his house. He was causing a lot of problems. He's burned himself out now, but he was kicking the hell out of the seat when we put him in there, as if he might be able to kick his way out of the car."

I shake my head at that. It's not the first time I've heard of someone trying that. "Found anything inside?"

"They just got started, so it's too soon to know anything yet."

"Mind if we go in?" I ask as I pull some shoe covers from my pocket.

"Be my guest. I'm sure you know all the protocols for an active scene." Her words are almost a question.

I nod and indicate for Lucas to follow me. We weave our way around the officers flowing in and out of the house. The colonial is two stories with a basement, and I know it'll likely take them a while to search everything. The air inside the house is stifling, thick. There are too many people in here, making it feel like I'm wading through hot breath. It looks like walking through a time capsule, the house firmly stuck in the eighties. There's a poster of Def Leppard on the wall, a Harley-Davidson jacket thrown on the floor next to it. Next to a cracked leather couch, there's a coffee table with so much trash on it looks like the table is vomiting refuse on the floor.

Bodies press against me as other members of law enforcement flow in and out of the different rooms. I skirt the kitchen, then find stairs that lead down. All around us, above us, I can hear footsteps, but the lights for the basement haven't even been turned on. I flip the switch and descend the stairs. As I reach the bottom, I realize I've lost Lucas somewhere in the house, but that's fine. Right now maybe we need some distance between the two of us.

My feet scuff against the dirt floor. The walls down here are dirty, mud and grime clinging to the rock walls. While the rest of the house looks like it was built in the early 1900s, this basement looks like it's been around since the 1700s. The air is thick, cold. The smell of earth floods my nostrils as I work my way through the small room at the bottom of the stairs. Behind me, there's a small opening leading to another room. I slip into it, noting the footprints on the floor. Someone was down here recently.

My heart pounds as I work my way from one small stone room to another, looking for signs that there might still be someone down here. Anxiety coils around my lungs as the apprehension grips me. What was Calvin doing in this house? And more importantly, what had he been doing at the farmhouse? The memory of the shackles flashes in my mind.

I turn the last corner, hoping to finally find the woman I've been seeking. But I just find a room with a broken dining room chair, an empty box of cheese crackers, small footprints that look like a rat or a mouse might have been in here. But as I look around something doesn't feel right. Above me, the house extends farther than this room, the wood continuing. I step forward, surveying the wall in front of me. And I swear, I hear something on the other side. I press my ear to it, and there's something like muffled cries.

I take a deep breath and start to press on the wall. There has to be a way through. This is a fake wall, something that Calvin built to throw us off. When I finally press the right stone, the wall shifts, a door opening up. The sound of a woman crying grows louder. I click on my flashlight, flooding the small space with light. It takes a moment for my eyes to adjust, to make out the shape of the woman shackled to the floor. There's a gag in her mouth, blindfold over her eyes. The sound of the footsteps above us echoes through the small room.

"It's okay. We've got you," I say, as I explain to her that I'm a police officer, that she's safe now.

I grab my radio and let them know what I've found. The woman is dirty, her clothes tattered. She's wearing an old housedress that's thick with grime. Despite her disheveled appearance, I recognize her from the missing posters that I've seen in town. This is Abigail Anderson. In just a few minutes, the room is swarming with activity, the woman being removed from the chains, the forensics team collecting the gag, the blindfold, the shackles. The woman clings to me as I take her upstairs, then get inside an ambulance with her.

"Thank you," she says as she sobs. "I thought I was going to end up like the others."

"You're okay now," I say, my hand still trapped in hers as she lies down on a gurney. There's a paramedic on the other side of her, checking her blood pressure, looking over her vitals.

"It was my fault that he took me. I shouldn't have been out. He told me that's why he took me. I made it too easy. He said that he wanted to lock me up to keep me safe, because only he could keep women safe."

"Did he tell you about the others?" I ask.

She nods. "He killed Mazie too. She wouldn't come with him..."

Getting Abigail to the hospital and checked out is all a blur. There wasn't a ton of information I was able to get out of her. She was weak and in shock, but from what I gathered, Calvin loved to talk about the past girls—the ones he collected. He liked to claim that he protected the girls, kept them at the farm where they belonged. A sourness rose in my stomach as she spoke. But also, the questions piled up. Calvin isn't old enough to have been responsible for the deaths of Lucas's mother and grandmother. So who was killing at the farm before Calvin?

29

Seeing a suspect sitting in the middle of an interrogation room, their arm cuffed to a metal chair, never gets old. His long greasy hair is disheveled, half hanging in his face. His whole body slumps against the chair, as if he were poured into it. With his eyes darkened and cast down, I could swear that he was just napping. Lucas and I stand on the other side of the two-way mirror. There's still tension between the two of us, and I hate it. The air is thick with all the words he's not saying, and I shift on my feet, trying to ignore it.

Finally, there's a knock on the interrogation room door and that's our signal that they're ready for us.

"You ready?" I ask Lucas, and he nods.

We walk together into the interrogation room. I've got a folder under my arm. It's got images, details of the crimes, the women that were found. Some of these I know aren't connected to Calvin since he would have been too young at the time to commit the crimes. But we know that he's responsible for the woman that was held in the farmhouse, and that she was moved to his house. There are enough similarities in the scene, and the fact that they're the exact same shackles doesn't help his case. We've got DNA and fingerprints in process, but those items take time. I want to see if we can get a confession today.

Calvin doesn't look up or acknowledge us as we enter the room. I scan his arms for scars, trying to see if there's any connection between what he's done and Carly or Aggie. But there's nothing. I take a seat across from him and Lucas takes a seat next to me. I hate that we're on the outs right now, and I really wish that I could smooth things over with him before digging into a suspect. But I can't delay this case for personal matters. We can work on our shit after we have a confession. That takes priority.

"Good afternoon, Calvin. Can I get you a bottle of water or something?" Lucas offers.

The man stays silent, his eyes still cast down. This will be fun. When he doesn't acknowledge Lucas, I decide to dig right in.

"So, Mr. Porter, as you know, we executed a search warrant on your home, and we found a young woman chained up in your basement. I'm sure you're not surprised by this information, since you had her over at Ackert Farm and then moved her to your property," I say.

I give him a moment to register what I've said, but he doesn't respond.

"Due to those circumstances, our office is prepared to proceed with charges of kidnapping, false imprisonment, attempted murder, battery, sexual assault, and five counts of first-degree murder," I say as I read all of the counts from the page. When he was read his rights by the New Paltz team, they'd Mirandized him with just the kidnapping and false imprisonment charges. Now that we've determined we can move forward with all the charges, so this guy can be locked away for good, it's my job to make him aware.

"I didn't kill nobody," he finally grumbles.

I raise a brow at that. "Okay, well, if you didn't kill anyone, then I need you to tell me who killed those women on the farm."

He finally looks up at me through a curtain of dirty hair. He doesn't bother sweeping it away. Shifting his head instead so he can see better, he just glowers at me through the strands.

"Hershel kept the first girls. He had them when I started working at the farm, two of them. Back then, he kept them in the basement of the house, chained up. Sometimes he'd get a fire lit under him and he'd move them to the root cellar because he was afraid that someone knew what was going on."

"So you knew that these women were being held captive on the farm?" Lucas asks and I start to question if he should be in here. This is a little personal for him. If Calvin was responsible for his mother at all... this may not go well.

He nods slowly. "Well, at first I didn't know they were being held captive. I was young. He told me that they were just workers on the farm but they did their work only at night. So I rarely saw them. I'd just happened on them by accident when I was at the farm early. The women didn't ask for help or anything. They didn't seem like they were being hurt. They just seemed scared that I'd found them. Then Hershel explained to me that they were his wives and that they helped him on the farm, but people wouldn't understand, so I should keep it a secret. He paid me really well to keep his secrets."

"You took money from him and kept it a secret that he was killing women?"

Calvin shifts his head in an almost animalistic movement, the kind of head snap you'd see from a predator as they scent prey in the air.

"He wasn't killing women. Those were accidents. Keely got sick, and Hershel didn't know how to make her better. She ended up dying in her sleep. Hershel was so sad about it. He loved his wives. He never would have killed them."

This is more twisted than I had imagined. He'd convinced

Calvin that he was a good guy who wasn't holding women captive or killing them, but that they were just married to him? I find this all incredibly difficult to believe. But then again, people lie to themselves every single day.

"Then Davida got pregnant, and Hershel was so excited. His first wife had never been able to give him kids and all he wanted was to have a family. But then as Davida got further along in her pregnancy she wasn't doing well, and she died in childbirth."

"Why didn't Hershel take Davida to the doctor?" I ask.

"I didn't think to ask. I was very young."

"So you didn't ask any questions about her death?" Lucas presses him.

"No. I didn't see her that frequently. Hershel mentioned it in passing as if it weren't a big concern to him. I don't think he saw them as people... I think he saw them as animals for the farm."

It's enough to turn my stomach. "And how did you see the women?" There's an edge to my voice, though I try to tamp it down.

"It was different. Abigail wanted to be there with me. She loved me." There's a wild look in his eyes that's alarming.

"She loved you so much that you had to shackle her to a wall?" Lucas spits the words out, anger hanging on every single syllable. I glance over at Lucas, noting his clenched fists.

"Hey, do you want to go grab us some coffee?" I ask him. His anger is rising, staining his cheeks pink.

Lucas looks at me, pain and anger swimming in his eyes. He shoves up from the table and storms off, the door slamming behind him. I wish that I didn't have to ask him to leave, but I know the path he's going down. I know that the rage brimming inside him will not ease during this questioning. It won't get any easier, especially as I have to ask questions about his mother and grandmother.

"I didn't shackle her because I was holding her captive. It was to keep her safe so that no one could take her from me. If Hershel had seen her, he would have taken her for himself. But she was mine. She knew she was mine," he says, his eyes bulging with every word.

I make a few notes about that. He's clearly delusional. Maybe growing up with Hershel as a role model twisted his mind or maybe all the makings of someone so sinister were there all along. Situations like this always linger in my mind, and I wonder every time I look at a stranger *what are they capable of?* Does everyone have the capability for evil?

"So tell me, where did you meet Abigail?" I ask. I need to get the background on where he met her, how. While Abigail gave me some of the details, I need his point of view. I need to know how much of this was his planning and how much of it was Hershel.

"Hershel always told me if I wanted to get my own wife, I'd have to take steps. I'd have to watch a woman from afar, to make sure I picked the right type of woman. He said that some women would fight, some would try to get away and wouldn't see what good husbands we could be. So it was about finding the *right one*. I always heard that when you found the one, you'd know. And that's how I felt when I saw her. She was working in the pet store. I saw her going into work. I didn't have an animal, but I started going in there, trying to spend some time with her." He pauses for a minute and smiles, like he's picturing what happened.

"You went to visit her often?" I ask when he's quiet for too long.

He nods. "Yes, and she was so nice. She tried to suggest a few pets for me. But she was the pet that I wanted. We got on friendly terms after a few weeks. We had coffee together. Then I brought her out to the farm when I knew she was ready."

My blood turns cold as I imagine it. Did she go willingly

because she trusted him? Because she'd known him from town? And then suddenly he turned on her, locked her up.

"We took a walk around the property, then I took her into the house. She was so curious about what it looked like on the inside. That was the sign, I knew. So I brought her down to the basement, and showed her where she'd be staying. At first, she was upset that she wouldn't be staying in the house with me. But I explained that once she proved to me that she could be good, then we'd be together in the house. It took her only a month before I realized she was ready for the house. Whenever I was here, we were together in the house. A few times I took her over to my house."

"How often was she shackled?" I ask.

"Only when I had to leave. I took good care of her. That was my job as a husband," he says as he tries to cross his arms, but the cuffs don't really allow it. They clink as he settles his hands back into his lap.

"Did Hershel know?"

He nods. "Of course he did. I called to get his opinions on if she was the right one, and how to get her to come with me. He talked me through the whole thing."

I force myself to remain stoic, even though I'm absolutely disgusted. I reach into the folder and grab the images of Lucas's mother and grandmother. I slide them across the table. "I know that you met Davida and Keely. Did you ever meet these two women?"

He squints as he looks at the pictures. His brows are furrowed, shadowing his eyes. "No, I never saw them. Who are they?"

"These two women were found in a cabin on the far edge of the farm's property," I explain. "Do you know anything about that?"

He shakes his head.

"So, Hershel didn't have any other *wives*?" I ask, nudging

the images a little closer. I want to be sure that he takes a hard look at the images. If Hershel introduced him to the other wives, why wouldn't he introduce him to these two?

"No, not that I ever met. But after Davida died, he moved away. He wasn't at the farm often anymore. He sold the farm. He wasn't here as often as he used to be."

"But he did come back?" I press him further.

He nods. "Yeah, I saw him at least once a month, maybe a little more."

The way he says it makes me wonder if Hershel really left New York at all. Flying back every month or more frequently just to check on the farm, which wasn't producing much anyway, seems like a stretch.

"Hershel never lived on the farm to your knowledge, correct?" I ask.

He nods. "Yeah, he had a house in Clintondale."

"Tell me what happened to Mazie," I ask. That's the last piece of this. I need to know what happened to her.

"I was driving past the farm, and Mazie was walking. It seemed like a sign, like she was being offered to me. So I slowed down and asked her if she wanted a ride home. She got in my truck." He stops talking and chews the inside of his cheek for a moment. "I wanted to see how good of a wife she would be. I touched her, and she started screaming. She tried to fight me. It was an accident. I was just trying to make her stop, to get her to calm down."

"So you strangled her?"

His cheeks go red. "I didn't strangle her! It was an accident!" Flecks of spit fly out of his mouth with the words as he hurls them at me.

"I need to check something—I'll be right back," I say as I shove up from the table. I can feel him staring at me as I leave the room. But I've got to check a gut feeling I have on the computer. In a few steps, I close the distance between the interrogation room and my laptop. I then navigate to the state property records database and search for Hershel. Sure enough, when the results load, I see that Hershel still owns his property in Clintondale. He never sold it. So he very well could have been staying just ten minutes away, visiting women he held prisoner in secret at the farm.

I print out the information regarding Hershel's property, then return to the interrogation room. It takes me a few more questions to finish up with Calvin. But when I head out of the room and scan the bullpen for Lucas, he's nowhere to be found. Sergeant Ortega strolls over, and glances from me to the interrogation room.

"How'd it go? Did you get everything that you needed?"

"Not everything, no. But I got enough," I explain and then show her the paper. "My hope is we can use this information along with what we know about Keely and Davida to force a confession out of Hershel. Unfortunately, Hershel owning a property in close proximity to the farm is all circumstantial and it'll be difficult to try to track down travel logs or information about what state he was really in going that far back. Our best chance is to give this information to the state of Florida and hope that he confesses after he's apprehended."

Her lips purse. "I hope you can get everything you need. Are you all done with Calvin? If so, I'll have one of the guys grab him."

I nod. "Yes, I'm all done. As far as I can tell, Calvin has no connection to Carly or Aggie. So, I'm not sure if there's any other digging to do there."

"For now, Vick isn't in town. We were mistaken apparently. We'd seen his brother. I've been watching his place, and a friend up in Albany told me that he registered with a parole officer up there. So I guess that was a false alarm," she says. "I called the parole officer and confirmed that Vick has been up there since release, and he doesn't have access to a vehicle to get down here."

"I'm glad," I say.

"I've got to get back to Abigail to make sure she's okay," she says.

"Good luck with her, please tell her I send my best."

She nods. "I will, thanks."

It takes me about an hour to write up the warrant for Hershel, enter it into the National Crime Information Center, and track down the sergeant for the Villages PD to notify them of the warrant. Though we're going to ask for extradition, that will take time. Especially in cases like this.

30

NINETEEN YEARS AGO

Sneaking out of a hospital isn't as hard as I thought it would be. Though the detective told me that someone would be at my door, watching, making sure that my mother and father didn't come, there are hour stretches where my room is unguarded. It's during one of those breaks that I slip from the room, my clothes pulled on under my gown. When I'm sure no one is watching, I strip off the gown and shove it into a trashcan. It's late in the evening, the sky outside already inky, dotted with a few stray stars.

My heart pounds as I weave my way through the halls, past a few nurses that don't even glance my direction. I've got my hair swept over my eye, hiding the bruise there. Finally, I reach sliding doors that hiss open in front of me. I step out into the cool night, the crisp air enveloping me. The hospital is a ten-minute drive from my house, so I know the walk will be long. But I need to get home, to grab my things. I heard the doctors and the cops talking about how they were going to hand me over to CPS, that I may end up in foster care. I'd rather run away. I'd rather be on my own. But to do that, I need to get my stuff, the money I've squirreled away.

When I finally make it home, the house is abandoned. Neither my mother nor my father is here. Tension blooms in my chest. Where are they? My mother never leaves. She's always sealed up in this house like it's her tomb. I climb up the trellis on the side of the house to the second floor, then skirt across the roof to my window. I drag it open and climb inside. Even though I've slept so much at the hospital, I'm so tired I feel exhausted all the way to my bones. I glance at my bed, feeling the pull of it. Maybe I should sleep for just a few hours, then I can go. It's already past midnight. There's no way that my mom or dad will come back here tonight. I walk over to my door, lock it, and climb into the bed.

Sounds deep in the bowels of the house awaken me. At first, I think it's my mother and father fighting. I open my eyes, the memories finally registering. I realize that they shouldn't be home. My pulse kicks up as I shove off the bed. It's still dark outside, but the flicker of red and blue lights on my ceiling catches my attention. The cops are here. I swallow hard, but there's a lump clogging my throat. It blooms there, threatening to choke me.

I grab my backpack that I've already got my clothes and money in and sling it over my back. There are footsteps downstairs, the cacophony of voices, orders being given. I creep to the window, knowing the best path to move so that the house will keep my secrets. I shove open the window, then slip out, closing it behind me. I'm not sure if they know that I've left the hospital yet, that I'm missing. Is that why they're here?

Darkness envelopes me, and I shift closer to the edge of the roof so I can hear what's going on. That's when I see it, the police dragging my father out into the night. My heart seizes when I see him, his hands in cuffs, his shoulders squared. He's not fighting the cops, but he's also not making it easy on them.

He's got his head held high, as if he's done nothing wrong. Tears sting my eyes as they open the squad car door and he ducks to sit inside. They slam the door, and I swear I can feel him looking at me.

I did this. The reason he's in that squad car is because of me. I told. I didn't keep his secrets, and now he's going to be gone forever. They won't leave me with my mother, not after her last attack. So where do I go? The words from the hospital, the warnings about sending me into foster care, bloom in the back of my mind. I feel like I'm going to be sick as a cold sweat pools on my flesh.

You have to keep moving. My father's words are sharp in my mind. And I know it's just my imagination. Still though, I shimmy over the rest of the roof, climb down the back trellis, and I don't look back before I let the woods swallow me.

31

Nothing feels right as I pull back into the hotel. I feel my time here winding down, the case close to being done. There's a limbo, an uneasiness that comes over me when we close a case— though this one still feels unfinished, and likely will until we have Hershel back in New York. We need to get his DNA and match it to Lucas's sister. That will really give us solid evidence that Hershel knew about them and held them captive. Being at the end of this case should feel good. I know I should get some kind of dopamine rush from finishing this off, from having all my questions answered. But that never happens. Instead, I look for the next thing, the next distraction, the next scene. I know what my father would say, that I'm seeking out distractions so that I don't ever have to face my feelings. He'd be right, and that's fine. I'm not going to change. I don't think I can face what's inside me. My trauma has grown into its own entity inside me, a layer thicker than my skin.

As I pull in, Lucas walks out of the building, as if he was waiting for me. My stomach is in knots as I look over his face, but I can't read his emotions, his energy. He's too stoic right now, which isn't at all like him. I square my shoulders and ready myself. I know the conversation isn't going to be pleasant. We haven't spoken since I kicked him out of the interrogation room.

"I can't fucking believe you," he seethes as soon as I get out of the car. "That was my moment that I could have gotten closure. I could have asked him all the questions that I needed to know the answers to."

"He never met your mother," I say. I understand his anger, but right now it's misplaced. If the tables were turned, he would have kicked me out of that room too. There's no way that he could have stayed objective and calm during that questioning. And if he went after Calvin, if he asked the wrong things, set him off, that could have jeopardized the entire case. While I will do everything in my power to help Lucas come to terms with his past, I will not let a killer walk free.

"You don't know that he's telling the truth. He's probably lying," he says, and there's an edge to his voice. He wants to rage at me, he wants to yell. If it'll make him feel better, I'll let him. It's not as if I don't have plenty of practice being on the receiving end of someone's rage.

"I've questioned a lot of suspects. He was very open about what he did to Abigail and Kaley, so I don't see why he'd lie to me about your mother and grandmother. He met Davida and Keely," I explain. "If I had any reason to believe he knew more about your family, you know I would have pressed more. But Hershel is the man who took your mother, your grandmother. He's the one who's responsible. Florida is already working on hunting him down and bringing him in for us. As soon as there's movement there, I'll let you know. We're going to bring him in," I promise.

His fists clench at his sides. "You're kicking me off of my own case. I should be involved in bringing Hershel in. This isn't your life, Harlow. This is mine. You had no right to take this from me."

A headache awakens in the back of my skull as the octave of

Lucas's voice hitches. A vein throbs in his temple, punctuating his anger. I know right now, despite him yelling at me, that this anger isn't really focused on me. I'm not the person he wants to be yelling at, but I robbed him of his opportunity to yell at Calvin, so now I have to stand in his place. Something prickles on the back of my neck, and even though I can feel Lucas's rage distinctly in the air—I can feel something else too. There's someone watching us.

"Lucas, I'm not taking your case from you. But you couldn't be objective in that moment. I stepped in. You can be involved in whatever capacity you want to be. But Dirby told me that if you were getting too emotional that I would need to take the reins."

"Oh, so you two are conspiring together to take this from me. What the fuck, Harlow? I thought that we were a team, that you were my partner. I didn't think that you'd go behind my back like this."

I suck in a deep breath through my nose and try to settle myself. Whenever someone screams at me like this, my body tenses, expecting to be hit, because that's how it always played out with my mother. Screaming led to abuse. Always.

"Lucas, I'm not taking your case. I'm not conspiring against you. But we need to make sure that we follow procedure here and that we don't put the case at risk. You know that if we make a wrong move here that Hershel could go free. It's difficult to lock down suspects in cold cases and I want to make sure that he's held accountable for what he did. That's all I'm doing." I try to keep my words as calm and even as I can. My hands tremble at my sides, and I shove them in my pockets to try and steady them. When that doesn't work, I cross my arms.

"I hope that you and Dirby are very happy working together. I'm off the case. I may just leave the team altogether. I don't need this shit," he says as he turns and storms back toward the hotel.

Part of me wants to follow him, to smooth things over. But I know that he needs time to decompress. Lucas can be a bit explosive when he gets angry. Usually though, if I let him breathe for a few hours, he feels better and we can talk things out. I grab my bag, sling it over my shoulder, and head inside the hotel. For tonight, I'll let him be mad. I'll smooth things over in the morning.

32

___

It's still dark when I climb out of bed. It took me hours to fall asleep—my mind was racing the entire night. I questioned over and over again if I should have handled things differently with Lucas. He's the only person that I've got on my side, and by following protocol, for doing what's best for the case as a whole, I've pushed him away.

I drag on my boots, throw on a jacket, and head out of the hotel. It's a few minutes' walk to the coffee shop near the hotel, so I decide to enjoy the crisp air rather than burn some of my gas. The streets are empty as I turn into the coffee shop. I grab two lattes and some donuts for Lucas. While he may still be mad at me, he has an intense sweet tooth, so with the right combination of donuts, I know I can start to smooth things over between us.

With the paper bag of donuts tucked under my arm, and the carrier of coffee in my left hand, I leave the coffee shop. The bell dings behind me, echoing through the abandoned streets. It's odd that no one is out yet this morning. I glance at my phone, wondering if it's a holiday that I've forgotten about.

I walk into the hotel, the sounds of life finally rising around me. There are people in the lobby, some checking out of their stays, some grabbing breakfast at the small buffet. I head to the elevator and take it to the third floor. Lucas's room is toward the back, next to the stairs. That's where he always chooses his hotel rooms. Though he won't talk about it, I know he's uncomfortable in elevators.

As I approach his door, something seems off. There's light pouring from a crack in the door. And I realize that it's propped open. The latch that's usually used to secure the door from the inside has been lodged between the door and the frame, keeping it open. Tension blooms around me as I push the door in. My mind blurs as I take in the scene. His white duvet is thrown to the floor, splattered with red and brown stains. Splashes of blood stain the carpet, the walls. His gun is on the ground, partially obscured by the duvet.

The coffee and the bag fall to the floor at my feet as I rush into the room. I take it all in. The blood. A broken lamp.

Lucas is gone.

33

NINETEEN YEARS AGO

It was too bright outside. The afternoon sun was bearing down on Lucas, prickling on the back of his neck with a warning of the sunburn that would come. But he couldn't go inside yet. His mom still hadn't come home, and his dad wanted him to play outside—and inside it was too quiet. Lucas wasn't allowed to turn on the TV or to do anything, really. Lucas was just so sick of it. His mom would be back soon. He knew it in his heart. Even though it had been days already, nearly a week.

He sat on the driveway, the heat of the concrete hissing against his legs. But he wouldn't move. Four multicolored Matchbox cars were abandoned in front of him, half of them flipped over, having lost all of their appeal. The wind picked up, brushing his dark hair away from his forehead for just a moment, the way his mother would always sweep it away. It was enough to make him look up.

A car rolled down the street, and Lucas watched it. As the car slowed in front of the driveway, he tried to make out the shapes in the back seat. A woman, he thought, with dark hair and pale skin. For a moment, his heart skipped a beat, then he shot up from the ground.

"Mom?" The word left him involuntarily.

The car stalled, then picked up pace again, rolling down the street. Lucas moved, walking toward the end of the driveway. He screamed in his mind for the woman to look at him, to notice him, but she stared forward—as if he didn't exist at all.

"Mom!" he shouted, the word tearing from him viscerally. It was as if the sound brought up razor blades with it.

His eyes stung as the car kept moving. The heat wrapped around him, tightening his chest, making it so hard to breathe. She had to have heard him, he was sure of it. There was no way that the woman in the car wouldn't have heard. But she did not move, the car didn't slow. He picked up his speed, chasing after the car, but he couldn't keep pace. The harder he pushed himself, the faster the car went.

"Mom!" he screamed again, his emotions pouring out with the word. She just had to come back. She had to stop the car, and to get out, and to tell him that everything would be okay again.

His foot caught on something and tripped him. All at once it was if someone had pulled the world out from under him. He landed hard, his knees skidding against the pavement, the hot rocks slicing into his skin. All the air escaped him, forced from his lungs. When he finally looked back up through the tears clouding his eyes, the car was gone.

She was gone.

And Lucas knew, no one would ever tell him that everything would be okay ever again.

A LETTER FROM DEA

Thank you so much for reading *Their Final Cry*. I hope that you enjoyed the third book in the series.

If you did enjoy the book and want to keep up to date with all my newest releases from Bookouture, sign up at the following link. Your email address will never be shared and you can unsubscribe at any time.

www.bookouture.com/dea-poirier

If you loved this series, please consider leaving a review. If you have a few minutes to drop a short review on Amazon, it would be very much appreciated. Every review—no matter how short or long—helps!

Thank you for reading.

Dea Poirier

dhpoirier.com

facebook.com/dhpoirier

twitter.com/DeaPoirierBooks

ACKNOWLEDGEMENTS

I am so thankful for my incredible editor, Laura Deacon, and the amazing support team at Bookouture (thank you all so much for everything that you do!), and my agent, Jill Marsal.

To my critique partner, and the best friend I could ever ask for, Elesha Halbert-Teskey, as always, I appreciate you. You're the best ♡.

To my readers, thank you so much for joining me for another book. Your support, kind words, and reviews are wonderful.

To my family—thank you for everything. Kiss noise.